Based on a novella by the same author: "Time Scope" it was rated highly by one Amazon reader: "What an intriguing concept! A time scope capable of looking into the past is a new twist on the time travel idea and one that has plenty of possibilities. Once I started reading this, only duty could stop me. Like everyone, I have a few of those to slow me down, but the story stayed with me even when I wasn't reading. The only thing that held me back from a 5-star rating was that I feel like there's more story to tell, more stories within the story, and I'd love to read an extended version. Every character in the story had elements that could be further explored." - So I did what she has asked for. The result is this novel.

This is an unusual story: starts as a science fantasy and then turns into a political thriller. The science parts are not meant to be realistic, or believable, they are merely the framework of the political part that should be thought-provoking regarding our existing reality.

For Vera

Acknowledgment

Special thanks to the person who helped me enormously in the writing and editing of this novel

Vera Mont, my wife, my best friend, and my merciless editor who never lets me get away with anything. From the original concept of the story, through the development of the plot and the final editing, she made invaluable suggestions and contributed colourful details to my characters and their dialogues. Without her participation, this would have been a significantly less polished novel.

SAVED
IN
TIME

SAVED IN TIME
An escape story

a novel

by

Francis Mont

Contents

EARTH 1

Zack Dougall stared at the gizmo on the garage sale bench. It looked weird. A plywood box of about 2 feet cube, with an old-fashioned CRT screen at the front, and a row of control buttons under it. The back was open, revealing an interior jammed full of electronic circuit boards and a wire-mesh of a peculiar pattern attached to two walls and to the top.

"What the heck is that?" he asked the old man sitting in his garden chair behind the bench.

"I wish I knew. It's from the estate of my tenant who used to live there." He poked his thumb in the direction of a small clapboard building in the back of his property.

"What happened to him?" Zack was curious. Taking a closer look at the device, he saw seven controls, labeled 'Power', 'Time', 'Space', 'Zoom', 'Speed', 'Scan', and 'Track'. Some were pushbuttons, some rotary dials. He also found four small buttons with arrows pointing left, right, up, and down. He expected volume control and channel selection but found none.

"He passed away last month. Brain cancer." The landlord sighed, shaking his head sadly. "Was still very young, no more than twenty-six, twenty-eight. People shouldn't die that early."

"What do you think this thing is?" Zack prompted. "Did he ever tell you about it?"

"Oh, he talked about it all the time. The big invention that was going to make him rich."

"What's it supposed to do?"

"That, he never said. He was very secretive about it but kept telling me to be patient with the rent because once he sold it, he'd pay me tenfold."

"And you believed him?"

"I was sorry for him. You see, he was invalided out of the engineering corps, got wounded in Iraq, and retired on a VA pension. I'm a vet myself, have seen quite a bit of action and I know how hard it can get. I cut him a lot of slack."

"He was an engineer?"

"They trained him in electronics when he joined up after he dropped out of the MIT Physics program. Thought he was too smart for them".

"Did he leave anything besides this gadget? Notes, diagrams - some clue as to what this is supposed to be?"

"There is a box full of crap like that left in his workshop, nothing valuable anymore. Those I already sold."

"Such as?"

"An oscilloscope, instruments of all kinds. Most of them I couldn't name, but someone picked them all up. The rest is just junk. I was planning to take it to the dump today after I closed down here."

"Do you mind if I have a look?" Zack asked eagerly.

"Be my guest, but don't take too long."

"Thanks. Please don't sell this to anyone until I come back. I might buy it myself."

As the old veteran said, the house and the workshop were empty, except for a big cardboard box on a workbench. It contained all kinds of things thrown in randomly. Components, circuit boards, cables, metal brackets, soldering kit, and many sheets of paper with hand-drawn circuit diagrams, lots of notes, and a badly stained and scribbled-over manuscript.

He picked it up and looked at the title. "E for Effort" by T. L. Sherred.

It was a stapled photocopy of a science fiction story Zack had read as a child. He gasped because now he knew what the inventor had been attempting to accomplish. He wasted no time returning to the front yard.

"How much do you want for it?" he asked, out of breath.

2

"I don't know. Make me an offer?"

"I'll give you fifty bucks." Zack hoped he had picked the right amount, not too high to make him suspicious, not too low to be rejected.

The old man chuckled. "You must be some kind of nut. You can have it".

Zack handed over the cash and, with some help, loaded the device in the back of his van.

"Do you mind if I take that junk too?

"Not at all, son, saves me a trip!"

The old man watched with amusement as Zack staggered from the workshop to his car under the weight of the box.

"Now, drive safely!" He laughed out loud, shaking his head as Zack drove away.

~

Zack had a long drive home from Farmington, Connecticut where he found his prize - yet one more funky electronic device acquired on his latest cross-country hunting trip. Not that he needed any more. His house in DC, his basement, even his garage was chock full of quaint gadgets and contraptions – some of them clean and labeled, some still dusty and unidentified, just as he'd found them at one garage sale or another. Zack's hobby was collecting 'antique' technology. He was a passionate tinkerer and prided himself on making old machines work.

He did not dare to think that this one could function. His driving became a bit erratic as he kept twisting his neck to look back at the big box winking at him with its lifeless screen.

That was science fiction, and this is real life. Stop your silly dreams and focus on driving, before you end up in a ditch! Now all the controls make sense. That man was trying to build a 'Time Scope', a device that could be tuned to any space and time coordinate and observe the events as they took place.

The background of the inventor sounded right: Physics at MIT, electronic engineering training at the army, he had the prerequisites. But to build a time machine, even if only a limited viewing device, seemed too fantastic. Zack could hardly wait to get home and try it out.

On second thought, he couldn't. He pulled into a McDonald's parking lot and collected the sheets of paper, notes, and diagrams from the jumble of small tools and components in the cardboard box. When he had them all, he went in for a coffee, taking the papers with him.

Some of the notes were test results, all suggesting success. Others were specifications on the power supply he would need. Several sheets were covered with tightly written differential equations. He recognized Einstein's space-time diagram, transformation formulas for momentum-energy, and electric and magnetic fields. The Lorentz Transformation Formulas were prominent on every page. Some were plans on marketing it to the highest bidder, once the final touches were complete.

Zack could hardly breathe, wiping sweat off his forehead.

Holy crap, this might be happening!

~

Tired by the time he got home, he forced himself to put off further investigation until the following day. He woke just after dawn and spent hours patiently wiring together power supplies and transformers, then testing and starting over, to find the right combination. He also needed to hook up an oscilloscope and a digital signal generator for calibration. Without the wiring diagrams in the notes, it would have been impossible to figure out.

When Zack finally turned it on, little dials over some of the controls were illuminated as if waiting for him to input a desired setting. He decided not to change the time and space dials for the first try and pushed the 'Scan' knob.

The picture tube came alive, focused and, after a few minutes, started showing a silent movie. A huge, badly dressed crowd in a wide public square, waving flags and placards Zack couldn't read faced a podium with a skinny bearded man on it, moving his mouth and gesticulating. Using the 'Zoom' knob, he identified the speaker as Vladimir Lenin. The 'Time' dial showed September 3, 1917.

He needed confirmation. Quickly. He set the 'Space' dial to New York and the 'Time' dial to September 11, 2001. He finessed it forward to morning. It showed the World Trade Center standing tall and proud on a clear bright September morning. And then came a low-flying jumbo jet and Zack watched in horror as it plunged into the wall and burst into flames. Fifteen *actual* minutes later, he could track the second plane careening toward and striking the south tower, all in eerie silence.

One more try before he dared allow himself to be convinced. For the 'Space' setting he looked up the GPS coordinates of his own address. For 'Time' he picked Aug 28 of last year, two days before he had sold his used Hyundai. Then he pressed the 'Scan' button. On the TV screen, his house and driveway appeared, with himself out front, taking an hour to wash and wax the car.

He couldn't have any more doubt. He had acquired a goddamn, functional time machine. Zack felt slightly dizzy with this unexpected opportunity that fell in his lap. He was aware of the magnitude of this discovery, the limitless uses, good and evil, it could be put to and was frightened of the implications. What if someone found out and killed him just to get hold of it? Should he alert the government? No, that wouldn't do, they would just confiscate it and start spying on their political rivals. It better to keep it a secret for the time being and find a way that he could somehow use it himself.

Further testing familiarized him with all the controls on the device. What he liked most was the 'Track' option that enabled him to focus on one person, animal or vehicle via the 'Zoom' feature and then, by pushing the 'Track' control knob, have the 'Time Scope' automatically adjust the space and time coordinates, so he could follow the movement of the selected subject wherever it went. He could even speed up, or slow down, the tracking by the 'Speed" rotary control. The man who invented this was a genius, no doubt about that!

Why, I can spy on anyone, anywhere, any time – *maybe even look into the future and learn the lottery* *numbers for the next draw or pick a high-yielding stock* *and get as rich as I want.*

This second idea, however, did not seem possible. No time coordinate beyond the current date was available.

~

His ruminations were interrupted by the doorbell. *This* *must be Suzy, she said she would drop by this afternoon.*

Zack quickly covered his gadget with a plastic sheet, and left his workshop, closing the door behind him. He wasn't ready to discuss this unexpected event with anyone – least of all Susan. He knew how aggressive she could be. Until he decided how to handle it, he wanted to keep it secret.

He opened the door and felt the usual dizziness on seeing her face and gorgeous body – he could never have enough of either. She wore cut-off jeans and a low-cut tank top, her blond hair swirling freely around her face. But that face was serious now, not her usual impish smile.

"Zack," she demanded, "have you shaved yet today? Look at you - you look like a bum!"

Zack inspected his reflection in the hall mirror and saw nothing wrong. He was tall and lanky, with a narrow face and black, curly hair that seemed to defy all attempts to be kept in some recognizable shape. The worn-out work clothes he usually had on in his lab did not improve the image.

That's the way I always look, so what's her problem?

"We need to talk," she declared, giving him pause; he wasn't used to her stern voice. "I'm not crazy about the way things are going between us." Zack started to protest but she silenced him with a gesture. "Let me finish. You have been out of a job for over a year, you are cooped up here, playing with your weird toys, living on god only knows what…"

Her boyfriend tried to stop the tirade, but she wouldn't be stopped. Not this time. "…and you are dragging me down with you. Our relationship is going nowhere, and I'm tired of this stagnation."

"But Suzy…" he tried and got slapped down again.

"Zack, this is an ultimatum. Unless you start behaving like a regular guy with a regular job, we are finished. Go out and find some work. Call me when you have."

With this last demand, she turned and flounced out of his house. Zack was stunned. He had not expected this.

Two things were unthinkable in his universe: life without Suzy and a regular job. So far, he had managed to survive on his dwindling inheritance, and he knew it wouldn't last much longer. His tinkering hobby was eating up way more than he admitted to himself and he had to do something to get hold of more funds if he meant to keep both his girl and his hobby. He wasn't quite sure in what order.

He shuffled slowly back to his lab and absent-mindedly pulled the sheet off the 'Time Scope'.

The germ of an idea began forming in his mind. *What if I can use it to lay my hands on some serious money?*

He knew that spying on the future was out. What if he spied on the past? How could he make money with that?

Blackmail was an obvious possibility, but he knew he would never sink that low. What else could he do?

He remembered a newspaper article that suggested a connection between Senator Hopkins and the infamous Mafia boss, Joe Petuccini – an allegation that the senator vehemently denied. The headline was: "Senator Hopkins meets with Joe Petuccini – questions asked".

The paper referred to 'sources' claiming that the senator interfered with a criminal police investigation, concerning one of Petuccini's associates, and raised the question of influence-peddling. An appointment in the senator's office, on September 14th, was on record. The article speculated on subsequent meetings but admittedly had no evidence of any. The paper showed their two photos, side by side, which was a nasty insinuation by itself, Zack thought.

Zack didn't believe a word of it. He respected Senator Hopkins, knew him to be an honourable man, and rolled his eyes at how the muckraking media were going after Hopkins. *They like to stir up shit about anyone if it helps them sell papers! Maybe I could use this device to prove them wrong?*

Zack realized all he needed to do was tune his 'Time Scope' to the senator's office and use the 'Track' option to follow him around. He did not need to track continuously but could skip ahead as the situation allowed. He would find out if there was a second, more clandestine meeting between the two. If there was, he could see for himself, and maybe show the world what really happened.

Hey, I should set up as a detective agency and use the device to solve crimes. I bet there is a substantial reward for some of these cold cases and it might be a steady income from an unsteady job I could do at home! This project would also be a good exercise in learning to use the machine!

~

It was the most boring week of his life, glued to his 'Time Scope', tuned to 5:00 PM every day of the past two weeks when the senator left his office. Zack quickly zoomed in on him and then pushed the 'Track' button. The 'Time Scope' worked like a charm. He leaned back in his chair and watched the senator going about his daily routine, all the way through town, stopping here and there, meeting with people, none of whom` was Petuccini.

Zack spent maddeningly slow days watching Hopkins arrive home, eat his dinner, read a book, sip his tea, light his pipe, scratch his neck, and do other mundane things.

Won't he do anything interesting for a change?

He almost gave up the idea when, on the fifth day of his vigil, he saw the senator walk outside and get into his car. The 'Time Scope' followed him along M Street to Georgetown Mall. He drove down the ramp to the underground garage. When he got out, a dark blue Caddy that had followed him pulled up alongside and stopped. A burly figure emerged from the backseat and walked up to the senator – Zack couldn't believe it – he saw Joe Petuccini's familiar face.

Holy crap! They did meet, and in an underground garage, late at night! I wouldn't have expected this! Quickly picking up his cell phone, he focused on the screen and started filming. He had no idea what they talked about, but whatever it was, it didn't last long. The senator shook his head and abruptly walked away toward the elevator. Zack copied down the date and time: September 26, 8:36 PM.

This looked like an encounter unexpected by Senator Hopkins and could prove his innocence. Zack already had the senator's email address and now he sent a very short message with the video clip attached.

He'll find it tomorrow and I'll be ready for his call.

~

Senator Hopkins enjoyed a quiet afternoon in his office, spent mostly on opening mail, both e and otherwise, from his constituents. He liked to deal with ordinary folks' problems, questions, and requests. It made him feel that he was doing something useful, away from the frustrating political infighting that came with his job.

But now he was confused. The email he'd just opened contained a video clip of him and Joe Petuccini, in the parking garage. The text only said: "we need to talk" and a phone number. The clip was legitimate, showing a scene that had really taken place. If this became public, he could be ruined. Nobody would believe how innocent he was.

Gordon Hopkins was a man in his late sixties, with picturesque silver hair, blue eyes, and an engaging smile, both serving him well in his re-election campaigns, but he was also a rarity, an endangered species in Washington: an honest, principled, and, most of all, incorruptible politician. In a career of almost thirty-seven years, he had avoided temptations, scandals, even the slightest suggestion of impropriety, until recently, when those speculations started about him and Petuccini.

They had first met when the casino tycoon came to his office, asking Hopkins to intercede on behalf of one of his 'associates'. The man, according to Petuccini, was wrongfully arrested, presumably to put pressure on himself. Hopkins served on the senate judiciary committee, so Petuccini assumed that he had influence. The senator briefly looked into the case, decided that he had no jurisdiction, and forgot about it.

Shortly after that, the rumours started. Senator Hopkins had a pretty good idea who had started them. His unscrupulous rival, Jack Cringe, must have heard about the case and wasted no time in using the appearance of collusion against him.

Then, a week ago, when he had driven to his usual shopping mall for groceries, he was accosted by the alleged gangster in the parking garage. He told Petuccini that he could do nothing to help him and walked away.

And now this!

Who on earth could have taken that clear, sharp clip in the under-illuminated garage? He had to find out. Reluctantly, he dialed the number. After making sure that the person who answered was the originator of the email, he said: "You have a 3:00 PM appointment in my office this afternoon," and hung up.

Zack was shocked by the summons. *Maybe he thinks I'm trying to blackmail him?*

He knew the senator would demand to know how he had acquired the video and he wasn't prepared to reveal that. *They'll take the 'Time Scope' away! It's mine and I want to keep it. My future professional income, never mind my love life, may depend on it.*

He decided to say that he had been sitting in his car, waiting for a friend, when he'd seen the senator and Petuccini together and, on an impulse, he shot the video for his celebrity collection. With this cover story ready in his head, and not a little apprehension, he drove to the Senate building.

Hopkins was all smiles; he invited Zack to sit on the padded leather chair across from his desk, then asked point-blank: "Mr. Dougall, I need to know how you acquired the video clip you sent me."

Oh my God, Zack groaned inwardly, *he already knows my name.*

He quickly rattled off his prepared speech and, strangely, the senator seemed to accept it.

"Well, then," Hopkins said, "what do you intend to do with this?"

"Senator", Zack blurted out, surprising even himself," I've been thinking of starting my detective agency, so I set out to prove your innocence. Partly because I'm certain you are, partly because I hope to use your reference in advertising."

"Zack... may I call you Zack?"

"Oh, sure, if you like," Zack stammered.

"Zack, that was very noble of you, wanting to help clear my name and I am sure I wouldn't mind returning the favour in the future, but first I must deal with my own problem. Let me ask you: were you there all the time that Petuccini and I were together? How long would you say that event lasted?"

"Not more than a minute, Senator."

"And, during that minute, did you see anything inappropriate? Did anything pass between us? Any document? Any object?"

"Oh, God, no sir, nothing like that, I 'm quite sure. I had a clear view and you were not standing close enough to hand over anything".

Zack relaxed. The senator didn't seem to be after his hide; rather, trying to save his own.

"Look here son", Hopkins continued, "there are these nasty rumours going around about me, and I know who started them but, until now, I had no way to counter them."

He smiled at Zack reassuringly: "However, now I have a witness to the only other brief meeting if you can call it that, I had with that man. So, what I suggest: *We* call a press conference and present your video clip, and your story, to the reporters. That way we nip any further rumours in the bud."

Zack wanted to protest, but the senator held up his hand: "I am sorry, but your participation is necessary, and you won't get into trouble, I promise. After that, you may use my name as a reference for your business. This is my price."

~

Joe Petuccini watched the press conference on TV and was not amused. Senator Hopkins told the assembled reporters about the video clip in his possession, explained how he had acquired it, and briefly showed it on his tablet computer. He also introduced the witness who gave him the video and could be called to testify if the need arose.

Petuccini was perplexed. He wasn't sure what he should do. Could that video get him into trouble? What else did the senator have on him? What else did the photographer snap pictures of? He knew that he was safe from another annoying investigation because after he had broken with his family, he restricted his activities to running his casino in Ocean City. All legitimate business, even if sometimes he had to be tough with various players trying to muscle into his enterprise. He shouldn't worry about someone spying on him, nevertheless, he found it annoying.

~

Zack saw the news item as well and was not at all pleased. He suddenly found himself in a dubious position, expecting the press at his door any minute. It turned out it wasn't reporters he needed to worry about.

The knock came late at night. Opening the door, he found himself face to face with Joe Petuccini, the infamous crime boss, and two tall, muscular men standing behind him.

"Hello," Zack said in a shaky voice, "can I help you?"

Petuccini smiled.

"I sure hope you can," he said sweetly, "for your own sake. May we come in?"

Senator Hopkins arrived an hour later.

He had never meant to visit Zack, but something in the back of his mind just wouldn't stop nagging, until he took another look at that video clip. The more times he watched, the more convinced he became that Zack's story of shooting that video from his car was bogus.

It took him a while to realize that the angle was wrong. The image was taken from considerably higher than where a person, sitting in his car – any car – would be positioned. Actually, not even a tall person, standing up, could have achieved that angle. *What was Zack hiding? How did he really acquire that footage? He must have gotten hold of a security camera tape, but how?* Hopkins had to find out.

When the doorbell rang again, Zack jumped up to answer, but Petuccini waved him back to the couch and signaled one of his shadows to see who it was. He recognized the voice immediately from the hallway and called out in the voice of a jovial host.

"Come on in, senator, the more the merrier!"

Gordon Hopkins stopped inside the living room door to take in the scene.

Zack was huddled in the corner of a sofa, obviously scared, but unharmed, so far. Petuccini was lounging comfortably in one of the armchairs, with a quizzical look on his face. Two expressionless bodyguards stood behind him.

Petuccini was the first to speak. "Looks like we are both after the same thing. I bet you came to discover how this gentleman acquired the video clip you showed the journalists. I must admit a similar curiosity prompted me, as well."

Hopkins considered this friendly opening and decided to play along for the time being. "I see you've made yourself at home. Have you come to any conclusion as to how it was possible? Did this *gentleman* divulge his secret? He seems to be still in one piece."

"Oh, he was very cooperative," Petuccini said with a barely suppressed smile, "once he saw the alternative to cooperation. Only," he added, "I'm not sure that I believe his story."

They all focused on Zack, who so far had not uttered a word. During this exchange, however, he seemed to relax a little and his birdlike features took on a thoughtful aspect. He turned to the senator, as if for support, and said, "I have a very valuable secret, sir. Actually, it can be extremely valuable to both of you, but only until anyone finds out." He looked pointedly at Petuccini's silent companions.

Petuccini was intrigued, considered the implications, and then nodded toward the exit. His bodyguards quietly opened the front door and went outside.

"Happy? We are alone and all ears – and you still have yours. Make your pitch."

"I'd better show you, or you wouldn't believe me," said Zack and, confidently for the first time that night, stood up and led them to the other room.

It needed a minute for the other two to take in the electronic workshop, with built-in benches around the walls, a large table in the center, and a jungle of wires and cables connecting odd contraptions that surrounded what looked like a homemade television set on the central table.

Zack pointed to the TV. "What would you say if I told you that with this set I can spy on anyone, anywhere, any time in the past?"

The senator rolled his eyes.

Petuccini caressed his right earlobe. "I would say prove that assertion, or you will regret wasting my time."

"Very well," Senator Hopkins challenged, "I always wanted to know whether Oswald was really at the window when Kennedy was shot. If you can show us that scene, I will believe you, however fantastic this claim sounds."

Zack spent a few minutes acquiring the space and time coordinates from the internet and then started fiddling with the knobs and dials on his outlandish device.

His two 'guests' were mesmerized, watching him fine-tune his contraption as he zoomed in on the sixth floor of the Dallas schoolbook depository.

Nothing happened for a while, but then they saw a window slowly open and the barrel of a rifle protrude through the crack, with a shadow holding it, barely visible inside the dark room. They couldn't identify the man on the view-screen but clearly saw flames erupt from the rifle. Since the 'Time Scope' did not provide sound, the effect of these silent shots was even more dramatic.

Zack looked up from his seat at his stunned visitors.

The senator sat down heavily on the only other chair in the room, while Petuccini emitted a low whistle, rubbing his temples with both hands.

Minutes passed before anyone spoke again.

Senator Hopkins was in shock. The existence of this time-travel TV set opened limitless possibilities in his mind. Witnessing Kennedy's assassination made him realize that it could be used for clearing up so many historical mysteries and settle centuries-long debates. They could prove once and for all if Jesus really existed or if Hitler really committed suicide at the end of WW2. His head was reeling with the implications. However, he was also aware of the evil practices a spying machine could be used for. The big question was: did anyone else know about it?

"Zack, who knows about this machine? Did you invent it?"

"No one else knows about it, sir, because the inventor died before finishing it. I found it on a garage sale bench. The landlord of the inventor had no idea what it could do, he wanted to cart it off to the dump if nobody bought it."

Finally, Petuccini found his voice: "Gentlemen, it appears we have both an opportunity and a problem."

"Yes. Oh, yes," Hopkins croaked. Clearing his throat, said, "This thing," he pointed at the TV with a not-too-steady finger, "could be extremely dangerous in the wrong hands."

"To whose hands are you referring, senator?" asked Petuccini softly, raising an eyebrow. "I believe we must come to some agreement here. Obviously, only the three of us can know about this."

"Three?" asked the senator, looking at Zack who was struggling with conflicting emotions. His fear was gradually giving way to resolve.

He said, somewhat petulantly: "There is no way either of you could operate this device without me. It's built into my lab that provides the very delicately calibrated power it needs." To drive home this point, he added, "And you need me to control it because it's awfully hard to tune correctly. So, whatever agreement you make, count me in."

Petuccini looked at the jumble of wires and nodded. "He may be right about that, senator. It seems we do need the young maestro to play this instrument." After a thoughtful pause he added, "And, I'm sure, you wouldn't dream of cutting *me* out, because you know that if either of us mentions our secret outside this room, we both lose our chances forever." He chuckled without genuine amusement. "It wouldn't take long for the FBI, CIA, NSA, and all the rest of the alphabet to swoop down and make it disappear. Maybe us, too."

Senator Hopkins considered his options. Finally, he said: "I'm willing to agree on one condition. That neither of us is allowed to use it for any purpose whatsoever that the other objects to." Petuccini tried to interrupt, but Hopkins raised a peremptory hand. "If Zack can set it up in such a way that operating it required us each to enter an encrypted password, then we both would have to be present before it could be turned on."

Zack, for the first time since the senator had arrived, exclaimed confidently. "Sure! I can hook up the power supply through the computer and hardwire a relay switch directly into a programmable circuit board to close the switch only when passwords are recognized." He said it, eagerly – maybe a bit too eagerly.

"Yes, I'm sure you could," remarked Petuccini, "but what would prevent *you* from using it any time you want to, for god only knows what nefarious purpose, like what you tried to pull on the senator here?"

"I didn't pull anything! I was only trying to help him clear his name!" Zack almost shouted, then added more calmly "I guess you'll have to trust me..." but stopped when he saw Petuccini's face.

"I guess we won't," said Petuccini, in a very firm tone. "Instead," he continued more softly, "I'll arrange my own kind of security. I'll have a lock installed on this room so that you can't get in unless I open it." Zack, who started to protest, was silenced with a glance. "Make sure you remove everything from here that you can't live without, except whatever this... machine needs. One of my servicemen will call on you tomorrow morning to do the work."

Zack knew when to shut up. He didn't have a choice.

The senator, however, wasn't satisfied yet.

"I know what I want to use it for, and we can discuss it later, but I must tell you, Mr. Petuccini, that I won't agree to anything criminal. If you wish to do research that does not involve anything illegal, we can have a deal."

Surprisingly, he met no argument.

"I knew it had to be something like that. I have a few personal questions, particularly as regards the comings and goings, during the last few weeks, of my less than trustworthy mistress."

Hopkins could not suppress a smile at that revelation – the feared gangster was jealous!

Petuccini added, "If you can go along with that, and I promise no physical harm comes to her even if I find my suspicions confirmed, then, yes, we have a deal."

Senator Hopkins considered this an acceptable price for the information he so desperately desired, concerning his own party's presidential nominee. Hopkins suspected a dark, hidden agenda behind that man and he needed to know whether his election would lurch the country onto a dangerous course.

Finally, he said: "Agreed. Now we only need to determine which of us will use the machine first. As I don't think it would be a good idea to run simultaneous research projects, I propose to do one at a time. Shall we flip a coin to decide?"

Petuccini immediately pulled a silver dollar from his pocket, ready to toss but the Senator stayed his hand: "Zack, do you have any change?"

Zack produced a quarter and tossed it. Petuccini won. They agreed on a day after the locks were installed and Zack had done the computer hookup, to meet again.

Joe Petuccini, driven off in his limo, wondered whether he really wanted to know the truth about Maria. *So, what if she is having some fun on the side?* The trouble was, he liked her too much. Depended on her too much. N*eeded* to know how far he could trust her.

~

Senator Hopkins was on his way home. He knew that he had an opportunity, a terrifyingly dangerous one to make a decisive difference, for the first time in his political career. An opportunity to save his country from a frightening change of direction. He had been unhappy with the way things were going. If he were to make a list of all the things wrong with his country, it would be a very long one.

On top of this list was this anger and resentment that seemed to permeate the news he read, the interviews he heard, the daily rallies and demonstrations against another incident of police brutality, the seemingly random mass shootings. The mood of the country was ugly: people were fed up and wanted change. *Any* change. That was the big problem. When there is a wave, you will always find those who ride it to personal success, regardless of consequences.

It was happening all over the world, unscrupulous politicians and rabble-rousing demagogues were popping up everywhere, fueling fear, hatred, suspicion – setting themselves up as the only ones who could save the frightened and angry population. The news of the world disturbed him, but Hopkins was primarily concerned with his own country, and within that, with his own party, and its new leader.

By the time he got home, Hopkins was determined to follow through with this crazy scheme. But first, he needed to discuss this with Muriel. She was his oldest friend and confidant. If anyone could give him sound advice, she was the one.

They had been married back when they were both too young to know what they wanted to do with their lives. It had taken fifteen years to figure out that their career paths required different settings: his in Washington, hers in Vermont. He had become a politician; she, an artist. The divorce had been amicable; they had no dispute over property and no children.

They reconnected from time to time when either needed a trusted friend to help to work through a difficult problem or dilemma, and Hopkins realized that now it was his moment to call her.

~

When the phone rang, Muriel was busy carving the cedar log she had salvaged from her woods that morning. *Let it ring,* she thought. *Can't be important!* Then she heard Gordon's voice leaving a message. She dropped her mallet and chisel and scrambled to get to the phone before he could hang up.

"Gordon," she gasped, out of breath from running across two rooms, "what kind of trouble are you in now?"

Hopkins chuckled. "I love you too, Muriel, how have you been?"

"I guess I must do," she admitted grudgingly, unable to stop a furtive glance in the wall mirror over the hall table, unaware that her hand flew to her hair in a vain attempt to smooth down her cowlicks.

"I've been fine. Busy as usual. I just managed to drag home a beautiful cedar log thick enough to carve that turtle I'd been planning."

Hearing Gordon's suppressed laugh, she added hastily: "...but I guess you didn't call me about turtles."

Hopkins appreciated her quick understanding. "No, Muriel. I need to talk to you about something very important that just came up."

It was Muriel's turn to chuckle. "Tell me one thing in your life that's *not* very important! Well, what's today's earth-shaking emergency?"

"Not over the phone, Muriel. We have to meet, and the sooner the better. If it's all right with you, I'll catch the evening commuter flight and be there in a few hours."

Muriel was flabbergasted. "Then it must really be important. If you give me the flight number and arrival time, I'll pick you up".

After he rang off, she reflected on how strange their relationship had grown over the decades. She had to admit to herself that Gordon was the only human being she trusted implicitly. She respected his integrity and dedication to doing as much good as he could.

It must be a serious crisis, for him to drop everything and fly up here, at a moment's notice, just to consult his old friend.

Gordon Hopkins' heart missed a beat when he caught sight of Muriel at 'Arrivals'. She was tall and erect, her pure white hair tied in a girlish ponytail. Under the inevitable layers of years, the oh-so-familiar face was as lovely as he remembered it from college.

After they hugged, they walked in silence to her car, then navigated slowly out of Montpelier International Airport. Muriel lived only an hour's drive outside the city, in a log house on a hundred wooded acres.

They didn't talk about his mission until they were comfortably seated in her living room, looking at the dark trees outside the floor-to-ceiling windows that covered one entire wall.

"Okay, Gordon, tell me," she opened the serious discussion.

"What would you say, Muriel," the senator started, "if I told you that I have access to a device that could spy on anyone, anywhere, *any time* in the past?"

"I would say," Muriel responded with her eyebrows high on her forehead, "that you're still hung over from one of those liquid lunches at the Senate Building."

"It's not funny, Muriel," Hopkins replied without a hint of a smile. "It's deadly serious, and I need your advice on what to do."

When Muriel said nothing, he continued. "I'm in a position to save our country from a potentially devastating tragedy, but the ethical considerations are so huge, I'm overwhelmed with indecision."

He proceeded to recount the whole story about Zack, the 'Time Scope', Petuccini, the experience of witnessing Kennedy's assassination, and their agreement. He concluded by pointing out that he could spy on the past activities of Norman Brady, their party leader, and perhaps confirm his suspicion of this man's dictatorial ambitions.

"Muriel, help me sort this out in my head. There is no one whose judgment I respect more." He gazed into her face hopefully, but by now, it had lost all expression, as if carved from stone.

"Damn you, Gordon," she said very softly, almost inaudibly over the crackling of the fire in the huge

Franklin stove. "I don't need the responsibility of helping you with this one." She added with some bitterness, "this is the kind of thing that destroyed our marriage twenty-four years ago. Do you want to risk our friendship as well?"

Gordon Hopkins didn't reply. He knew that he had to wait for Muriel to make up her mind. He was prepared to go home without discussing his problem any further if this is what she wanted. After a while, he saw her shoulders sag in defeat. She took a deep breath and looked him directly in the eyes.

"All right, then, if you must. What's your dilemma?"

EARTH 3

Zacharias Dougall, known to his friends as Zack, was pissed off. After he had installed the computer hookup for the power supply, programmed the computer to randomly generate two passwords, and activate the relay switch only when they were entered correctly, he was unceremoniously locked out of his own room by Petuccini's 'serviceman'.

He knew that he had trapped himself into this situation, which did not make it any easier to tolerate. He was between a rock and a hard place, not quite sure which of his overseers was which. Both the senator and Petuccini were forces way beyond his level of competence. He just had to wait and see where all of this would lead.

He briefly considered discussing his situation with Suzy, but quickly changed his mind: that could be the last straw his girl needed to become his ex-girl.

Just wait, he told himself, *both of these 600-pound gorillas need my help and, if I play my cards right, I might get out of this not just alive, but even with something to show for all this shit I have to put up with.*

He had to deal with it one day at a time, and today was the first. The senator and the mobster were due to arrive soon, to run Petuccini's experimental 'research' on the newly configured system.

~

Petuccini was first, unaccompanied by his bodyguards.

"Hello, Zack," he greeted the morose young man. "Let's see if I can open this door for you?" He proceeded to insert a very peculiar-looking key into the new lock and, without further ado, marched right in. Zack followed, not hiding his resentment over being a second-class citizen in his own home.

"Now, show me how this setup works. I would appreciate expediency, as my time is quite valuable."

It was all very simple. They had to turn on the power bar, which started all kinds of transformers in the room buzzing, then booted up the laptop now wired into the network of cables that connected everything. The computer then displayed input boxes for the two passwords and, below them, a 'Start' button.

Both Petuccini and Hopkins had already had their own passwords generated and emailed to them by Zack's program. Of course, Zack had no problem finding out what these were, but he could not use them himself because he was locked out of the room unless this overbearing guest was present.

Hopkins soon arrived, deep in thought as usual. He was worried about another meeting with Petuccini, even at an obscure residence in the suburbs. *"What if a journalist finds out?"* He could never discount this possibility, but he thought it was worth taking this small risk.

His consultation with Muriel convinced him that he must proceed with the plan. Unfortunately, Petuccini had won the coin toss and he was forced to wait. Hopefully, it wouldn't take too long for 'Romeo' to find out what he wanted about his girlfriend, and then it would be his turn.

~

Before leaving Atlantic City, Petuccini had instructed Maria Montrose, the assistant manager of his "Dreams Come True Casino", to keep a close eye on the shop. Two problems were brewing in the background and he wanted to make sure that nothing would come to a head while he was in Washington. He had told her that he would be away for a week, not a long time for her to pull double shifts to ensure that everything was running smoothly, and that nobody was causing any trouble.

He trusted her loyalty on the job since it was Maria who had alerted him to the manager's improper handling of the slot machines and undisclosed phone conversations with one of Petuccini's business rivals. There was no solid reason to doubt her sexual fidelity either - except that he never understood why she was attracted to him. He was middle-aged, and in reasonable shape, but no movie star. She was an absolute knockout, gorgeous thirty-five years old, she had an accounting degree, a solid career, and no need for his money. Then *why*? Good-looking hunks were abundant on the casino circuit and Petuccini wouldn't be surprised if Maria, being confident and adventurous, decided to sample all that his world could offer. Maria didn't object to his request, which was reassuring, but now he wanted to be sure that her nights had been as innocent as her very busy 16-hour workdays.

After the two passwords were entered and the machine came alive, he instructed Zack to tune the 'Space' dial to the GPS location of Maria's bedroom, and the 'Time' dial to 1 AM, on the day after he'd left town for his visit to Washington.

When the Time Scope showed the scene, they could clearly see the bed occupied by one person and Petuccini recognized the sleeping face of his girl, her long dark brown hair spread out on the pillow. He watched her lovely face for a few minutes with deep satisfaction.

So far, so good.

He told Zack to hold the space coordinates but keep changing the time randomly from midnight to 7 AM, one day ahead each time until they arrived at this morning.

On the second try, they caught her getting ready for bed, preparing to undress and change into her nightgown. Petuccini hastily ordered Zack to look the other way, while Senator Hopkins had already turned his back. Petuccini enjoyed watching her voluptuous body slowly released from her elegant pantsuit and far too quickly obscured again by her nightgown.

Repeating the random search, his two companions soon lost interest, because the result was always the same: Maria sleeping peacefully in her own bed at any time they looked throughout the night.

Petuccini was satisfied. He knew that Maria had a demanding job at the casino, a job that kept her busy all day and evening, in full public view or in the office with its security system, with no privacy at all, except during the night and, as he had just learned, her nights were as innocent as could be.

He stood up with a big sigh of relief, shook his head in wonder a few times, and then laughed, maybe a bit too loudly, to hide his embarrassment. "Gentlemen," he announced, "I realize that my worries were unjustified, and now I have to ponder how to deal with my newfound situation."

Hopkins and Zack gazed at him with uncertainty, waiting for specifics.

Petuccini obliged. "I propose to set a date next week for the senator's session. I have some business to attend to in New Jersey that cannot be postponed."

"I hoped to do it sooner than that," Hopkins protested. "For me, every day increases the danger."

Petuccini was sympathetic but unbending. He ordered Zack to shut down the system and suggested they all leave the room so that he could relock it.

After a brief hesitation, Hopkins accepted the decision and followed the others out of the room. The loud click of the lock emphasized the end of this incredibly unexciting time travel session they had experienced.

~

After a bumpy one-hour flight, Joe Petuccini was greeted by Maria at Ocean City Airport. She thought that the brewing crises at the Casino required Joe's immediate attention and wanted to start reporting on business the second he arrived. However, her carefully prepared opening had no chance, because Joe was uncharacteristically emotional. He picked her up in the air and twirled her around, in plain sight of everyone.

"Babe, I missed you so much!" Joe enthused "What do you say we go straight to bed and make up for lost time?"

"What's got into you?" Maria gasped the words out and wriggled from his tight embrace, "It's only been a week!"

"A week, a day, who cares?" Petuccini dismissed her objections, and declared solemnly, "At my age, sweetheart, a week can seem an eternity without your sweet lips. Let us adjourn to my sanctum and correct this huge omission first. Then we may talk."

Maria was too impressed with her lover's enthusiasm to protest any longer. She wasted no more time but drove him home to resume their mutually satisfactory relations. Petucinni derived a little secret pleasure from imagining himself on the other side of the time scope, looking in.

~

Hours later, after immediate emergencies were taken care of, she tried again to talk sense with him. "Joe, you have a problem here and you need to take care of it. John is really screwing you with the slot machines and may be trying to sell you out to the Markos consortium. At least, I've caught him a couple of times, making secretive phone calls, while you were away."

Joe sobered up quickly. He had suspected something like this, but now Maria seemed to have some evidence, though not solid enough.

What should he do about it? Obviously, the same thing he had had to do, year after year, with upstarts who had become too bold for their own good. Suddenly, he felt overwhelmed by boredom - the "here we go again" kind that usually arrives on the doorstep of successful businessmen. They have seen it all, done it all before and there is no challenge left; no novelty to enjoy and look forward to.

Did he need more of this? How long was he going to keep repeating the same pattern? Is this the way he wanted to spend the rest of his life?

Here he was, in bed, with this fantastic, intelligent, loyal woman who, for some unfathomable reason, was attracted to him; who offered him a relationship such as he had never had before, and he was twisting his brain into a pretzel, trying to figure out how to deal with low-life vermin that did not deserve a minute of his attention.

He decided to sleep on it and enjoy the rest of the night in his own bed, in the arms of his own mistress, with his own secret of knowing everything about anyone's past if he so wished. He would need to think this all through.

His mind wandered over to the 'Time Scope'. What was it that the senator wanted? What was important enough to risk associating with a notorious character like himself? The senator had mentioned danger, but never explained what danger he meant, from what quarter.

According to their agreement, he had a right to know, and veto power over, the other man's purpose. He resolved to call the senator in the morning and move the date of their next session up a few days, to discuss the project and the procedure they were to follow. His domestic problem could wait a bit longer. He found this new situation very amusing, how the three of them, such drastically different personalities, found themselves allied in some kind of conspiracy. With this final thought and decision, he kissed Maria good night and emptied his whirling mind, ready for much-needed sleep.

~

Senator Hopkins didn't find sleep as easily as his exhausted 'partner'. He kept going over his worries regarding Norman Brady. He had no solid grounds for concern; only rumours, news reports, the man's own campaign speeches, and - most importantly - his last conversation with the nominee.

At the end of a long night strategy session at party headquarters, Hopkins was reasonably sure that Brady was sounding him out on the possibility of sharing the ticket. He had been more open and forceful in his questions than ever before, and those questions were deeply troubling.

Perhaps Brady had been a little bit drunk at the time; maybe he wasn't aware of how much he'd revealed about his intentions, when, not if, he won the election and became president. He had demanded to know how Hopkins felt about governance, democracy, and leadership.

"Gordon, what do you think is the biggest problem in our country?" Without waiting for a reply, he'd answered his own question. "Lack of strong leadership. All this stupid hand-wringing over civil rights, legal jurisdiction, and due process has paralyzed this country."

Hopkins waited for clarification.

"I don't mind admitting that I've always admired strong leaders. Sure, some of 'em were misguided, took the wrong direction. But they got things done, by God, and the government fell in behind them, or else! They unified their people."

Hopkins wanted more, so he asked: "For instance, Norman? Give me some examples."

"Don't take me wrong," Brady continued. "I despise some of the decisions they made, and I know a couple of 'em went overboard, but you've got to respect the strength and the grit. Because those guys achieved what they had wanted to achieve."

Hopkins started to have a very bad feeling about this. But Brady wasn't finished. "Just for their efficiency, and not their aims, I give credit to America's favourite whipping boys, like Saddam Hussein, Vladimir Putin, and, even way back, before we knew any better, even Hitler and Mussolini had their moments. *Somebody's* got to make the trains run on time, eh?"

Gordon Hopkins was flabbergasted. He stared into the other's belligerent, alcohol-soaked glare and couldn't utter a sound. Brady must have sensed his shock, because he suddenly changed his tone, as if a switch was thrown, and laughed loudly at Hopkins.

"Gordon, you should see your face!" he guffawed. "You don't really think I'm serious? I was just kidding around, man!" He slapped Hopkins heartily on the back and walked away, shaking his head and chortling all the way to the bar.

Hopkins managed a weak smile and uttered an uncertain "No, I suppose not", to nobody but found himself still reeling from the sudden revelation of the man's potentially terrifying intentions.

That was the end of their interview if it was what he thought it was, and they never spoke of it again.

EARTH 4

Susan Turnbull was lonely. The last time they met, she'd been quite harsh with Zack. She had wanted to jolt him out of his rut, not to hurt or discourage him. She really cared for him: his quirky ways were endearing and made her laugh, and the sex was terrific.

She had not seen him for over a week and he had not even tried to call once in that time. How had he reacted to her ultimatum? Was he trying to find a regular job? Or had he given up? Was she going to lose him? She decided to drop in after her shift at the "Geraniums" flower shop, where she was employed, nine to five, like a normal person. She hoped things were still OK between them.

When her boyfriend opened the door, Suzy was startled by his appearance: more unkempt than ever and no sign of his characteristic good cheer.

"Hi Zack, will you let me in? Unless you don't want to see me anymore after the way I talked to you?"

"Suzy! I do want to see you!" The words tumbled out of Zack in a rush. "I didn't expect it but I'm happy you came. Boy, am I *ever*! Come in!"

"What's wrong?" Susan asked, not quite sure what gave her the impression that he was in some kind of trouble.

Zack led the way back to his living room and sat down on his usual spot on the sofa, while Susan took the chair. She looked around the room, searching for clues to his morose demeanor, and almost immediately noticed the shiny new deadlock on his workshop door.

"What the hell, Zack?" she exclaimed. "What do you need *that for*?"

Zack emitted a big sigh, realizing that he had no choice but to tell Susan everything. All through his exposition, her eyes grew larger and larger, her expression slowly changed from suspicious incredulity to something near horror.

"So, I am locked out of my own lab by a senator and a gangster," Zack concluded his tale, "and I have no idea what's going to happen." He added softly. "I'm a bit scared, kind of pissed, and super frustrated. I don't know how to get free of these guys."

It took her a while to digest this incredible story, but the lock on the door and Zack's worried, almost grown-up, face convinced her that it was for real. *A time-scope? Spying on people's activities anywhere, any time in the past?* If she believed that, she'd believe anything.

Her practical, no-nonsense mind finally prevailed over her emotional turmoil and began to consider the actual situation. "Why do you let them push you around?" she demanded. "Didn't you tell me that they couldn't use it without you?"

"Yes, I know, but..."

"Don't be such a wuss, for crying out loud!" Suzan exclaimed. "Have you tried to set your own terms?"

"What terms?"

"I don't know, You're the genius with the gadget. *You* found this time scope or whatever you want to call it. *You* figured out how to use it. You're the one who can operate it."

"That's all true, but..."

"Well then, it makes sense that you should get some benefit from it, not just be a servant to those big important bozos. I hate to see them walk all over you!"

"Yeah! So, how do I do that?"

"Think, Zack! What could you use it for? Trying to blackmail a senator was the dumbest idea you ever had, and that's what dropped you in this pile of shit."

"Hey! Be fair. I did *not* try to blackmail him!" Zack protested. "I only wanted to help clear his name, so I could use him as a reference."

"You mean, for a job?" she asked hopefully.

"Um, no. I was thinking of, maybe, setting up a private detective agency. Solving crimes and mysteries that nobody else could. I'd have no competition at all."

Susan was impressed, seeing the potential in this scheme.

"That would kill several birds with one stone," she admitted. "You wouldn't have to hold down a regular job, you could do most of your work at home, tinker with your toys, and pull a fairly steady income."

"Suzy, I love the idea," he confessed, "but how can I start? I'm locked out and can't do a damn thing without their permission. I can't get them off my back."

"Zack, be a man. Stand up on your hind legs!" Suzy replied angrily. "Next time they come, tell them that you won't help their research anymore unless they let you do your own." Seeing Zack was ready to object, she added hastily, "Make sure they understand that you'll only use it for legitimate business, that they can monitor everything you do, but that's the deal – take it or leave it."

"Do you think I could get away with this?" Zack asked with a glimmer of hope appearing on his lugubrious face.

"What have you got to lose?" his girl asked in exasperation, which evaporated as she thought of a possible answer. "Anyway, you'll never find out unless you ask."

"I guess you're right," Zack nodded slowly, combing his long fingers through his hair in thought. "So that's what I'll do." He was silent a moment, then shyly asked: "Is the couch too uncomfortable to fool around on? You know it's been... a while."

Susan rolled her eyes. "I thought you'd never ask".

~

Petuccini and Hopkins arrived almost at the same time. Zack greeted them with great apprehension, but was fully determined to follow Suzy's advice: she had made him promise to stand up for himself, with dire threats concerning their relationship if he didn't.

He looked at them defiantly and declared, in a somewhat shaky voice: "Before we do anything, I have to clarify my role in this enterprise."

The other two stared back at him.

Petuccini appreciated the humour in the situation: it was as if a chair had spoken up and demanded fair treatment. "You are in no position, young man, to clarify or negotiate. Your role is to avoid jail, or worse."

Zack had had enough. His boiling point was unusually high, but the frustration of the last two weeks and then the contempt in Petuccini's voice pushed him over the top. "That goes for all three of us, I believe, unless you mean to make me disappear, so I can't testify against you for spying and god only knows what else you're planning here."

Petuccini burst out laughing at this unexpected show of temper. "Senator, would you believe this? The young fellow has spunk."

Hopkins wasn't amused. The illegality of what he had been contemplating weighed heavily on his mind and he didn't care to be reminded.

"Maybe we should hear him out?" he suggested and, after a few seconds of considering, Petuccini agreed.

"Okay, let's humour him if it doesn't take too long. We have important topics to discuss. All right, kid, you have the floor. Tell us concisely what you are after."

Zack was grateful to the senator and for the first time since they arrived, he actually saw hope.

"It's very simple," he started. "I found this device, I managed to make it work, I understood what it was for and how to use it, so I believe I'm entitled to some benefit from it, instead of being treated, in my own house, like a slave."

"You should have considered your options before trying to blackmail a US senator," Petuccini responded. "Let alone spying on me."

Zack shouted defiantly: "I was *not* trying blackmail! I never asked for money and cooperated with the senator from the start. And I never spied on anybody except your girlfriend."

Hopkins couldn't deny this: "It's true. Zack did nothing improper. He offered to help me, and I promised to help him."

Still, Petuccini wasn't pacified. "He should have known better," he muttered.

Zack had only one card left, and he was very reluctant to play it. Whichever way he put it, this would sound like blackmail, or extortion, as Petuccini would recognize instantly. He had to try something else first, before resorting to his final argument. "Okay, so, I'll go on helping with your research, as much as you like, but I want to be able to use it myself, too. Legitimately, of course. I've got to make a living."

Now Petuccini was curious – he couldn't imagine a legitimate business connected to a spying machine.

Zack declared proudly: "I intend to start up as a private eye and work on unsolved crimes and mysteries. With this device, I could follow clues back in time and find out exactly what happened."

"I'll be damned!" Hopkins exclaimed, unable to hide his surprise and the sudden realization of how well-suited this innocent-looking TV set was for criminal investigation.

Petuccini, in his turn, burst out laughing, unable to stop.

"Kid," he declared, "you *are* a genius!"

"Does that mean," Zack asked hopefully, "that you'll let me use it?"

Petuccini and the senator looked at each other, the first still amused, the other in a thoughtful way.

"We need to think about it, Zack," Hopkins finally spoke up. "I don't think that your request is unreasonable, but we need to make sure that we have clear rules on who, when, and how can have access to this device."

Petuccini seemed to agree, or at least he did not outright veto the idea, so Zack felt encouraged to carry on.

"What I suggest, for a start, is that you remove that lock from my workshop door because I can't get started without unlimited access to the very foundation of my plan." Before either of his 'guests' could interrupt, he added hastily "However, I'm here 24/7 – something that neither of you can afford, so I can help with your own research and collect data on a regular basis for both of you – if you tell me what you are after."

"Now that's an idea!" Petuccini admitted.

"This way," Zack continued, "I can be your research assistant even while working on my own investigation."

Hopkins thought that this was a tremendous idea. Being a good judge of characters, he was tempted to trust Zack. Also, he'd never felt good about meeting regularly with Petuccini; it was only a question of time before some nosy reporter followed him to the house and noticed the other visitor. "I'm inclined to go along with this," he said, looking over at Petuccini expectantly.

"Very well. I'll give it a try, young man," his 'partner' looked at Zack sternly. "but you would very much regret trying to pull a fast one on either of us."

Zack's sigh of relief could have launched a commuter flight.

"I won't let you down, either of you!" he promised. "I'll be an enthusiastic assistant in whatever plans you two have." He couldn't resist elaborating, "Much better for all of us if I don't participate with reluctance and resentment."

"Okay, kid," Petuccini decided. "The lock stays until such time as we ascertain that we can trust you." Before Zack could protest, he added, "but I won't lock it anymore unless," he raised a warning finger "you give me a reason to do so."

~

Norman Brady was livid. These goddamn journalists were picking up every fucking scrap of gossip they could lay their hands on. Nobody appreciated what a miracle he had achieved by securing his nomination, in their stupid faces, despite all their educated guesses and projections.

Everybody kept parroting that the people wanted change, and, by God, he was going to give them change – the kind they had never seen before in America. No more bullshit excuses, no half measures, he was going full out and nobody could stop him.

His followers were enthusiastic, pumped up, and motivated. All you had to do was appeal to their fear, greed, and, most of all their hatred of anything you told them threatened their grubby little existence.

Brady knew what made people tick and what they wanted to hear. No point telling them what they didn't want to hear. Truth had nothing to do with it. Politics wasn't about telling the truth, it was about scoring points on your opponents.

But the fucking journalists just kept coming after him, questioning his credentials, his accomplishments, his methods. It was infuriating that he had to tolerate them a little while longer.

He'd have to decide very soon on a running mate. His plan for Hopkins fell through when he realized that Gordon was too much of a boy scout. Too bad, because a boy scout would have looked good on the ticket, and would have mollified some of his critics.

Anyway, time to think about going to bed, it was nearly 3 AM, he'd just finished updating his Facebook page, sent out his last emails, and could call it a day. The fundraising was going well and even some of the party brass started to fall in line. All in all, it was looking good.

~

Muriel spent a sleepless night after Gordon's visit. His shocking revelation about their party leader, coupled with the fantastic news about a spying machine, deeply disturbed her. She had been a politician's wife long enough to realize how much damage a rogue president could do to the country and, for this reason, she encouraged Gordon to pursue his investigation.

Which was not without danger, she realized. Whatever Gordon managed to discover about Brady's past activities, how on earth could he make it public? He couldn't just announce the existence of the 'Time Scope', they both agreed. Without that evidence he had no case and would only make things worse – the backlash would be devastating. She fully realized the quandary he was in. Could he find out something that might compel Brady to withdraw from the race? Maybe just letting him know, anonymously, that somebody was on to him?

Muriel still deeply cared for Gordon and wanted to help him through these difficult times. What if she put her own projects on hold and traveled to Washington to be with him for moral support? One problem though: she had two dogs whom she wouldn't put in a kennel. Bearcub and Daisy were very attached to her and she couldn't contemplate leaving them with strangers.

However, Gordon was also very fond of dogs and he did live alone in a house with a little yard; there might be room for them. She decided to leave it up to him, and quickly, before she could think better of it, sent off an email message to him:

"Gordon, I have some business in Washington this coming week and, if you think you could put me up for a few days, with two of my dependents, please let me know."

She had done all she could, the rest was up to him.

Gordon Hopkins, United States Senator, wasn't sure what he'd gotten himself into. He wasn't supposed to be here. He could face severe punishment if it ever became public. Yet, he couldn't leave. The stakes were too high. He had to know the truth about Brady.

All Hopkins found out, even after extensive research, was that Petuccini had never been in prison, had never been indicted; though he had been investigated, there was no criminal record on file. He was third-generation Mafia, his ill reputation seemed to come from his family connections, rather than what he had actually done. He had kept himself busy for years, running a major casino and convention center in Ocean City, and was not involved in anything else, as far as Hopkins could tell. The only allegations of underworld activity appeared in gossip columns. Not enough to scare Hopkins away, but certainly not something a US Senator could advertise in his next re-election campaign.

According to their agreement, he was duty-bound to explain his project to Petuccini, and he had no idea of the other's political leaning, or how he would react. Still, it had to be done, and he briefly outlined the background to his worries and the information he needed.

To his surprise, Petuccini was enthusiastic. "Senator, you may find it strange that a man like me is interested in politics." He shook his head as if trying to dislodge some nasty insects. "As a matter of fact, I am not," he continued, "but nor am I altogether oblivious to what transpires in this country."

Hopkins raised an inquiring eyebrow.

"That poseur, your party's nominee, his braggadocio about being a self-made man, that makes my blood boil!" He almost shouted the last sentence. "I could tell him something about self-made men – people who don't start out with a trust fund from their papa!"

There was no doubt in Hopkins' mind whom Petuccini was talking about.

"He claims to be tough on immigration and crime, but all he wants to do is make poor people's lives harder, while he and his confederates grow even richer." He stared at Hopkins intently, as if trying to convince him of something the senator already knew. "It's easy to talk tough when one has an army at his command and no gun in his own face. If you want to dig up any dirt on the bastard, I am all for it."

"That's settled then." Hopkins sighed with relief and proceeded to lay out his plan. He wanted to start a thorough investigation on Brady's comings and goings and even his home activities. He asked Zack to film meetings that Brady had with everyone who visited and any private conferences he had. Hopkins would review the footage once a week and give Zack further instructions as required. When all the questions were answered and all the clarifications given, Hopkins and Petuccini left, a few minutes apart.

~

Zack had been locked out of his workshop for so long that he couldn't wait to step inside. Everything was exactly as they left it, except that, without the stultifying presence of his two chaperones, it felt roomier. Finally, he was master in his own house again, not a criminal on probation.

He walked over to his 'Time Scope' and gently placed his hand on top of the box, caressing it affectionately. He would start working soon after he had called Suzy. She had made him promise that this would be the first item on his agenda the minute his visitors left.

"Hi Zack, how did it go?"

"Amazing! I still can't believe it - we *won!* They went for the deal and I didn't even have to use blackmail!"

"That's great! So, what are you going to do now?"

"I really want to try that private eye business, but I don't exactly know how to get started," Zack admitted reluctantly.

"Why don't you Google unsolved crime rewards?" Suzy suggested, giving Zack the impression that she had already considered the same question at some length. "That way you can have a guaranteed income - assuming you produce the evidence and collect."

"That's a great idea, Suzy. I'll get right on it."

"You want me to come over?" she asked, a bit too eagerly for Zack's liking.

"No, Hon, not this time. I want to try it on my own. You've been a terrific help, but I need to figure things out for myself."

"Okay. Let me know how it's going," she said and rang off.

~

When Hopkins got home and looked at his email, he found Muriel's brief note about a visit to Washington. Good thing he was sitting down; this was a shock. They had not slept under the same roof since their divorce twenty-four years ago and he wasn't sure what her message implied.

The "business in Washington" part was too much of a coincidence to believe. Therefore, he could imagine only two possible explanations. Either Muriel wanted to rekindle their old love, which he was sure still lingered under the ashes, or she believed in his dangerous plan and wanted to give him advice and a shoulder to lean on. For his own peace of mind, he chose to believe the latter.

He had been introduced to the dogs on his recent visit and had no objection to having them around for a few days. He looked at the open email one more time, and then replied:

"Dear Muriel, I'd be delighted to put you up for a few days and don't worry about your dependents. Bring whatever they need, or I can lay in some dog food if you tell me the brand. I'm sure we can find dishes around the house. Let me know when you plan to arrive, and I'll pick you up at the airport."

Rereading it one more time, he clicked on the 'Send' button and watched the slider bar delivering his message. For better or worse, now he was committed.

~

Zack was just about to start searching for his first client when the doorbell rang. Would Suzy come over on a weekday? he wondered. He was disappointed to find Petuccini on his doorstep, smiling mysteriously.

"I guess you didn't expect me back so soon, kid," the big man said. "I must remain in Washington a few days longer and I have a business proposition for you."

Zack was taken aback. The change of demeanor in his feared persecutor was unbelievable. He barely managed to stammer out: "What are you talking about? What kind of business?"

Petuccini pushed past him into his living room, and Zack had no choice but to follow. His visitor sat down in his usual armchair and looked him up and down appraisingly as if trying to determine whether he could be entrusted with a job.

Zack sat down on his sofa and waited.

"I know that it's the senator's turn," Petuccini began. "However, there is nothing in our agreement prohibiting a separate contract between you and me."

"Like what?" Zack blurted out, losing patience.

"You will be doing the senator's research but, you could also investigate something for me."

"You don't mean you actually want to hire me as a private eye?" Now, this really was a change in their relationship!

"Yes, this is precisely what I do mean." Petuccini continued, "and there is a financial reward if you find the evidence I require."

"Money?" Zack's eyebrows ran up to his hairline. "How much?"

"How does five grand sound?"

Zack was speechless; he could only nod several times while swallowing hard.

"I take it," Petuccini smiled," that your nodding means 'yes'. Then, I shall indicate what I am after."

Zack fished out the notebook and pen he always carried in his shirt pocket.

Petuccini explained how he had deep suspicions that his manager was conspiring with a rival to sabotage his slot machines and trigger massive financial losses that would force him to sell at a loss. He needed proof on videotape that the two men, John Wasserman and Jose Markos, had met secretly, more than once, during the last month. He gave Zack both office and home locations, two snapshots, and the time to investigate. He suggested tracking Wasserman as the easier mark.

"I'll need it fairly soon if you do secure evidence," he concluded. "This is my mobile number," he gave Zack a business card. "Call me when you have something."

~

Reading Gordon's invitation, Muriel almost lost her nerve. *What am I getting into?* She asked herself, and then repeated the question to Daisy, who joined her at the desk, placing a warm muzzle on her knee, in a reminder that it was time for their daily romp in the forest.

Muriel wasn't ready yet. Gordon asked for a flight number. But that would be too stressful for the dogs, who had never been in an airplane. She looked up the Montpelier to Washington route and learned that it is 583 miles via the I-91; the estimated travel time 9 hours. With judicious speeding, she could cut it down to include necessary stops to walk and water the dogs. A whole day's drive: if she left early in the morning, she could get there by late afternoon or early evening.

The idea of having her own car on the visit appealed to Muriel: she would be independent, and not have to rely on Gordon, public transit, or taxis for transportation.

Besides, the long drive would be an excellent opportunity to mull things over. She had to determine which was more important to her: to spend time with Gordon again, after so many years apart, or to provide encouragement. Apparently, Gordon wasn't the only one who needed it.

Decisions made, she dashed off a reply to Gordon, advising him of the day and time to expect her arrival, by car instead of a plane; that saved him a trip to the airport.

"Okay, Daisy, *now* it's time to go." She stood up and followed her out to the front porch where Bearcub was already prancing in place under the leashes hanging from their hook. "If I get into trouble, kids," she admonished, "it will be your fault. You didn't talk me out of it."

~

"I'll tell you the whole story," she addressed her two companions on the back seat, who were hanging on every word. "Gordon and I met at Johnson State College, in residence. He was in the Bachelor of Science program; I was in Fine Arts. We were both far from home, shy and lonely. He was charming and intelligent and not bad looking so, as time went by, we became good friends. Very good friends. We planned, after graduation, to build a house outside town on some nice treed lot and live happily ever after.

"It worked out fairly well. He got a job with Honeywell in Montpelier and I started selling a few landscapes, getting commissions... sculpture went even better, and once I began working in wood – well you know how that's going! Then, things got complicated. Gordon became involved in politics. He felt passionate about one issue, then another. Seeing all the unfairness and inequality, he had to do something. He ran for councilor, then the state legislature, and finally got elected into his current position: Senator for the state of Vermont.

"Are you two still with me?"

Daisy and Bearcub almost nodded their heads in unison.

"Okay, then, I'll go on," Muriel said, trying to determine how much she wanted to admit to her two friends, or maybe even to herself. "That's when our problems started. Gordon wanted to move to Washington, as his job required, and I was horrified at the prospect of leaving our beautiful house in the woods for a big city. My art would have suffered, and I would have had to give it up. I flatly refused to go, and he had to choose. For a while, he kept coming home on weekends and summer vacations, but these became fewer and shorter as the years went by."

"That was a very long time ago," she explained, "way before you were born. Eventually, we realized that living apart had become a permanent arrangement. Neither of us wanted to be dishonest. We decided on divorce to free us to find more suitable mates, without trauma or guilt. Years, then decades went by, but we managed to stay good friends. Even though we had other romantic attachments in our lives, we never really stopped caring for each other."

She added with a sigh:

"Now we're both free again and I have to admit I'm a bit lonely without a human companion. You guys can't make up for the stimulating intellectual conversations I enjoyed with Gordon. The big question I'm asking myself - and you two as well, so pay attention: Will I let myself get involved with him again? If I do, beware, that is not without danger. The conflict of interest is still there: he's still a senator, and I would never leave my house in the woods, so you can relax. What do you think?"

Her furry friends on the back seat, after a brief consultation, responded that as long as they could get out of this noisy, stinky car, they would go along with anything she suggested.

EARTH 6

Zack wasn't sure where to start. He had two assignments, one paid, the other voluntary if you could call it that. Thinking about it, he realized that Petuccini's task was the easier: he had to find out if those people had actually met. How hard could it be with his Time Scope?

He looked up both addresses on Google Earth to obtain the space coordinates, then set up a random search pattern at the two locations, at different times on different days, hoping to get lucky and spot either one leaving or arriving.

After two days of staring at the monitor, Zack decided to automate the process and save himself from the crimped neck that was fast developing. His computer had face-recognition software, so he scanned in the two photos Petuccini had given him and aimed the computer's high-resolution camera at the screen of the Scope. Programming the software to sound an audio alarm if a match was found was no problem at all. Now he could relax and let his gadgets do the work. He was warming up his TV dinner when the phone rang.

"Hi Zack, how is it going?" Suzy's voice was full of excitement and anticipation.

"I just got started and it's too early to tell, but you won't believe what I'm working on!" He couldn't resist bragging about his first paying job.

"Zack, that's wonderful! I'm so happy for you!" she enthused. "Can I come over and watch? Please? Pretty please?"

Zack didn't have the heart to say no; besides, he was ready to resume their activity on the sofa a few days ago. She arrived half an hour later.

Zack explained the setup and how it was automated, so they would have time for some fun while the computer watched the screen.

"That's men for you," Susan sighed in exasperation, "they'll do anything to avoid work!"

"You don't think 'fun' could be work? I think it's hard aerobic exercise. Good for your health!"

Before Susan could answer, a loud beep from the computer made them rush over to the Scope. They got there barely in time for Zack to zoom in on the moving figure and press the Track knob.

John Wasserman walked across the parking lot and got in his car. The Scope followed him to a nearby strip mall, apparently to buy something at the pharmacy, and then drive back to his office in the casino.

"That sucks!" Susan sounded disappointed.

"You can't expect to hit the jackpot on the first try," Zack cautioned. "this will take some time. I've been watching this guy for two days now and it might take another two before I catch him red-handed."

"Or not," Susan was still morose, seeing no immediate result. "I guess you just have to keep doing it. At least you don't get gum on your shoes with this setup," she giggled. "So, what do you want to do now?"

"You know what I want to do now," Zack rolled his eyes, liberated two bottles of Labatt's beer from the fridge, and turned on the music as he passed his stereo. He had prepared for her arrival the minute she said she was coming.

This became an enjoyable routine for both in the following evenings, only interrupted by the occasional beep from the computer when the software recognized one or the other of his quarries on the screen.

Before each new session, Zack adjusted the space and time coordinates, alternating between the two addresses. If Petuccini's suspicion was justified, sooner or later, he was bound to record some action. It took two more evenings of diligent watching before something happened. They were tracking Markos as he drove to a different plaza from the one where he usually shopped. They saw him pull into the parking lot, and then sit in his car. After a short while, a dark green Toyota parked beside him and the driver, a young man with blond hair, joined Markos on the passenger seat. Before they could identify the face, the computer beeped again. It was Petuccini's manager. They had confirmation of the meeting; all they needed now was to prove it.

Zack didn't know if he could zoom close enough to the windshield to see both faces together, but he tried and finally got a clear picture. With his camera already mounted on a tripod, he filmed the two in animated conversation.

"If only I had lip-reading software," Zack shook his head regretfully, "I could find out what they're talking about."

After a few minutes of filming, he saw the men shake hands and part company. Zack quickly panned back and had a good shot of the two cars side by side, making sure it included a clear image of both license plates. From the Time knob, he copied down the actual date and time when the meeting took place.

"The money's in the bank, Suzy," Zack said mischievously. "what do you say we celebrate in style?"

Suzy chased him to the sofa and jumped into his lap, kissing his triumphant face. "Don't you have another assignment from the senator to start on?" she teased. They both knew that they had other plans for the rest of the evening.

~

Petuccini was impressed. The video Zack had given him was conclusive evidence of his manager's betrayal. Now he had to decide how to handle it. Suddenly, he realized what he wanted to do more than anything: discuss it with Maria - preferably after the reunion they usually enjoyed following a trip of more than a few days. Three hours later, back in his own bedroom, he did exactly that.

"That low-life! That rotten snake!" she exclaimed. "He owes you everything after you gave him a job when nobody else would! You trusted him and this is how he repays you!"

After a few minutes of calming herself, she asked the simple question that Petuccini had been asking himself all the way home from Washington. "What are you going to do?"

"I don't know, Maria, I can't make up my mind and that's what bothers me most."

"Well, how about: you fire the bastard, put Carlos in charge for a couple of weeks, and go away with me on a vacation, so you can really think it over without undue haste? "

"A vacation? I haven't had one of those for a very long time," Petuccini said wistfully. "Do you think it would be wise?"

"Wiser than making an impulsive decision that may affect your whole life," Maria replied. "It's almost winter and I've heard that Porto Vallarta is particularly pretty this time of the year."

"I have to think, but it sounds very attractive," Petuccini admitted. "First I have to kick that creep out and then choose someone to put in his place temporarily. Carlos is a good idea; he will do for a few weeks. I have already got my choice for a permanent replacement."

"You *have?*" Maria's eyes opened wide. "Do I know him?"

"It's a *her* and you know her every time you look in the mirror," Joe chuckled at his own witticism, enjoying Maria's open-mouthed reaction to the announcement he had been planning for the last two weeks.

Finally, when she found her voice again, she asked more timidly than Joe had heard her speak before. "Are you sure? You think I can handle it, and not because we're... you know?"

"There is only one way to find out, cara, and you better not let me down."

"I'll do my best, but I think we really ought to take that vacation. After, we'll both start with a clean slate and a clear mind."

"Amen!" he agreed and that was the end of serious discussion for that evening.

~

Gordon Hopkins kept looking at the wall clock in his living room. He expected her any minute now and still wasn't sure how he would react to this exciting, disturbing, and downright scary event that was about to take place. Muriel, in his own house, and no telling what it could lead to. They were in their late sixties, living alone. *Do we have to stay that way? What if old feelings still have a chance? What if Muriel feels the same way? What if she doesn't?*

He looked at the clock again, wondering where she might be when the doorbell rang. He jumped up and hurried to the front door, expecting her, but found himself face to face with two large dogs, anxious to get inside, even if it involved knocking him off his feet.

Muriel tried to hold them back, but she was no match for Bearcub: a hundred-and-twenty-pound Great Pyrenees wasn't going to be stopped by a hundred-and-fifteen-pound old lady.

"I'm so sorry, Gordon!" she apologized. "You better let them out to the yard, before they go through the wall. They've been cooped up in the car so long that they need to be free for a while."

Gordon saw the wisdom in that and opened the patio door to two very eager dogs, who wasted no time getting outside to water his lawn.

"Come in Muriel," he invited. "Can I help with your luggage?"

When everything was inside and carried upstairs to the guest room, he offered her the drink he knew was badly needed after such a long journey. One large scotch for himself, and a gin and tonic for Muriel, took only a minute to pour, and finally, they sat on his leather couch, facing each other. Each waited for the other to start talking, and then they both spoke at once, leading to an embarrassed laugh that broke the mood of apprehension.

"Isn't it like old times?" she asked and then added, "with one big difference: we're both a lot older and wiser."

"I don't know about the wiser part," Gordon confessed, "but I agree about the older bit: my knees and my back tell me daily."

They had some idle chit-chat about her trip that gave them time to compose and organize their faces and their feelings.

"Tell me what's happening." Muriel started.

He briefly explained the new arrangement with the other two conspirators, adding that he now had a research assistant, so his exposure became significantly smaller, not having to meet with Petuccini or visit Zack's house more than once a week.

"I instructed him to look into Brady's activities and meetings for the last month, to find anything that I should know."

"There must be something," Muriel commented, "because the way he's been talking on the campaign sounds wilder and scarier every day."

"I know. It sounds to me, and to a lot of my friends on the hill as if he were gearing up for some kind of war, or revolution or I don't know what. His supporters are so crazy, anything can happen if he becomes president - as seems more and more likely." Gordon acknowledged with deep creases on his forehead, throwing his hands up in the air. "I'm preparing for the worst. He seems unstoppable unless Zack finds something that I can use."

"Let's hope he does," Muriel sighed. "But we can't do anything about it tonight."

Gordon suddenly remembered: "I haven't asked if you're hungry! I can warm up something."

"Thanks, I had a quick dinner on the way, so all I need now is sleep."

"Oh, you must be very tired," Gordon apologized. "Flying all the time, I forget how long a drive that is. Go straight to bed!"

"Yes, that would be wise, only, I need to feed the dogs first. Would you mind letting them sleep in my room? They'd feel insecure unless I was within sight and smell."

"No problem, I just put an old rug on the floor, so they can lie on it more comfortably than on the bare wood."

"Thanks. I hope we won't be too much trouble. Tomorrow we can discuss everything else we need to, but I admit, right now, I'm really bushed."

With that, they felt they had said everything that they were prepared to say, and, after a shy and cursory hug, they went about their evening ablutions.

Tomorrow, they both thought, *maybe tomorrow we discuss this very strange experience of being together, under the same roof again, after almost three decades.*

Norman Brady was increasingly annoyed with his campaign manager. Trevor Smythe was OK with organizing events, but he didn't have a clue how to motivate people. He wanted to play it safe, like everyone else, the same traditional shit people were fed up to the teeth with.

"Look Trevor," Brady tried one more time. "let's be clear on who's running this show."

"I thought I was in charge of the campaign. I assumed that was my job." Trevor rubbed his forehead with the back of his hand, trying to steady his nerves.

"Your job description says," Brady chuckled, "I know because I wrote it: to do what I tell you to do. Now I'm telling you to get off my back."

"So, you won't change your speech for tonight's rally?" Trevor was aghast. "You'll scare them to death!"

"Or I'll whip them into a frenzy they haven't seen since World War Two."

"But, how will it affect our allies? And what about Russia? And China? They'll be outraged at your foreign policy initiatives."

"Let 'em be outraged," Brady shrugged. "At least my actions, once I'm president, won't come as a complete surprise. It's time someone stood up and had some guts. We've been asleep too long, it's time to show them what we can do".

Trevor was shaking now. His boss frightened him more and more as the campaign progressed from one fiery speech to the next. He saw that it was hopeless, trying to steer Brady into a more moderated strategy. He began to wonder if it was too late to bail out.

"Trevor, you don't understand. You're not a general." Brady tried to explain to this clueless civilian. "I am. Four stars. I know what it takes to get results, and it's not pussyfooting and fence-sitting." His voice rose in pitch as memories of past frustrations came back to him. "I was restrained far too many times by chickenshit politicians! When a little courage and perseverance would have led us to victory, we had to endure humiliating defeat or stalemate."

"But do you think it's wise to alarm people? You could lose a lot of votes!"

"If I give them a vision of greatness, I motivate them. They'll vote for me".

"I know, but…"

"Have you noticed, Trevor, this is how you start most sentences lately?"

"What do you mean?"

"You've become a 'yes-I-know-but' guy and I'm tired of the 'but' part. Cut it out!"

With that order, Brady turned his back on his befuddled manager, leaving Trevor to see himself out.

Once alone, he went down the back hall, unlocked his private office. He reviewed the conversation in his mind and nodded with satisfaction. He'd controlled his voice sufficiently. Trevor had no idea of the depth of his disgust with the system he had served under for so long.

Being yanked back on the leash, like an impotent attack dog, by incompetent civilians, when I was on the verge of victory!

The thought was accompanied by a burning hatred for those with no right to call themselves leaders.

When I'm president, I'll show them real leadership. Just wait a bit more, push the right buttons in the right sequence, and then I'll be able to make a difference. My kind of difference.

He turned to The Map and resumed work on it.

~

Gordon and Muriel sat in silence in his breakfast nook, watching the two dogs sniff around the cedar fence surrounding the small back yard.

"They can't help it," Muriel said apologetically. "They're used to more running space where we...where I live."

"What did you say?" Gordon, startled from his reverie, tried to reconnect with the present. "Sorry, I was thinking about Brady's speech last night".

"I can't blame you, it petrified me too!" Muriel sighed.

"What was he thinking? Has he gone mad? You can't say things like that in an American Presidential election campaign! What's he trying to do, start World War Three?"

"I wouldn't be surprised if the Russians were preparing for it right now." Muriel shook her head and picked up the morning paper and read a quote from Brady's speech at the Orlando rally.

'It's time to assert ourselves as the only superpower left on the planet and stop the cowardly acceptance of rogue states like North Korea and Iran.'

What the hell does he mean by that?"

"Or this one." Gordon took the paper from her hand.

"The American military is the most powerful in the world, but we've had to fight with our arms tied behind our backs all through history. We must acknowledge our superiority instead of apologizing for it. We should use it to establish peace and order on this chaotic planet for the prosperity of our own people!'

This sounds like he's planning world conquest!" Gordon shook his head in disbelief. "And you know what frightens me most? His supporters loved every word and seemed ready to attack anyone he pointed a finger at."

"You and your spy boy had better dig up something to use against that dangerous lunatic, or nobody may be able to stop him," Muriel said in a hushed, somber voice Gordon had not heard since the Cuban missile crisis.

~

Zack slept in. After the previous night's celebration with Suzy, dancing around the table with Petuccini's cheque in the middle, he was still groggy, having only a vague recollection of how the night ended.

Senator Hopkin's voice on the phone woke him up fast. He had almost forgotten about the assignment he had been 'volunteered' for.

"Zack, I need to talk to you today," Hopkins said in a serious tone. "I'll be calling on you after lunch," he announced and hung up.

"Who was it?" Suzy asked, coming out of the bathroom, wearing his shirt and nothing else.

"I didn't know you were still here. Don't you have to go to work?"

"Are you still drunk?" Suzy asked, "it's my rare weekend off, and you did ask me to stay over."

"Oh, sorry, it's coming back to me now," Zack confessed sheepishly." that was Senator Hopkins. He's coming over. I've got to do some work on his project, double-quick, and I don't think you should be here when he arrives. Might be classified info," he added with a wink.

Susan rolled her eyes. "You guys and your secrets! Don't worry, I have better things to do with my weekend than cloak and dagger stuff."

Gordon Hopkins found Zack ready to proceed, sitting in his workshop, computer and the Scope turned on, notepad and pen in hand. He was pleased by the young man's sudden attention and serious demeanor because he wanted to impress upon him the importance of his assignment.

He briefly explained what to look for and why and pointed out that Zack was in a position to avert a major disaster for their country.

Zack, not much aware of political reality, nevertheless perceived the danger posed by the quotes from Brady's speech that Hopkins read out to him. He promised to start immediately and record everything suspicious.

~

58

Petuccini and Maria were doing something neither had ever done before: riding horses. In a Mexican forest, following a bunch of tourists uphill, toward a spectacular waterfall. At least, that's what their Mexican guide promised. He'd even shown an old black and white snapshot of the falls, with the cross of a diving figure in front of it, arms outstretched, halfway down to the small pool at the bottom.

"That's me, jumping!" he announced proudly. "You and I jump together," he grinned and nudged Petuccini in the ribs. "Great fun, you see!"

Petuccini laughed in a carefree way Maria had never heard before.

"I think I will watch you do it," he told Santos. "It will be safer!"

He must have impressed the guide when he had asked for straight tequila, instead of the various mixed drinks other tourists ordered on the boat ride across the bay. With a mysterious smile, Santos brought out a full bottle. He unscrewed the cap and dropped a small pebble in, then handed it to Petuccini.

"You get pebble out, you keep whole bottle," he challenged.

"How?" Petuccini asked.

"I show you," Santos said. He tilted the bottle up to his lips and, after a second, showed it to the American. The pebble was gone. Santos spat it into his hand, then dropped it back into the tequila. "Now you do it."

Petuccini tried. He raised the bottle as Santos had, waited till he could feel the pebble against his lips, cautiously opened his mouth - and promptly got his face washed with tequila. But the pebble stayed where it was.

"Neat trick, I have to practice it at home." By that time many of the other tourists were watching the show and laughed good-naturedly at Petuccini's failure. He joined in.

"Joe, I've never seen you this happy before," Maria remarked when everyone stopped listening. "You should seriously consider doing this more often!"

"I have been thinking the same," her lover admitted. "What's the point of being rich if I don't take the time to enjoy the benefits? I will give it more thought when we get home, I promise!"

The two weeks went too fast and they reluctantly boarded the plane to New York. Petuccini wasn't sure what they were returning to. *I wonder how the senator's research is going* was the last thought in his mind before he dozed off, leaning back in his comfortable first-class seat.

~

Senator Hopkins was wondering the same. He had been getting daily reports from Zack on his so far fruitless research into Brady's activities. Boring, endless meetings; drives across the country in a campaign bus; eventless flights surrounded by journalists; exactly what you would expect from a political campaign. Nothing to confirm his suspicions, nothing he could use against Brady.

Finally, he instructed Zack to concentrate on Brady's home and film any meetings with visitors. The theory was that Brady would want maximum privacy if he had anything, or anyone, to hide. A couple of days later an excited call came from Zack: "Senator, I think you should come over. You want to see this as soon as possible."

When he arrived, Zack had a dazed look on his face.

"Do you want to see the film clip I took, or watch it in real-time? I first saw it this morning, when I was tracking his movements last Wednesday.

"Show me in real-time, Zack." Hopkins nodded; his throat constricted with anticipation.

The 'Time Scope' was already tuned to the right coordinates. When it focused, they saw Brady talking to another man, stepping in menacingly close and gesturing angrily. When at last he turned away, Hopkins recognized the pale, stricken face of Trevor Smythe, Brady's campaign manager. After a few moments' hesitation, the young man quietly left the house. Brady walked briskly to the back hall, where he unlocked a heavy door. The Tracker followed him into a room furnished as a military operation center. Zack fiddled with the knobs and panned across the entire room, finally coming to rest on the longest wall, entirely covered by a map of the world, showing different icons pinned on various countries. Some of these icons were American flags, some were tanks, fighter planes and ships. Two were mushroom-shaped clouds. They could see clearly: one over North Korea, one over Iran. Zack adjusted the controls to scan the adjacent shorter wall, that displayed a gallery of portraits, all framed and hung in a neat row. Zack zoomed in on the images one by one: Julius Cesar, Alexander the Great, Napoleon, Rommel, Goering, Hitler, Stalin, Patton, Sherman, and MacArthur. At the end was a self-portrait in full military regalia.

The camera moved back to Brady, who walked to a closet and opened the door to display sets of different military costumes, hanging limp, waiting to be favourite of the day. They watched in shocked silence as Brady pulled out a jacket and donned it over his shirt and slacks. It looked very much like the Wehrmacht uniform of Hermann Goering, complete with medals. He walked up to Hitler's portrait and saluted smartly. It was the Nazi salute. Zack focused on Brady's expression which frightened them both: his face was distorted in a hateful rage, devoid of sanity.

"You have the film of this?" Hopkins asked once he was able to speak again.

Without a word, Zack handed over a small memory card.

"Thank you, Zack," Hopkins put his hand on the young man's shoulder. "You may have just saved our country, probably the whole world. All I need now is to decide how to use it to stop this madman."

"Good luck, sir, and I mean it!" Zack matched the senator's tone with a mature voice of his own. "I hope you succeed."

On the way home, Hopkins reflected that he would never forget this moment. The images were etched onto his retina and into his brain with frightening intensity. He was sorry that he would have to subject Muriel to the same shock.

"What are you going to do?" Muriel asked after she saw the clip.

"I'm not sure. I must do something, but I must think it through. I have only one shot at this, and if I blow it, tragedy is almost certain." Gordon replied.

"Maybe you should have a conference with everyone in the Time Scope project and hear all opinions and ideas."

"You mean Petuccini and Zack too?" Hopkins looked surprised. "You think?"

"They know about the device and the danger," Muriel seemed more and more excited by the thought. "What can it hurt to hear their thoughts as well? You need all the help you can get."

"True, but I don't have much time. If I'm to stop Brady, it must be soon, while there is some hope for sane minds to prevail. Okay, I'll send a message to Petuccini to get in touch with me ASAP. I'm told he's home and has had a few days to clear the vacation mist out of his head."

"Do that, Gordon," Muriel said softly, "and, if it's not too much trouble to host me and the dogs until this is resolved, I'd like to be included as well."

"I wouldn't dream of doing it without you."

They didn't need to say anymore, they were a team again, just like old times. Common danger brought them closer together.

"I'm only sorry for the dogs," Muriel added. "I'll have to take them for long walks every day, maybe the new smells will cheer them up."

"I can help you with that," Gordon volunteered. "I need the exercise."

~

By mutual agreement, they met at Zack's house, partly because the Scope was there and they might need it to make their plans, partly because Senator Hopkins still wanted to meet Petuccini in a neutral and private place.

The others were already in Zack's living room, sitting in their usual places when Hopkins and Muriel arrived. They had seen the video and were past the shock. Not past enough to take the danger lightly.

"What do you all think I should do with this information?" Gordon opened the conference and looked around the table. "The objective is to make Brady withdraw from the race."

"Too bad he has so much security protecting him all the time, or I could take care of it," Petuccini muttered.

"How about if we email him the video clip and threaten to make it public unless he stops?" asked Zack.

"He would just claim it was filmed in Hollywood by his liberal enemies," Gordon dismissed the idea, "and his supporters would believe it."

"What if we contacted Homeland Security, show them the video, and explain how we obtained it?" Muriel asked. "Never mind," she amended, "this is a dumb idea. I shudder to think what they would use the 'Time Scope' for, after."

"They'd never let me keep it!" Zack was alarmed. "I need it for my private eye career!"

"Relax, Zack," Petuccini chuckled. "None of us wants the feds to get hold of it."

"The biggest problem I see," Gordon explained, "is authenticating the video, without revealing the source. We *must* have direct eyewitness observation of that room. Preferably by journalists, for maximum exposure."

"Suppose," Muriel rubbed her chin thoughtfully, "someone in his camp invited the press to Brady's home? Preferably when he's far away, on a campaign trip. Show them around, including the 'war room'. It should be someone we could convince to cooperate. Maybe by showing him or her the video and explaining the risk?"

"I know Trevor Smythe, his campaign manager," Gordon picked up the thought. "He's a decent guy. He can't possibly know Brady's true colours. Problem is, Brady keeps the room locked."

"That's no problem," Petuccini sounded confident. "Give me ten minutes and I will take care of that lock."

None of them being able to offer a better idea, they agreed to leave it with Hopkins and hope that he could recruit Trevor Smythe to their cause.

~

Trevor Smythe thought it only slightly odd to get an invitation from Hopkins. They belonged to the same party and had met occasionally. He thought the Senator wanted to pump him for information about the status of the campaign. At *his home? Maybe he doesn't want to be overheard.*

His first surprise was Muriel. He knew of her and thought it was strange that Gordon's ex-wife would be present, but it would have been rude to comment. Anyway, estranged couples make up sometimes. Very soon that surprise was dwarfed by the real one they had in store.

"Trevor, I'd like to show you a short video. I ask you to look at it very carefully and think of all the implications before you react." Hopkins said and clicked the 'Play' button on his notebook. They watched the scene without speaking and continued silent for minutes. All the while, Trevor kept rubbing his forehead, unaware of doing it.

Finally, he found his voice and croaked out: "Where did you get this?"

"I can't tell you that, Trevor, but I assure you, it's authentic."

"How can I be sure?" Trevor was clutching at straws now. "Maybe somebody photo-shopped it, or whatever they do to create fake videos!"

The senator and his lady exchanged meaningful glances. She nodded encouragement, and he leaned forward to look hard into Trevor's eyes.

"Have you seen this room in his house before? Are you in his confidence?"

"No, I haven't. It's at the end of the hall and I never had any reason to enter it." Trevor said defensively.

"If I can arrange for you to see inside, would that convince you?" Hopkins asked earnestly.

"How could you do that? If this video is authentic, Brady would never let me in."

"Doesn't he trust you?"

"Not with sensitive material. Actually, he doesn't think all that much of me...."

"Then, we'd have to look when he's not at home," Hopkins said thoughtfully. "unfortunately, that's illegal - a serious crime. But consider the alternative."

"Assuming it's true, what would you want me to do?"

"We need you to call a press conference at Brady's house. When the journalists arrive, and the candidate doesn't pretend that you'd mixed up the dates, apologize and then show them around, including that room."

"Basically, you're asking me to choose between my boss and a felony. Some choice!" Trevor summarized their situation. "But if this is true, a felony might be the lesser of two evils. Before I give you an answer, I must see the inside of that room with my own eyes. Arrange that, and "I'll consider your proposition."

"I understand," Gordon didn't argue. "When would it be possible?"

"He's flying to Seattle the day after tomorrow, I'm to join him Friday," Trevor replied, after briefly looking at his cellphone to confirm Brady's schedule. "That works for you?"

"I'm sure we can make it work." Gordon stood up and looked Trevor in the eye. "Let me know what time and we'll meet you there."

"This was a major shock to me, senator," Trevor admitted, his voice not too steady. "I've been worried about the general for some time, but I never suspected anything this sinister. Don't think I'll sleep tonight."

"Join the club. We haven't slept much since we first saw that video." Gordon accompanied his guest to the door and clasped his hand in parting. "I'll be waiting for your call, Trevor."

"Goodbye, Senator Hopkins. And God help us all!"

~

Trevor had the security code to Brady's house, as he had to fetch papers, a speech, or a change of clothes for his candidate. The door to the back room, however, was always locked. Petuccini, true to his word, had it open in less than ten minutes. Skills acquired in his misspent youth were still at his fingertips.

The three men trooped in, turned on the light, and stopped in the middle of the "war room" – there was no other way to refer to it unless you wanted to call it a 'bunker'.

Trevor walked around slowly, examined everything carefully, without touching. He spent a long time in front of the map, studying Brady's plan for world conquest. With the end of his necktie on the handle, he briefly opened the closet to assure himself that the uniforms existed, then proceeded to the 'gallery', all the time shaking his head in disbelief.

"The son of a bitch really means it!" Petuccini exclaimed as he viewed the display.

Hopkins just stood there, by the table in the middle of the room, finally realizing that the scene wasn't a nightmare to wake up from.

There was a computer on a desk and scattered papers with handwritten notes. "Maybe Zack could hack into his computer and see what other excrement he can dig up," Petuccini suggested, but Smythe shook his head. "No need for that, I've seen enough."

Hopkins touched his arm. "Trevor, I know it's a shock, a lot to take in. But time is short. Are you with us?"

67

"Let me talk to the general, just once," Trevor pleaded. "I've got to assure myself that I've tried everything short of stabbing him in the back."

"I would call it saving your country from tragedy," Hopkins muttered.

"Maybe it's just a fantasy, a hobby. Maybe he doesn't mean any of it!" Trevor was almost in tears. "I must be *sure* I'm doing the right thing."

"All right, Trevor, but time, as I said, is *very* short. We're entering the final phase of the campaign. You know the election is in only four weeks."

"I'll talk to him in Seattle on Friday." Trevor's voice had a tone of finality.

They left the room and Petuccini carefully relocked it.

"I'm awaiting your call, Trevor. I hope you'll be strong enough to do the right thing. And please make sure you don't let slip that you're aware of his little fantasy!"

"Don't worry about that. If he really means ... all this...," Trevor said as they walked to their cars, "the bastard doesn't deserve my loyalty."

~

"You can be sure that I fucking mean it!" Brady barked at Trevor, who had spent the last five minutes trying to convince his boss to moderate his rhetoric on foreign policy. "I thought you had more guts than that, Trevor. It's not too late to replace you with somebody who's got a backbone!"

"I'm not worried about what you'll do as president," Trevor lied. "I want to see to it that you get enough votes to *become* president!"

"Don't worry about the votes, you chickenshit. Just make sure you organize the last four weeks with your usual efficiency. *That's* what I recruited you for, not psycho-babble."

"Still, do you think the possibility of a major military confrontation is going to win votes?"

"Have you heard the crowd respond? The whistles, the cheers, the clapping, and stomping? My people are ready for bold action!"

"How about the general public? The millions who don't attend your rallies. You need their votes too!"

"And I'll get them, don't you worry!" Brady was shouting now. "It's time to be *decisive*. I wish those ninnies at the end of world war two had more guts. We could have kept on going and demolished the Russkies. We had the bomb then and they didn't. Now it's too late, but we still can clobber the uppity kaffirs in Iran and North Korea!"

Trevor didn't need to hear more. He had his proof. After reassuring Brady that he would be his diligent and reliable soldier, he returned to his own hotel room and called Hopkins. All he said was: "I'm in."

~

The newspaper headlines three days later were in the largest font the papers could muster. "Presidential Nominee's Bunker"; "War Hero Closet Nazi!"; "Shocking Revelations about Front-runner!"; "General Plans Word War Three" and on and on and on.

The FBI announced an immediate investigation into Brady's foreign connections; Homeland Security denied any knowledge of Brady's secret Nazi leaning; Brady's party convened an emergency meeting. It was unthinkable to support their nominee after these revelations; he would have to withdraw. They had three weeks to replace him. There was no historical precedent.

Nobody worried about how the discovery had been made. Trevor Smythe's explanation of mixing up the dates was brushed aside as irrelevant. The photos of Brady's 'war room' and the viral video clip of Brady saluting Hitler's portrait, swept aside any argument. General Brady disappeared from the public eye, presumably hiding from the army of reporters who all wanted a piece of him.

When Gordon Hopkins was summoned by the National Committee, he didn't know what to expect. He couldn't imagine how they might have discovered his role in this mess, but he was still a little concerned. He was unprepared for what they had in store for him.

"Gordon, sorry for the urgency," Mike Sutherland, the party chairman, greeted him. "But we are desperate. We have three weeks till the election, and we need a new candidate. We can't start a new process at this point, must go with the most popular ranking party member. We overwhelmingly voted for you. Do you accept?"

Gordon needed to sit down. This was something he had never aspired to; never dreamed of. All he wanted was to retire and leave this constant drama behind. Suddenly, in his mind, he saw the Vermont forest with the log house, Muriel at her carving bench, happy dogs chasing each other outside on the leaf-covered lawn, and knew, beyond a shadow of a doubt that he did *not* want to be president.

~

The three conspirators met for the last time in Zack's living room. They had a decision to make regarding the 'Time Scope'. Zack owned it, but they all felt it was their common responsibility.

"So, kid, what do you intend to do with it?" Petuccini asked. There was more respect in his voice than he had ever shown that young man.

"You know my plans," Zack replied. "I'll start searching for my first...ahem... second client tomorrow morning."

"It's not that simple, Zack," Gordon explained gently. "This is a very dangerous device in the wrong hands and, now that we are aware of it, we want to make sure that it's used only for legitimate purposes."

"You can trust me on that by now." Zack objected, but Petuccini interrupted him.

"I have thought of a possible solution if you both agree." He turned from one to the other. "What if I hire you, Mister Dougall, as a technical expert in my casino, with salary and flexible hours, to supervise our security system maintenance and upgrade?"

"You're kidding!" they both exclaimed, but Petuccini wasn't deterred. "Most of the time you would pursue your own business activities, but I could keep an eye on you and on what you do with the gadget."

Zack was speechless, but Hopkins wasn't. "I have a counter suggestion. What if we set up a company for Zack, invest in it financially so that he can get a decent office and all the equipment he needs? Then we *both*," he looked pointedly at Petuccini, "can keep an eye on him, his device, and his activities? Would that suit you, Zack?" He turned to the kid, who kept swiveling his head from one of his 'mentors' to the other.

"That would be a lot better for me," he enthused. "I have no intention of moving to Ocean City or getting involved with a casino. If you help me start up, I'll give you unlimited access to the Scope and all three of us can make sure that it's used properly."

"Well, that's a thought... and a disappointment," Petuccini admitted. "But there is some logic and justice in this plan. Count me in."

"That's great, Zack because I would like to do some research for a book, and I need to check historical facts." Hopkins laid out his own agenda.

With all three in agreement, the rest of the meeting was devoted to discussing the new premises Zack would need.

EARTH 9

Norman Brady stood in front of Hitler's picture in his war room. "What would you do?" he asked his hero staring at him from the wall, looking smug, being the Fuhrer of a master race. Of course, the photo was taken at the height of his short and violent career, no wonder he looked smug. Brady knew that the confidence was justified: Hitler rose from obscurity to be the conqueror of the world and that was no small feat in post-war Germany. However, he had the ground prepared for him: the anger and resentment at the time were not unlike what the US population experienced now, so Brady should have been able to exploit it.

He was so close, only a few weeks away from final victory, before that horrible betrayal by his trusted campaign manager, Trevor Smythe, ruined all his plans. He had obviously underestimated that degenerate traitor, both in his political leanings and his resourcefulness and cunning. He still couldn't imagine how it was possible to film him in his war room. There was no trace of cameras, even removed cameras, anywhere in the house, so how was it possible? The angle of the shots suggested cameras installed high, just under the ceiling, but no matter how hard he looked, he could find no sign of anything attached to the wall or the ceiling - the paint was smooth without even a scratch or a nail-hole anywhere. He had to find out what Trevor did.

He must have had expert help; the idiot was too clumsy and inept to have accomplished all that on his own. He had tried to call Trevor, both at home and at his office, but his calls remained unanswered - for obvious reason. The snake was in hiding from his previous boss's predictable vengeance. Brady had to use less conventional methods to have access to Trevor Smythe.

He lifted his phone and dialed a number he had not needed to call for a long time. When the call was answered on the third ring, he recognized the voice immediately and, after identifying himself, he said "Matthew, we need to talk. Come by this evening, I'll need your help again." After his request was acknowledged and confirmed, he ended the call and went back to his war room, planning his next move.

~

Matthew Brewster, or Mad Matt, as he was referred to by the few people who knew him well, was a 6'2" ex-football player, with the build still visible under the layers of fat he accumulated after retiring from professional sport. His face showed signs of the rough profession: several scars, a broken nose, and mangled ears gave him a frightening appearance. He usually wore a leather bomber jacket, heavy boots, and a leather cap that covered most of his bald head.

He was pleased that the General wanted to see him. Lately, he found it harder than usual to secure paying assignments and he knew Brady was very generous if the required results were delivered. He had a pretty clear idea what the assignment was: the revelation on the U-tube video of his Nazi bunker couldn't be missed and he was quite sure that the General was after revenge of some kind. He couldn't blame the man, since he had been betrayed by a trusted employee and he wasn't the kind of man that would just let it go at that. He had no doubt that he could do it again, no matter what was required of him.

When he arrived at the address, well remembered from previous assignments, the General was waiting for him. He was shocked by Brady's appearance: the ramrod, proud military man he remembered was replaced by this shadow of his old self, who seemed 20 years older than he had looked the last time they had met. It was his eyes that bothered him most: The General avoided eye contact, even though his eyes kept shifting around the room as if he was looking for something. But the voice was still the same when he gave Matt his assignment:

"I want you to bring that bastard Smythe here, so I can find out who helped him and how he managed to have that video filmed in my locked command center. I don't want you to hurt him, unless absolutely necessary."

This sounded like a simple job: just pick up the guy from wherever he was hiding and deliver him to his ex-boss. A nice, simple, clean job and the General offered $5000 for a day's work. Matt couldn't complain. After he was given the addresses where Smythe could most probably be found and a photograph cut out of a PR photo, he was dismissed with the last admonition:

"I don't care how long it takes, just bring him here. Call me before you come." And that was that, Matt whistled happily all the way to his car. He sure could use five grand right now; his newest girlfriend, Carmelita, cost a lot of money.

~

Trevor Smythe was worried. His phone answering system had recorded five calls from the General in the last day and he was pretty sure what the calls were about. He didn't regret what he had done; somebody had to stop that madman and he was the obvious choice. He was still wondering about the Senator's success in filming Brady in his locked vault. He now realized that he might be in some trouble if Brady came after him. However, he couldn't think of anything that Brady could do to punish him, so he went about his usual routine and tried to forget about it. So, he was surprised, and not a little bit frightened, to find a total stranger in his living room. The stranger was a big guy in a leather jacket with, scarred face and bald head. He moved unexpectedly fast to stand between him and the front door, cutting off his escape route.

Trevor quickly pulled out his cell phone from his pocket to dial 911 but changed his mind when he saw the expression on his 'visitor's face. It was discouraging, to say the least. He stammered out the obvious questions that anyone would ask under the circumstances, half expecting the answer. It had to do with Brady, he was sure

"Who are you? How did you get in here? What do you want?

"Who I am is irrelevant. So is how I got in here. What I want is simple: I want you to accompany me to Mr. Brady's residence, so he can have a chat with you. You can walk with me to my car parked just outside, or I can carry you, it's your choice."

From the frightening expression of the thug, Trevor had no doubt that he wouldn't have a chance if he tried to fight, he could only be badly hurt. With shaking legs, he started to walk toward the front door, closely followed by his 'visitor'. He was told to get into the backseat after his captor handcuffed his hands behind his back.

~

Petuccini, on his way home, was mulling over recent events and what he should do next. "*I know Maria has been keeping things together, very competently. However, it just might be time to take a closer look at my business and decide what I want to do in the long run.*"

As expected, she was waiting at the airport and it was obvious from the way she greeted him, that she had missed him too.

"Well, how did it go?" she asked.

Petuccini was uncertain how much to tell her. He had promised not to divulge the existence of the device to anyone. But he hated to keep secrets from her. Besides, Hopkins had already told his wife. In business, a person cannot trust very many people. Having broken with his family, Maria was Joe's only confidant.

"Maybe it's time to think about starting a family of my own, maybe it's not too late? I wonder how she would feel about that?" This thought kept persisting in the back of his mind, during the drive home, during their happy reunion in the bedroom, during the evening news that they watched in bed. *"We can't be any more domestic than this. Why shouldn't we make it permanent? What if I ask her right now?"*

The news was wall-to-wall coverage of the Brady scandal and Maria was mystified by how that U-Tube video could have been acquired. "Someone must have bugged his room with hidden cameras," she speculated. "Who could have had access?"

"Good question." Joe managed to say, feeling slightly guilty.

"I mean," she persisted," how could they come and go undetected? And there had to be two or three cameras if you look at the angles!"

"It's a mystery, for sure." Petuccini was unable to find a more appropriate comment without straight-out lying.

"You don't seem to have much to say," she prompted. "Have you thought about this at all?"

"I have had other things on my mind, honey. We might as well discuss them now." Petuccini decided to dive in at the deep end. "We have known each other for two years now and have been very close for most of that time. How do you feel about escalating things?"

Maria was speechless.

"I mean to make our relationship permanent. If you think you might like to team up with an old scoundrel like myself?"

"Joe, what are you talking about? Are you teasing me?"

"Maria, I'm an old-fashioned Italian. I don't joke about family issues. I'm asking you if you would consider marrying me and starting a family!"

There was a long silence from the other side of the bed.

"Did you hear what I asked?" Petuccini was nervous now. He knew if she said no, that would be the end of their relationship. He could not live with rejection, not at his age and position.

"I did, Joe, and I'm still in shock. Give me a minute to pull myself together. I don't think I ever told you that I love you, but I do. I never thought that you might feel the same way, so it's completely new to me. If you're really serious, then yes. I would be very happy to marry you and start a family."

Now it was Joe's turn to be speechless. This is what he had hoped for and dared not expect.

"Joe, tell me now if you weren't serious!" Maria almost shouted the question. "If you weren't, we can pretend that this conversation never happened and go back the way we were, but I need to know your answer NOW!"

Joe finally found his voice.

"I was serious, Maria, and, unbelievable as it is, we seem to have just agreed to get married."

The rest of the evening and most of the night was spent planning their life together. Nothing else was said about the Brady scandal that night.

~

Trevor looked into the belligerent face of his erstwhile boss. He was handcuffed to a metal chair, down in the war room he remembered so well. After Brady's thug delivered him from the car and immobilized him in the chair, Brady dismissed him with a curt thank-you and a thick envelope that was, presumably, the fee for his capture.

Brady stared at him for a long time, his face a mask of hatred and barely controlled rage. Finally, he seemed to have come to a decision and forced himself to resist the urge of strangling his betrayer right where he sat.

"I want to know everything about who helped you, how it was done, who else knows about it."

Trevor, unexpectedly, felt a surge of anger replace his fear.

"Don't you want to know why I did it?"

"I don't care why you did it because I already know. You are a chikenshit closet liberal and you planned to betray me from the start. But I know that you had to have help because you are too dumb to pull it off by yourself. This needed expert help and I want names and addresses. Now."

He moved menacingly closer to the shackled man, barely controlling his rage. Trevor with a shaking voice shouted back at his tormentor.

"I am not a liberal and I served you faithfully until I found out what you were up to. I did it to save my country and the whole world from a dangerous madman who could have got us all killed!"

Brady lost all control he had barely managed to force on himself up to this point.

"You fucking bastard, you spineless, gutless coward, you destroyed my chance at greatness! I could have been one of them in those pictures" He pointed at the wall with the portraits of his heroes. "I won't let you get away with this, you rotten snake!"

Brady was a big man with powerful arms and when he hit Trevor across the side of his head with his fist, Trevor's head snapped back with a sickening sound and then hung down with blood seeping out of his nose and mouth.

Brady grabbed him by the hair, yanking his head up, shouting in his face:

"Names and addresses at once or you'll get some serious treatment!"

Trevor didn't respond and, when Brady let go of his hair, his head lolled to the side, making him look like a rag doll.

That's when Brady started to panic. He quickly touched the neck of his lifeless captive looking, in vain, for a pulse.

He stared at the dead man, suddenly sober, realizing that he had just killed his only chance of finding out who his enemies were.

He pushed the growing regret out of his mind, realizing that he had to deal with the body before doing anything else.

He picked up the phone, dialed Matthew Brewster's number, and left a short message, instructing his helpful associate to call him back for another assignment.

~

Zack and Suzy argued. Zack told her about Petuccini's offer of a job and how he had refused.

"Are you out of your mind?" Suzy couldn't keep her voice down. "This sounds like a once-in-a-lifetime opportunity and you *refused*? I can't believe it!"

Zack looked at his girlfriend with calm, steady eyes, something Susan wasn't used to. He somehow seemed to have grown up during the last month. He acted with a quiet confidence that was new to her. New, and very attractive.

"So, it looks like we'll discuss it now," he said. "I know that you always wanted me to have a steady job, but that wouldn't be me. I like my freedom too much. I don't want to be under anyone's thumb. An independent businessman is what I want to be, and now I have the opportunity. This is who I am. You might as well accept it because I won't change."

Suzy wanted to interrupt, but Zack wasn't finished. "Besides, you liked the idea of starting a detective agency. With the help of the Scope, that's what I'm going to do".

"Well, I guess, if that's what you want, I can't stop you. But how will it affect us? I can't change who I am, either. I need stability and commitment in my life. Now I don't have either!"

"I have thought of that," Zack said calmly, "and I have a proposition to make."

"A proposition, or a proposal?" Susan couldn't keep the sarcasm out of her voice.

"A little bit of both," Zack continued undeterred. "What I'd like to do is start searching for my next client, and I could use your help."

"My help?" Susan was surprised. "How?"

"I can't entirely rely on the Scope. There's an awful lot of legwork to do, and I think you'd be good at interviewing people – you know, like witnesses and suspects. With your mind and body, you can charm anyone into revealing information they'd never give me."

"Oh, sure, you think that flattery will melt me into a puddle?!"

"Seriously, Suzy, I would like you to consider moving in with me and quitting your job. With financial assistance from Hopkins and Petuccini, plus what I have left from my inheritance, we could live modestly for a year or longer even if no other money comes in."

"Seriously." She echoed. "You want me to move in. Aren't you afraid that I might never move out when you change your mind?"

She was still not quite sure how far she could trust him. This calm and confident Zack was new to her; maybe temporary.

"You should know I'm crazy about you. I've never looked at another girl since I met you. Next to the Time Scope, even way more than that, you're the most important thing in my life."

Susan was floored. She had not suspected this intensity of feeling from Zack; she had always thought that their relationship was a casual one, not for keeps: he was too immature.

"I need time to think about it, Zack." She gave him a brief hug as if to reassure them that they were still the same two people. "In the meantime, how about going to Google to start searching for rewards? If I see that this madcap idea has a future to base a life and a relationship on, I will consider it. Seriously."

"That's fair," Zack conceded. "But do we have to do it right away?" he asked with an attempt at a straight face. "We haven't had our aerobic exercise for a few days, and I may be losing my touch".

Susan rolled her eyes.

"Oh, you men never change, it's always pleasure before work with you."

"Let's find out how we can combine the two." Zack laughed and went to his bar to pour drinks and turn on the stereo.

There must have been something in the air that night because Gordon and Muriel were also having a heart-to-heart discussion in his home, as they watched the evening news together.

The big drama was over, Brady had lost his nomination, and a major disaster had been averted. The country was in the grip of anxiety over the upcoming election, with the conclusion almost certain. One party being without a credible candidate, the opposition's victory was guaranteed. Still, endless discussions and merciless soul-searching occupied the pundits. Questions of why no one had suspected for so long, and how the truth finally came to light would keep journalists busy for months to come.

Gordon and Muriel knew that their role was over and were happier for it. They didn't need this level of excitement and were ready to put it all behind them.

"Have I mentioned the caucus asked me to accept nomination for president?" Gordon had reluctantly decided to tell her, embarrassing though it was.

"No, you have not. Obviously, it slipped your mind! Such an insignificant tiny item of news can easily fall out of your head, at your age." Her eyes twinkled saying this and it took Gordon a second to catch on. "And did you?" she continued in the same semi-serious tone "Have you written your acceptance speech yet?"

"Take it easy, Muriel! You know damn well that they asked out of desperation. That nomination could only ever be a lead balloon, and they knew it."

"Weren't you even tempted? It would have been a feather in your cap anyway, win or lose, and the exposure would have greatly enhanced your career!" Muriel was now completely serious, offering Gordon an opportunity to talk about his plans.

He didn't waste it. "This career is over. I've made up my mind to retire from politics. I've had a long run, had some fun, won a few victories, made things a little easier for a few people. It's time to close the account."

Muriel raised an eyebrow. "And what are you going to do with yourself in retirement? I can't see you in a rocking chair, twiddling your thumbs for the next twenty years."

"You're right about that." Gordon plunged ahead, hoping for a sympathetic and supportive response. "I'm going to begin serious research into the history and meaning of the US Constitution for a book. It's time people understood the foundation of our country and our government."

"Why, that's great! Gordon, I can't imagine anything you'd be better suited for!" As an afterthought, she added. "Could you use Zack's gadget for that research?"

"As a matter of fact, I'm planning to do exactly that. And, incidentally, make sure the kid stays on the straight and narrow."

"So, are you ready to dive in and transform your house into a writer's lair? You should have a roll-top desk, I always admired those."

"Actually, I was thinking of a vacation before my term ends, somewhere quiet, to think things through in peace. My life has been somewhat hectic of late," Gordon said ruefully.

"I have an idea, for you to consider," Muriel's voice was hesitant and cautious. "Why don't you come up to Vermont and spend a couple of weeks? Plenty of quiet in the woods, and the dogs hardly ever bark."

"Do you mean it, Muriel? Don't you think it might lead to complications?"

"The only complications I can imagine are those that we consent to. We're adults; we know each other well enough. I will trust you if you do the same."

There was nothing more to say. They both knew where they had come from, where they were in their lives, and where they might end up again - if things worked out as they hoped.

~

After Matthew Brewster left with Trevor's body and another fat envelope, Brady was left alone with his regret over the lost opportunity. He cursed himself for the uncontrollable temper that robbed him of his only chance of finding Trevor's associates. Who helped that idiot to bug his war room and film him in his favourite ritual of saluting one of his heroes? It was just bad luck that they caught him saluting Hitler's image. That cost him the presidency.

If only he could have controlled himself a little while longer, Smythe would have confessed to everything. The man was no hero, he could not have held out very long against Brady. This hapless civilian had no military training and he would have a very low pain threshold.

Now he was gone and had taken his secrets with him and Brady was at a dead end. His career and his ambitions were in ruin and he had no idea what he could do with the rest of his life.

He looked through his heavily curtained front window and could see the reporters were finally gone. After days of camping out, waiting for him to emerge, they gave up their vigil and missed their opportunity to notice Matt's arrival and, most of all, his unmistakable carrying a limp body from Brady's house to his van. Luckily, his house was far away from his neighbours, at the end of a long driveway obscured by densely planted cedar bushes on both sides, so no prying eyes could have witnessed all the commotion outside.

What should he do? The only goal he could set for himself now was revenge. He had to find out who was behind Smythe and make them pay for the harm they had caused him. Was there any other way he could find out? The only thing he could think of was to get hold of Trevor's phone records for the past month and find out whom he had contact with. Maybe that way he would have a new lead. He knew exactly whom to call for help, he had contacts in military intelligence and had a friend there who could do it for him. The man owed him for his last promotion, so Brady had no doubt that he could call in a favour and get hold of those records. Whether they would reveal anything useful was still unknown, but that was the only lead he could think of. So, after looking up the number in his computer's address book, he picked up the phone and dialed.

~

Joe Petuccini and Maria were deep in conversation regarding their plans. After a few days of celebrating their momentous decision, it was time to deal with practicalities. While Maria was planning their wedding, having been given a free hand to organize the event, Joe was busy thinking about his own future. His earlier feeling of being tired of it all had returned with a vengeance, coupled with the memories of their vacation in Mexico, Joe was seriously considering retirement. It was time to start a brand-new chapter in his life, without all the hassle and headache of business worries sapping his energies and robbing him of the opportunity to enjoy his considerable wealth.

Joe always fantasized about owning a small island in the Caribbean and now he was in a position to fulfill that life-long dream. So, while Maria was busy talking to wedding planners, he started two research projects. First, he had to find a buyer for his casino empire, and then he had to find his island.

Finding a buyer should be no problem because the Markos consortium that his manager had conspired with had already contacted him with an offer that could be negotiated to reach acceptable terms. Finding his island that would satisfy his needs, and one that he could afford, would be more difficult, but with hundreds of Internet listings on real estate websites, he would have no problem narrowing down his search. But, before he did that, he decided to call around, in case one of his associates knew something available at a reasonable price.

After several calls, he got a lead. It was from his cousin Domingo, who knew of an island near Barbados, that sounded ideal for his needs. It was about 130 acres, with forest covering most of the gentle hills and it had a sandy beach. It also had a good size house and a natural harbour that was suitable for anchoring medium size boats. The only drawback was a rumour Domingo had heard that the island was used by arms smugglers. It was remote enough, far from the others in the archipelago, so it could be an ideal place for illegal trafficking of any sort. Petuccini needed to find out if this was true. The only way that he could be sure was to watch the night activities around it for a few nights. He knew exactly how he could accomplish that. If the result was negative, he could make an offer to the owner, otherwise, stay away.

~

Zack had some time to kill because Suzy wasn't ready yet to make up her mind to quit her job and move in with him. They had searched the Internet for unsolved crimes that offered rewards but had not found anything yet promising success, so they agreed to wait till one came along. Zack kept looking but got bored after hours of fruitless search and decided to investigate one of his own questions regarding the inventor of his Time Scope. He wanted to meet the guy who created this incredible machine and watch him build it.

"Maybe," he thought, "I can learn some new tricks about the Scope by watching him put it together and use it. All I need to do is get the exact space coordinate of the genius's workshop and then go back in time and watch the process of construction."

That meant another trip to the old man's house in Farmington, Connecticut. The place was 350 miles via I-95, a 6-hour drive if he remembered correctly. If he left early enough, he could get there, copy the coordinates off his GPS and make it back home by nightfall. He called Suzy to let her know that he would be away for a full day.

Suzy was curious about his trip.

"I thought you were working full time to find us a client?"

"I have been doing that for a week now, Suzy, and I need a break. I want to research the Scope to find out what else I can do with it and the only way I can accomplish that is by watching the inventor put it together and use it."

"What are you talking about, Zack, the inventor is dead, so how can you...oh, I see, you want to watch him on the Scope, and you need the space coordinate of his workshop."

"You got it babe and I'm happy you understand."

"Well, drive carefully and call me when you got home. I'm also curious to meet this guy and, if you don't mind, I'd like to watch it with you, at least for a while."

"I'll be happy to share this hunt with you; I think it will be a lot of fun to meet Mr. Inventor.

Zack rang off and started preparing for his trip when his phone rang. Senator Hopkins was calling him for an appointment to start his research for his book project.

Zack told him to come by in a couple of days after he rested enough from the long drive.

A few minutes after he hung up, his phone rang again.

"Never rains but pours!" Zack was rolling his eyes and picked up the phone.

It was Petuccini.

"Hey Zack, how's it going?"

"Busy like hell, Joe" Zack had decided to return the first name address in a similar fashion, except for the Senator. He wasn't confident to call him Gordon, besides, he was an old man and a Senator, so Zack thought he had to maintain decorum, out of respect.

"Listen, kid," Petuccini continued "I may have another assignment for you soon so let me know when you are free to discuss it."

Zack could smell money coming his way again and he wasted no time in telling Petuccini that he would be free all next week, except for one day when he had to meet with the Senator. That day wasn't fixed yet, so Zack suggested that Petuccini coordinate with the Senator and agree on the days convenient for both. Zack was completely free, so it was up to them.

"OK, kid" Petuccini agreed, I'll call you back when I have the dates."

Zack put down the receiver and stared at it for a few seconds, wondering if it would start ringing again. He liked the idea of people beating a path to his door because it meant money coming in. Besides, he liked both of his 'mentors' and owed them for helping him set up business.

~

Zack's trip was uneventful, he got to the place in good time and was lucky enough to find the old guy at home. The old vet was surprised to see him after he recognized Zack as the nutsy buyer who gave him 50 bucks for the useless gadget that he couldn't sell to anyone and was planning to take to the dump.

They had a brief chat about the inventor and Zack finally learned his name: Jack Bansky. Zack let the old man reminisce for a while but had to cut the visit short because, as he said, he still had a long way to drive, he only wanted to drop in for a minute to say hello, after he realized that he was driving through the same town where he had acquired his newest toy.

It was late at night when he got home and called Suzy to let her know he was safely back and invited her over for the next day to find Jack Bansky bending over his workbench, working on the Scope.

"I still can't believe this," Suzy confided her reluctance to admit that time travel was a possibility, even though she had seen it in action several times in the past month.

"Just make sure you don't blurt it out by accident to anyone besides our group," Zack cautioned her "because we might lose it forever."

"I'm not an idiot and you should know better than to worry about that" she retorted angrily but relented when she heard Zack's reply.

"I know that babe, and the only idiot in this conversation is me bringing it up."

"OK, so what time should I come over tomorrow? It's the weekend and I'll be free all day."

"Why don't you make it for lunch, I have a pizza in the freezer and beer in the fridge, we can watch while munching."

"Gourmet lunch, as usual, I see" Suzan laughed and agreed to the plan.

Zack was too tired to do anything else for the day, so he went to bed early and spent the night dreaming about meeting Jack Bansky.

~

Early next morning Zack had a hasty breakfast and settled down in his workshop, rubbing his hands in anticipation after he turned on the power to the Scope. He set the space coordinates to the values he acquired from his GPS during his trip on the previous day. For the time coordinate, he set it for two months before his first visit to see if Jack was still able to work there. He scanned the empty workshop with the Scope clearly visible on the bench but no sign of the inventor anywhere. He started going back in time in one-month increments, assuming that Jack would show up sooner or later if he found the right time before cancer incapacitated him. On his third jump, he was in luck: he found a young man at his workbench, fiddling with the controls of the Scope. Zack was tempted to continue scanning but decided to wait for Suzy because he had promised her to do it together. Since it was close to lunchtime, he took the pizza out of the freezer and put it into the oven so it would be good and ready when she arrived. He even set his dinner table with plates and cutlery and managed to find some napkins in a drawer. The setting was completed with beer glasses and he was ready for her visit.

He spent the next hour working out his strategy. He decided to keep jumping back in time to find the earliest moment at which Jack started building the gadget, to see every detail of the construction. Once he got there, he would start tracking forward, filming the entire scene to be reviewed later at his leisure. He knew that Suzy wouldn't be interested in the technical details, her curiosity went as far as seeing the young genius.

Finally, the doorbell chimed, and Zack rushed to the door to let her into his open arms. After a somewhat lengthy kiss, they proceeded to the dining room and had at the hot, steaming pizza ready in the oven.

Once lunch was over, they moved to Zack's workshop where Zack whisked the cover off his Scope to show Suzy the image of young Jack Bansky, in the last frozen image he had displayed before her arrival. Jack was seen in profile, with jet-black hair, steel-framed glasses, and a high level of concentration visible on his face.

"Suzy, meet Jack Bansky" Zack made the introduction. "Jack, this is Suzan Turnbull, my girlfriend, and we are both very pleased to make your acquaintance."

Suzy nudged him in the ribs playfully and told him to stop clowning and start scanning, so they could see Jack in motion as he went on testing his device.

"Zack, this is so exciting, I still can't believe we are spying on a long-dead man." She exclaimed in wonder and Zack couldn't disagree with her. This was a technological miracle and they were watching the man who had invented it.

The only regret Brady felt for killing Trevor Smythe was over the lost opportunity to get the truth out of him. Now the only other possible lead he had, a long shot at that, was Trevor's phone records for the last few weeks before the betrayal. He must have had help and they must have talked to coordinate things and telephone conversation was the most obvious way of contacting each other. So, when a few days later he received these records from his contact, he looked through them very carefully, searching for a name he recognized, one that could conceivably be a conspirator.

Most of the names were party contacts, a few numbers he tracked down were to family, friends and utilities, and such, none of them looked promising. However, one number he noticed, after looking it up was Senator Hopkins's, two days before the media marched through his house. That wasn't impossible. He remembered vividly Hopkins's reaction when he had sounded him out about the vice presidency. Hopkins's shock at Brady's comments about strong leaders was unmistakable. He was also highly intelligent and not without resources, so it might just be possible that he was involved, maybe even organized the break-in and the planting of the recording devices.

These days cameras could be as tiny as a button, easily disguised anywhere in the room, and safely picked up later, without leaving any trace. The more he thought about it, the more promising a possibility it seemed. The question now was how to proceed. Having an American Senator kidnapped was out of the question, Hopkins's disappearance would blow up into the biggest scandal in Washington, and no stone, including his own, would be left unturned.

What else could he do? Brady spent an hour wearing down his carpet with his nervous marching back and forth, trying to come up with a plan. Finally, he decided to have Hopkins followed, on the assumption that others must have been involved with the plot, others Hopkins might contact again. Trevor certainly didn't have the technical know-how required for bugging his house, filming him, and then removing the cameras. First, his war room was always securely locked, and he doubted that Hopkins, or even Trevor, would have the skills required to open that lock, also without leaving any marks. Hopkins (if he was the one) and Smythe must have had others helping them, and it was conceivable that they still had some loose ends to tie up, such as paying off some of their 'experts'. So, if he had someone follow Hopkins, chances were that they would spot some of these people. Once he had other suspects, picking them up would be a lot less dangerous than going directly after the Senator.

The question was: whom to hire to follow him around? Who had the skill to do it without being noticed? Matthew was all muscle and not much brain and subtlety wasn't his strong suit. He had another contact in military intelligence that would do and he was sure the man could be trusted, especially if a suitable reward was offered. Having arrived at this decision, Brady didn't hesitate, he looked up the man's number and dialed it on his cell phone. The ball was now rolling and all he had to do was wait and hope that his investment would pay off.

~

Zack was in eager anticipation, expecting Petuccini's arrival with high hopes for another well-paying assignment. He wasn't disappointed because Joe arrived with a folder that he thrust into Zack's hand as soon as he was inside the door.

"Here's your new assignment, kid, everything you need to know is in here."

Opening the folder, Zack found photos of an island surrounded by clear blue waters. He also found a paper with printed instructions on how to get to the island, including GPS coordinates.

"Joe, you want me to track this island back in time to see how it was formed by a volcanic eruption?"

"Very funny, Zack, I don't need you to go that far back. My interest in geological formation is minimal at the moment. What you need to do is find out about the people who live there, their comings and goings, and their visitors, especially during night hours."

"What is it that you are after? Anything special? Give me a clue as to what I should be looking for."

"I am considering purchasing that island for my retirement and I need to know everything about it. The present owner has a connection to some weapons smugglers, and I need to know if it is used for shipping cargo and transferring some of it to larger ships. It has its own harbour but not deep enough for really large boats, so it would make sense that the original shipment arrives there in small unobtrusive pleasure yachts and, during the night a bigger boat could approach the island and accept the transfer under the cloak of darkness and then take off to the final destination."

"Holy shit, Joe, you want me to spy on arms dealers?"

"Why the concern? Can anyone notice the time scope zooming in on them?"

"Not very likely, especially by gangsters who have no way to detect the minute trace of radiation, if there is any that the Scope would bounce off of examined objects. I have no idea how this Scope works, the theory was way over my head when I tried to understand some of it from the notes and diagrams that I found with it. By the way, I tracked him down three months before he died, and I even know his name from his landlord. He was Jack Bansky and I intend to find out everything about him and how he put the Scope together. Maybe I'll find new features that could come in handy in my detective work."

"Sounds like fun, and you are perfectly safe to do this job for me. If you find proof of secret shipments, I offer you another five grand. Even if you don't find anything, I can still pay you half for your effort."

Zack was only too pleased to promise Petuccini immediate priority.

"I'll call you as soon as I have the result, positive or negative."

Nobody could have recognized the jovial relationship from the way it started all those weeks ago.

~

Gordon Hopkins was worried about Trevor Smythe. Nobody has seen him since a few days after the big Brady scandal. He had dozens of appointments in party headquarters and he didn't keep any of them. What was even more worrisome, he had not canceled any of them and it was so unlike Trevor that people started to speculate about it. That's why Hopkins couldn't help wondering if Brady had something to do with it. That man was crazy and ruthless and was unlikely to forgive his campaign manager without attempting some kind of revenge.

The obvious way, for him, was to ask Zack to spy on both Trevor and Brady, and find out what happened. In case Trevor was in trouble, he owed it to him to help in any way he could. Originally, he meant to start research for his book, but this was much more important and much more urgent.

He found Zack with his shirt sleeves rolled up, as he came out of his workshop and the Scope was on, so he was obviously doing his own research or, maybe, something Petuccini had asked him to do.

He explained his worries to the young man and saw the concern in Zack's eyes when he understood the situation.

"This is scary, Senator. What if Mr. Smythe was kidnapped by that madman? Can Trevor lead him back to us? Are we safe?"

"We won't know for sure until you find out what happened to Trevor and if Brady is involved somehow. I believe it's in our interest to put top priority on this job and I'm sure Petuccini feels the same way. Please don't do anything else until you find out. Until we know for sure that Brady isn't involved, it's better to keep our distance. If you find that my suspicion is confirmed, call Petuccini with the information, instead of contacting me. I'm well known to Brady, but he has no way of knowing about Petuccini, so we won't inadvertently lead him to you and the Time Scope. If Brady is involved, then Petuccini can let me know after you tell him to contact me."

"I'll do that Senator, hopefully, our worries are unfounded, but it's better to be careful."

~

Two days later Joe Petuccini received a call from Zack. The boy was almost incoherent, his voice shaking, barely recognizable.

"Joe, Mr. Smythe is dead. The bastard killed him! I saw it with my own eyes! What are we going to do? Is he after us now?"

Petuccini was silent for a long time and Zack almost panicked about being left alone to deal with this secret, but Joe told him to sit tight and wait for his visit to discuss the situation.

"I'll be there in an hour and then we can look at our options. Don't contact the Senator until we know what we should do. The fewer of us are in contact, the safer we are. We don't know what, if anything, Brady found out from Trevor Smythe and we must do more research on what Brady did next. Your Time Scope is going to be very busy for the next few days."

When he arrived at Zack's, the boy was still pale, and his hand felt clammy when they shook hands.

"I had time to think on the way here," Petuccini tried to sound soothing and calm, his top priority was to reassure Zack.

"The first thing to find out is how much Brady learned from Trevor before he killed him. How long were they together?"

"That's the thing, Joe, it was only for a few minutes. A big bald tough-looking guy led Mr. Smythe into the war room and handcuffed him to the chair. After that, he received an envelope from Brady and left. I saw them shouting at each other for a minute or two and then I saw Brady hit him on the side of the head. His head lolled to the side and he remained motionless. I saw Brady touch his neck, presumably looking for a pulse, and then just stood there for a long time, staring at the dead man. It was obvious that he was dead, the way his head just lolled to the side, his neck must have been broken. "

Petuccini sighed with relief. "Looks like the bastard lost his temper before he could find out anything. Just to be safe, can you show me the entire sequence in case you missed anything?"

"No problem, Joe, I filmed it and it's loaded in the recorder. I'll turn it on now and wait for you in the kitchen, making something to eat and drink. I don't want to watch it again if you don't mind. Once was once too many."

When Petuccini joined him in the kitchen, Zack could see that he was satisfied.

"I have no doubt; he didn't have the chance to find out anything. His rage and temper got the best of him. The question is: what is he going to do next? He is not the kind of guy who gives up easily. So, our job now is to monitor him continuously from then. I suspect that he'll collect phone records from Smythe's last few weeks and see if they lead him anywhere. That means that he may come to suspect the Senator, but we don't know for sure until we have observed what he will do during the next few days, find out whom he contacts, and see if any of them might turn out to be a threat."

"Shouldn't we warn the Senator?" Zack was still worried, but he was also intrigued by the challenge of further detective work.

"Not yet, kid, we have to know more before we alarm him with news of possible danger. I don't think Brady would dare to kidnap a US Senator; he may have him shadowed to find out whom Mr. Hopkins is talking to. If it turns out to be true, then we can deal with the situation much better. Rule number one: don't make any move until absolutely necessary, keep your opponent in the dark as long as possible. Good practice for your detective ambitions."

~

As it turned out, Brady's hired spy wasn't as unobtrusive as Brady had expected him to be because the Senator did notice someone trailing him wherever he went. It didn't take him long to add two and two together and make the connection between Trevor's disappearance and his shadow showing up a few days later. He managed to lose him for an hour and used that time to make a phone call to Zack from a public phone in a crowded supermarket. His worst fears were confirmed when Zack told him about Trevor's murder and Brady's activities after that, including meeting a man in his house. The man matched the description of Hopkins's shadow. He was also told that Petuccini was making plans to deal with this situation and suggested to Gordon to take a few weeks vacation, maybe in Vermont, after Petuccini managed to get rid of his follower and before Brady could hire another one.

That sounded like good advice and Hopkins wasted no time making travel arrangements. The next day, walking from his office towards the same mall, he was joined by Petuccini, walking with him in the same direction.

"Senator, all is clear now, your tail is dealt with and we can talk without being observed."

"Mr. Petuccini, I don't want to know what you did, hopefully, nothing lethal."

"Don't worry about it, Senator, He was just misdirected by a friend of mine and he won't be around for a few days, long enough for you to leave on an extended vacation until I figure out how to deal with Brady."

"Thank you, for taking care of this for me, Mr. Petuccini, I'll breathe easier now that nobody is watching me. And now I'll call Vermont and announce my sooner-than-expected arrival."

~

Muriel was more than happy to hear from Gordon and even happier to be told that he was planning to arrive the same evening. When she asked him why he needed to leave earlier than planned, he only promised to explain everything once he got there. This sounded mysterious and maybe even a bit alarming, but she was sure that there was a very good reason for the accelerated vacation plans. Since she had a few hours before she had to leave for the airport, she went back to carving the turtle that she had left unfinished when she visited Gordon a few weeks

99

before. Cedar needs to be carved before it dries too much and she thought it was time to get started.

It was so much more pleasant to be artistic and creative. She didn't have to fight back nausea she often felt when dealing with the power establishment. She could only wonder how Gordon managed to deal with them for such a long time. However, she knew him well enough to realize that his passion for fairness and social justice motivated him above all else and the few small victories over the decades that he was able to wrest out of the Washington jungle, was enough reward to keep him going. And, finally, during the last few weeks, he managed to make a huge difference for the whole nation, indeed for the whole world. That could never be surpassed. Muriel knew that this final success justified, in Gordon's eyes, the retirement he was planning and the immediate vacation he was to start tonight.

After explaining all this to Daisy and Bearcub, she was ready for the one-hour drive to Montpellier Airport. Her quickening heartbeat told her how eagerly she anticipated his visit.

Brady was livid. He was stomping up and down in his war room. The detective he had hired to follow Hopkins failed to report after a day of training, didn't respond to calls, and his mobile phone was turned off. Brady couldn't imagine how it was possible unless the man was noticed by Hopkins or his associates and they made him disappear. He was more and more convinced that Hopkins was somehow involved and this latest mystery all but convinced him that he was right.

When no word reached him from Sam, his hired detective, for two days, he started calling his other friends, trying to find out what Hopkins was up to. What he found out disturbed him even more. Apparently, Hopkins left on vacation the day after Sam started following him. This could not be a coincidence. Brady had to find out more. Further investigation revealed that Hopkins got on a commuter flight to Vermont and that made sense: his ex-wife lived there, and they were still friends, so Hopkins must have moved there for the time being, out of reach. There was nothing else Brady could do but wait for his return. All he could do in the meantime was wait and fume.

Finally, after three days of absence, Sam contacted him, apologizing for his silence and explaining that he had been following Hopkins when an urgent family matter came up. He got word that his son got himself into serious trouble in an industrial park and, when he rushed there, he was directed to a set of containers where his son was last seen. While searching in one container after the other, some idiot locked him in by accident and he had to spend two days inside, without any way to communicate because his cell phone couldn't get through the metal enclosure. He was just released because someone finally had heard his banging and crying for help. He needed the rest of the day off to recover from the ordeal but was ready to resume his task the next day. Brady told him to wait for further instructions.

Norman Brady wasn't at all convinced about the family emergency; the obvious explanation was that the idiot was spotted and misdirected by the phony emergency so Hopkins could leave town without being followed. His enemies were on to him and now he had to find a new way to flush them out and punish them, whoever they were. At this moment all he needed was the patience to wait for the next opportunity.

~

Gordon Hopkins and Muriel were sitting comfortably in their leather chairs, facing the large Franklin stove that radiated heat at them from the blazing fire inside. They had drinks in their hands, accompanied by two large dogs listening to their voices as they discussed their situation. Gordon was in a blissful mood. After the last few weeks and the past two days, this was a peaceful oasis that calmed his frayed nerves and gave him a feeling of safety and sweet familiarity. It brought back so many memories from the past when they were happily married, their whole lives ahead of them, promising accomplishments and adventure. Muriel seemed to be in a similar mood, judging by the relaxed expression on her face and the dreamy look in her eyes.

"Muriel, I don't remember when I was last this relaxed" Gordon confessed, "and this is so surprising, because of what has happened during the last few weeks and days."

He had told her about Trevor's murder and that shocked her as any unexpected tragedy would but, by now she had accepted it as the evil their world was so full of. Yet, here in this house, in the middle of her 100-acre wood, none of it seemed to matter, none of it seemed real. They didn't talk much about the future, the present seemed to envelop them in a safe cocoon where nothing could harm them, nothing could disturb the magic of this place.

She responded to his confession, in a dreamy voice, almost hesitating to say the words that were in her mind ever since he had arrived.

"You could make it permanent, Gordon if you wish. after you retired. It's up to you if you wish to resume our old life together?"

There was a question mark at the end of her sentence, and she was prepared to accept whatever he said next. His reply was immediate, without hesitation:

"Nothing would make me happier, Muriel, if this is what you really want."

"I guess we have a couple of weeks to make the final decision, I only wanted you to know that I am open to this arrangement if it suits both of us."

Nothing else needed to be said and the rest of the evening was spent in a blissful mood of comradery they remembered so well.

~

After Hopkins' departure to Vermont, Petuccini visited Zack again. The kid still looked anxious, which was understandable, so he hastened to reassure him about their situation and inform him about new developments.

"So, the Senator is out of town and Brady doesn't know anything about us and the Scope, so you can relax. I suggest you look in on him once a day, just to keep an eye on him, but otherwise, you are free to resume other projects. Like the one I asked you about. Have you looked into it yet?"

"Joe, you must be kidding. I hardly slept at all since I saw Trevor's murder! I expected some thugs to break down my door any moment."

"Relax, kid, if Brady knew anything about you, that would have already happened. He wouldn't have wasted time following Hopkins around. You are in the clear. So, get on with my request because I want to make a move on that island, and I need all the information you can find for me."

Zack, feeling a lot better than he had for days, sighed in relief.

"OK, I'll start looking tonight, but I also have other projects that I want to pursue during the day."

"What projects? Do you have another client?"

"I am my own client this time" Zack explained, with a broad smile on his face - the first one Petuccini had seen on him since the Brady problem showed up, "I want to find out more about the Scope by watching the inventor build it and use it. Maybe I'll learn new tricks that would come in handy later."

Petuccini slapped him on the back while laughing heartily. "You geeks never change, curiosity trumps everything in your mind. Just remember what happened to the cat!"

"I'll keep that in mind, but I don't think it's the cat's fate I have to worry about. There is still Brady out there with vengeance on his mind that's hard to forget.

"OK, Zack, call me when you found out what I asked for!"

Zack saw him out and then returned to his workshop, trying to decide how to proceed. Petuccini's project was a paying job and he should start on that immediately but, ever since he had seen Jack Bansky working on his Scope, only witnessing a murder and being scared half to death stopped him from further investigation. He decided to look a bit more before starting on Petuccini's request. His last thought before turning on the Scope was "Suzy would be furious if she saw me wasting my time on mere curiosity."

~

Maria Montrose was up to her eyeballs, planning their wedding. Joe left it completely up to her and she was preparing a surprise for him. Even though Joe had told her that she had a practically unlimited budget, she wanted it to be small and intimate. Neither of them had any family or close friends, so a large reception was out of the question. Above all, she wanted to be as far away from their usual surroundings as possible and the only place that kept coming back to her mind was that place in Mexico where they spent their first vacation together. She saw him as the happiest ever in their relationship and she thought that their wedding should celebrate it for what it was: the single event that brought them suddenly very close.

She rented a villa overlooking the ocean in Porto Vallarta. She arranged for the whole house to be filled with tropical flowers, exotic birds, and butterflies and secured the services of a local guitar ensemble that she had found on the Internet. She had a Catholic priest standing by to perform the ceremony. The only task remaining was to set the date for the event and decide whom, if anyone, they wished to invite.

She had been putting off discussing this with Joe for the last few days because he seemed preoccupied with business decisions and she wanted him to be relaxed and open-minded when she told him her plan. So, she waited, watching his mood for signs of relaxation, indicating that whatever his preoccupation was lay behind him, finally resolved.

She didn't have to wait long, in a few days he seemed his old self again, as they were relaxing in bed, after a mutually satisfactory indulgence in their favourite activity.

"So, Joe, what do you think about getting married in Mexico?" she sprung the question and waited anxiously for his reply.

She wasn't disappointed.

"What a wonderful idea, Maria, I have very fond memories of that place. How long would it take you to arrange it?"

"My love, it's all arranged, only waiting for your blessing and setting the date and deciding whom to invite."

"You little witch, you have already done it behind my back, keeping it all secret. What if I hated the idea?"

"I knew you better than that, I have never seen you as happy as you were down there, I was sure you would approve."

"Approve? I love the idea and can't wait to be down there again. When would you want to do it?"

"If you are free in the casino for a couple of weeks and no other issues are outstanding, then we could do it next week if it's all right with you. We only need to decide whom to invite because they might not be as flexible as we are."

"What if we don't invite anyone? Make it our own, private, personal affair?"

"If that's what you want, Joe, that's fine with me. In that case, I can make the travel arrangements. Everything else is ready and waiting for us."

Nothing else needed to be said and they hugged each other passionately, feeling the closeness of their bodies and their souls, completing the long road behind them, bringing them to where they were now.

~

Zack was watching Jack Bansky on the Time Scope, making small jumps back in time, searching for the time when the young inventor started building the machine. He was making small increments, not wanting to miss anything, but he couldn't see any progress on the Scope, it looked exactly the same, even weeks before he first spotted Jack working on it. He was getting impatient, deciding to make bigger jumps back in time, and still, there was no change at all until, after the last jump, suddenly the Scope wasn't there anymore.

This was totally confusing, not what he had expected. Trying to pinpoint the disappearance, he started going forward again, in small increments, until finally, he saw the Scope back on the bench. He needed to know how it got there, so he started scanning back again, making very small jumps, until he saw Jack Bansky driving up to his clapboard house and taking it out of his trunk. It looked somewhat different. It didn't have the plywood box as it did now, but some kind of cover with a smooth surface and a much smaller viewing window.

This was a total mystery and Zack started scanning forward again, watching Jack carry it into his house and set it up on his workbench. Filming the next few days, he observed Jack building the plywood box with a regular-sized TV screen and placing the mysterious object inside it. He spent days connecting everything together, then turning it on, and it came to life, just as it was on Zack's workbench now.

Finally, Zack realized that Bansky had not invented the Scope, he only found it somewhere and made it work in his own workshop. So, where the hell did he find it? Zack needed to know. He could trace backward with the Scope in small increments but only if the location didn't change. He had no idea how to trace back a moving target. However, all he needed to do was set the time back by one day and then wait for Bansky to start driving to wherever he was going to get the Scope. Then he could track him forward again.

It did work as he had expected and the Scope followed Bansky through the streets of Washington, through Annapolis, across the Chesapeake Bay on Hwy 50, and then across Kent Island, changing to Hwy 90 at Salisbury and then turning south on 20 toward Berlin, where he left the major road and navigated along some dirt roads to an abandoned archeological dig.

He got out of his car holding a sheet of paper in his hands, looking at it intently. He seemed to be following a map to some dunes, one of which Zack could now see, had a cave-like opening. The Scope followed him in, along zig-zagging passages into a larger underground structure that looked like an abandoned laboratory with workbenches and strange-looking instruments. He seemed to be looking for something and, finally, found a bench with all kinds of gadgets lying on it. One of these gadgets was the Scope. He picked it up, turned it this way and that, examining it from every angle, then carried it to his car and put it in the trunk.

Holy shit, Jack had found it and now Zack wanted to know how it got there, who invented it, and why it was abandoned.

He started scanning back in time in small increments, with the space coordinate fixed on the lab, and every time he looked, the gadget was still there. He increased the increments from days to weeks, to months, to years and nothing changed. He didn't know how far back he would have to go to find someone leaving it there, so he decided to be bold and jumped back a hundred years. Still no change, He never saw another human being, the room with the Scope looked the same every time. What the hell is going on here? He started jumping back a thousand years at a time and each time it was the same.

He was ready to give up, suspecting a Scope malfunction. Maybe it couldn't go back beyond a point in time and he was just watching the same image over and over. However, after the last thousand-year jump, the image changed. Suddenly the room looked different, with orderly benches in neat rows, with human beings moving around purposefully. Zack couldn't believe his eyes and, looking at the time setting of the Scope he realized that he was 51,378 years in the past. He couldn't doubt it anymore: he had discovered an ancient, technologically advanced civilization, the real inventors of the Time Scope.

ATLANTIS 1

Ivo walked briskly along the lakefront path, looking forward to another pleasant day in the historical research library. It was the first beautiful spring day and he had to fight the temptation to take a day off from his study of the planet's deep history. He even stopped briefly, looking around the tree-lined promenade, watching the birds singing their little hearts out. He regretted not being able to do both and, with a deep sigh he resumed his walk toward the building he had already glimpsed in the distance.

He couldn't slow down his research when he was so close. He was convinced that their planet wasn't the original birthplace of his species. All the archeological digging failed to show any signs of 'evolution', as if they had arrived from somewhere else, already scientifically and technologically advanced. He was determined to find out where they had migrated from and why. How come there was no historical record of this migration? Only myths and legends and lots of speculation. What he needed was concrete data and solid proof.

Ivo was a middle-aged man, pushing 75, still in excellent physical shape, although his posture was slightly stooped from long nights spent in libraries, poring over ancient manuscripts. His dark brown hair had a few strands of silver woven in and his old-fashioned glasses gave him a distinguished look. That look, and his pleasant, friendly manner, made him popular among the ladies at the University. He was a bachelor and that status gave him an extra 'what if' value in the eyes of single women on the faculty.

He was almost there when he spotted Jenna approaching from the opposite direction. He waited for her at the entrance - exchanging pleasantries with Jenna was always an enjoyable pastime. She was slightly younger, and Ivo found her very attractive in an understated way.

Her attractiveness was mostly due to her intelligence and personality, rather than her looks. Ivo found it very relaxing to spend time in her company.

Her face lit up with a friendly smile when she spotted him and waved a cheerful hello.

"Hey, Ivo, what are you doing going into that gloomy building on a glorious day like this?"

Ivo smiled back at her, holding the door open. "I could ask you the same question, but I already know the answer: we are both nuts!"

"You are, of course, right and it's nice to have company in that distinguished group. So, what are you after today? Let me guess, you are still chasing the elusive original planet. Am I right?"

"You know me so well, I can't hide anything from you. How about you? Still trying to plan the perfect curriculum for your students?"

"The plan already exists in my head; all I need to do now is put it together and then find a volunteer to test it on. You wouldn't be interested, by any chance? I would offer a unique lunch in exchange if you can tear yourself away from musty documents?"

A lunch invitation from Jenna was something Ivo couldn't possibly turn down. Her knowledge of quaint, exotic food dives was legendary.

"Any time, Jenna, just say the word, I'll line up right behind you and discourage all the freeloaders who might follow us to one of your secret places."

"Shall we say early next week? I should have it in a presentable shape by then. Assuming you don't hold me up with glib chatter any longer!"

They smiled at each other and then parted company, both proceeding to their destination.

Ivo's was the research library on the second floor. Having come from outside, it felt gloomy enough, with little natural light filtering through the few windows not completely curtained. Individual reading tables were arranged on the floor in orderly rows, each with its dark green-shaded reading lamp and imitation leather insert on the surface of dark-stained wood. Half of them were occupied by students and faculty, their faces hidden by the shadows.

Ivo liked this place very much because it was so old-fashioned. For a historian it was an attractive quality: real books instead of the viewing machines all other libraries were equipped with, it made him feel more human, not a cog in some technological contraption.

One aspect of his research had always bothered him: how was it possible that there was no significant change in his planet's history over such a long time as 50,000 years? Not that he would want any; he couldn't imagine what could be significantly better than living here and now. The people were comfortable, happy, busy in their various occupations, pursuing science, art, sports, and exploration. Who would want to change that? They lived in well-balanced anarchy where things just worked out through peaceful cooperation.

If they had a disagreement about an issue, they considered the pertinent facts and available options. Soon a consensus would emerge that satisfied everyone. Rational thinking applied to scientific knowledge would always point to a natural solution. The planet had everything they needed: the population dispersed in small communities, technology that could have spoiled their world with its waste, and other unpleasant side effects like noise and pollution, had been removed to the two moons a long time ago. Food production was mostly taken care of by automated protein-synthesizing factories and large-scale hydroponic farms. Energy production was all based on solar, wind, and tidal wave generators, clustered around the large ocean that occupied almost half of the planet's surface.

The climate was mild and pleasant with enough variety of four seasons, so no one got too bored with unchanging weather, or threatened by extremes of one kind or another. Ivo couldn't see any reason anyone would

112

want to change all that. But it still bothered him because, if his theory of past migration proved correct, their ancestors must have given up on their original planet and taken to the stars in search of something better.

He wanted to know what caused it. For his peace of mind, he needed to know that no similar tragedy was lurking in their own future. However, he first had to find actual proof that such migration had taken place. With a big sigh over the magnitude of his task, he went to a research terminal and started a query for myths and legends pertaining to their history. He wanted to know if any existing document, hidden away somewhere, could explain the origin of these fables.

~

Unknown to Ivo, help for his research was already on the way. Two floors above him, in the Physics Research Library, a young man was trying to find some documents to support a rumour he had heard of an ancient invention that allowed time travel back to the past, in a viewing capacity, that would allow the operator to observe events as they took place. Judd was a scientist researching information dispersal and he was fascinated by the possibility of another great conservation theory to be added to the well-known laws of conservation of mass, energy, and derived laws like conservation of momentum both linear and angular. He was convinced that information was one of the conserved quantities in nature and, if this was true, it should be possible to retrieve dispersed information from the galaxy. He had come across the description of a very old device that utilized this conservation principle to allow adjusting space and time coordinates to pinpoint an event in the past and then trace the sequence of visual information through time and space as it evolved.

Judd was a young man of only 45, having just earned his second degree, eager to dive into actual research instead of the endless studying for exams. He had bright red hair, a long and narrow face that often fractured into a wide grin and he was well known for his booming laugh. He found most things and most people funny on some level, which motivated him to indulge in practical jokes and pranks that he was both admired for by his peers and dreaded by his victims. The only two things he was serious about were Physics and cave exploration.

At the moment it was Physics that occupied his mind. How could he trace down this elusive rumour? He needed a historian, experienced in researching ancient documents and he knew exactly how to accomplish this task. He would have to ask the entire faculty of the history department and see if anyone would bite. Of course, he had to do it in an unauthorized but creative way by introducing a virus into the database of the history research library, so the question would pop up on monitors any time someone entered a query. Judd was chuckling into his drink when he thought of the many responses he could expect, once the virus was active. Wisely, he never identified himself, only directed responses to an untraceable mailbox that he could examine later. Once a positive suggestion was made (that had nothing to do with his ancestry or his longevity) he would deactivate the virus and contact the sender of the mail. It would take him a few days to get everything ready and wait for the answers to start pouring in.

~

Ivo spent the day in a fruitless search and decided that enough was enough. He needed a break to clear his head and think of a fresh approach. That break manifested by the invitation he received from Jenna to the promised

114

lunch the next day. She was a bit mysterious about the location but promised it to be both educational and enjoyable. Ivo's curiosity was properly aroused by the time they met the next day, and he had thought he was prepared for anything. Little did he know. When they met at the promenade as had been arranged, she only asked one question.

"Ivo, let me know if you want the educational part or the enjoyable part first." Her question was accompanied by a mysterious smirk.

"I'm not yet hungry, so let's do the education part before I can really dig into some good food." Ivo laughed at the secretive arrangement.

"Are you sure it's wise?" Jenna laughed "because the educational part might spoil your appetite. You might want to eat first before risking my version of Physics demonstration."

"Who am I to argue, it's your show, lead on."

"Tell you what, I'll explain first what the demonstration would be about then you can decide with full knowledge of the risk involved."

"Now who is overly cautious this time? Ivo laughed.

"I am experimenting with a new way of teaching basic principles to freshman students and my theory is based on a practical demonstration. All my students have heard of multiverses where the laws of nature can be wildly different from this universe. I want to exploit this idea and will instruct each student to design a universe where one of our laws is replaced by a new one. This way they will learn from personal experience exactly what role each plays in our universe and what it would be like if it was different."

"Wow!" Ivo exclaimed "what an original idea! Question: How will you actually demonstrate what this altered universe would look like? Computer simulation?"

"Much better than that, Ivo, in my lab I set up an experiment where you can make the change in a localized way and see what happens. As a demonstration, my lab has a chamber that turns the law of universal gravitation on its head. It will result in a universal anti-gravity law where every material object inside the chamber will repel every other one. You want to try?"

"I see why you said that the educational part might affect my appetite." Ivo burst out laughing, wiping tears out of his eyes, while Jenna was waiting for his answer with a satisfied grin on her face.

"OK, you win, let's go and eat first, and then I want to see that anti-gravity chamber."

The restaurant they went to was a new place that Ivo had heard about but had never visited before. It advertised itself as a testing ground for new culinary ideas where each guest was required to enter a list of ingredients to his or her meal and any special instructions on how to prepare it. After that, the computer would generate a recipe and prepare the meal accordingly. After all the meals were prepared, the restaurant displayed them in a buffet arrangement and each patron was free to sample as many of the dishes as desired. When they were finished, they had to vote for their top three preferences and the top three overall winners would be included in the restaurant's permanent menu. This was a very popular game and you had to make a reservation for the once-a-week event.

This promised to be great fun and, for two hours they created and sampled the most exotic dishes anyone had ever heard of. Ivo's recipe of mushrooms, garlic, cottage cheese, and curry won third prize and lots of praise from the other guests. Jenna was particularly pleased with his enthusiastic participation and promised to invite him again to other venues he had never visited before.

"Well, now, are you ready for the educational part?"

"Absolutely, if you promise I don't have to do somersaults in your anti-gravity environment. My lunch might disagree with the exercise!"

"Not now, you overly cautious historian," Jenna laughed "this time you'll have the pleasure of watching others make total fools of themselves. It will be your turn next time."

Ivo sighed a huge sigh of relief, in an exaggerated way, but curiosity prompted his next question: "Who are the hapless experimental rabbits?"

"Who else? Have you ever thought of what graduate students are for?"

"I'm a historian, all I can do with my graduate students is make them index musty documents, as you called them."

"Then you are missing all the fun a Physicist can have with the poor slaves."

They arrived at her floor and walked down a long corridor to the labs at the back. The place they stopped at was the window of a chamber of about 10'x10'x10' completely empty except for two young students of the opposite sex who were circling each other in a grotesque swaying kind of way, trying to touch each other and failing miserably.

"They are not repulsed by the walls, the floor and the roof of the cage, so they don't float up to the center of the room as would otherwise happen, but they are gravitationally repelled by each other's bodies" Jenna explained "but their assignment is what I called 'the first kiss'. They will have to keep trying until they find a way to accomplish that."

Ivo didn't remember when he laughed so hard, watching the two young people desperately trying to bring their lips together, only to be thwarted in the last second. They tried to grab each others' clothes to pull themselves together, but the clothes were also repulsed from their bodies, ballooning out, and avoiding their grasping fingers. Finally, after fifteen minutes, the girl decided to pull out all the stops and wrapped her legs around his waist, her arms around his neck, and pulled with all her might against the repulsive force until their lips finally met.

Jenna started clapping and, pulling a remote out of her lab coat pocket, she pressed a button. Both students

117

gratefully sank to the floor and celebrated their release with a proper kiss and showed no sign of wanting to break it any time soon.

"So, what do you think about my way of teaching Physics?"

"I wish someone taught me Physics like this when I was an undergrad. I would have never chosen History as my major! Especially if a pretty girl was provided for the demonstration. I would have volunteered every time."

It was time to go back to their interrupted work. Ivo felt completely rejuvenated, ready to start a new line of inquiry. However, when he turned on his terminal and entered his research query, he got a bit of a surprise. The message displayed, replacing the expected acknowledgment of his request, simply read: "I need assistance from a historian who can help me find an ancient document regarding a long-forgotten invention, that allows limited time travel. Please volunteer by sending mail to the following address..."

This was either a hoax in very bad taste or a glimmer of hope for his own quest. Without hesitation, he entered his name and contact information and sent it off as requested. Now all he had to do was wait and see if this was a stupid joke or had any kind of possibility that he couldn't afford to miss.

Zack was determined to follow up on the newly discovered mystery. Who were those ancient people 50,000 years ago who invented the Time Scope? What happened to them? How come no trace of them had ever been found by all those archeologists digging all over the place? How did Jack Bansky get hold of the map that led him to the secret chamber underground? He was just about to launch a new tracking session when his doorbell rang. He was annoyed to be jolted out of his very enjoyable detective work and yanked the door open, ready to discourage the intruder, but he quickly changed his mind when he saw Suzy standing in the doorway. They hadn't talked since he had told her about Petuccini's request for another search on his behalf.

He felt a pang of guilt because he had not made any progress on it and was quite sure Suzy wanted to know how his investigation was progressing. So, he greeted her more effusively than usual, inviting her in and offering her coffee and cookies.

"Never mind the bribe, Zack, I want to know how your job is going."

"Well, Suzy, please don't be mad, but I haven't started it yet." Zack blurted out, with a sheepish expression on his face.

"Why not, Zack? It's been three days! What have you been doing all this time? I thought you wanted to convince me that this mad scheme of making a living with detective work had a future?"

"Suzy, you won't believe what I discovered!"

Zack went into an enthusiastic description of his search for the origin of the Time Scope and finding the ancient civilization that invented it. He kept looking at Suzan, hoping for a sign of matching enthusiasm, but all he could see were signs of anger mixed with worry over the implications of his confession.

"I was hoping that you had become more mature in the last few months, mature enough to base a future on, but I see you are still following your whims wherever they take you. This isn't what we agreed to when I told you I would consider moving in with you and starting this business."

Zack tried to interrupt her, but she held up her hand in a forbidding fashion.

"I'm not finished yet and I have a problem with your attitude. Based on the prospect of another paying job from Petuccini, I quit my job, ready to start working with you in two weeks time after the notice I had to give. Now it may be too late to change my mind about the nursery and I may have to start looking for another job, thanks to you!"

She was wiping a tear away from her face and Zack felt horrible about disappointing her.

"Please don't look for another job, I'll start working on Petuccini's project right away and promise you I'll take our future business very seriously. My curiosity about the Time Scope got the better of me and discovering that old civilization just about blew my mind. You have to admit, it is sensational news and I still don't know what to do about it but, believe me, its importance is miles behind my commitment to our future together."

Suzy looked at him with uncertainty, wanting to believe him, but worried about another relapse into immature playing with toys, instead of building their future. However, his discovery of that ancient world did impress her, despite herself.

"Zack, this is your last chance. Follow through with Petuccini's request and then we must sit down and map out our plan to build up this business. I won't withdraw the notice I gave my company unless I see another relapse. With that stern warning, she turned around and walked out of his house.

Zack was flabbergasted, jolted into a firm resolve to reassure Suzy that he was serious about their future. The ancient civilization had to wait till they were well into establishing the detective agency. He mused over the irony of his eagerness to follow up that mystery: "They could wait for 50,000 years; they can wait a bit longer" he thought.

~

Brady was ready to explode when the result of the presidential election was announced. The election that he should have won, would have won but for the betrayal of the late Trevor Smythe. At least the bastard wasn't around anymore to do more harm, but now Brady had to deal with this new reality: another bleeding-heart liberal Democrat was elected to become President. This was impossible to swallow; he would have to do something to save the country from this degenerate.

His failed attempt to find and punish the conspirators who had managed to thwart his political ambition made him even angrier. The frustration with being stopped made him determined to prevail over idiots, cowards, and traitors.

He spent the rest of the day in his war room, making plans, compiling lists of names and resources he would need to put his plan, once he completed it, into action.

~

Before starting his research into possible arms dealing on Petuccini's island, despite his solemn promise to Suzy, Zack had to do one more thing about his discovery of 'Atlantis' as he came to call the ancient civilization in his mind. He just had to tell someone, or he was in serious danger of his head exploding, so he called Senator Hopkins in Vermont. The Senator had given him his cell phone number in case there was an emergency with Brady.

Well, this discovery wasn't exactly an emergency, but Zack was sure that the Senator would want to know. He had no experience dealing with issues of this magnitude and importance and he wanted to pass it on to the only person he knew who could handle it.

When Zack finished explaining his discovery, there was a very long pause at the other end followed by a hoarse "Are you sure of this Zack?" betraying the Senator's shock at hearing this incredible news.

"I'm quite sure Senator, and I have no idea what to do. I thought you would be my obvious choice to tell. Now that I have, I don't intend to do anything more with this information, I'll trust your judgment whatever you decide. Right after this call I'll start working for my new client to shore up my fast-dwindling financial assets, so good luck to you sir, let me know what you decide."

With this final comment, Zack rang off, pleased with himself for passing this extremely hot potato to someone else, freeing his mind up for the much more immediate and practical task of earning Petuccini's commission.

He had the GPS coordinates of the island and set the time coordinate to 12 AM, one month before, and pressed the 'Scan' button. It took him a while to move his 'camera' in position at the island's harbour and adjust it to have a clear view of the entrance from the sea and the exit via land. At the moment no one was visible, the place looked dark and deserted. He could see one building by the road leading to the harbour, but all was quiet, all windows dark, no sign of any activity. He had not really expected anything else, so he programmed the computer to alert him if the camera detected any motion in the frame displayed, so he wouldn't have to watch it continuously. He turned on some music and retrieved a Labatt from the fridge.

Nothing happened during the night he was watching. He adjusted the time coordinate of the Scope for the next day and repeated the scan. He had to do this several times with the same result. This promised to be a long and boring night. He thought of jumping ahead in half-hour increments but was afraid of missing something, so he settled down to listen to music, sip his beer, and read his latest sci-fi novel. When he had finished with his drink and got bored with the book, he decided to Google the net for unsolved crimes with a reward offered. He had to think ahead and line up a promising client if Petuccini's job didn't end profitably. He was sure Suzy would approve of this initiative and trust him more with their planned life together.

The usual long list of Google entries (32,600 results) came up as soon as he entered the search string "Unsolved crimes reward" into the Google search box and the fourth entry caught his attention: "Major unsolved crime rewards not enticing tipsters". He opened the page and the first paragraph was very encouraging:

"Six years. Sixty-six cases. Nearly $10 million was offered in rewards. And not a single conviction. The Nova Scotia Department of Justice created the Rewards for Major Unsolved Crimes Program in 2006 to encourage more people to come forward with information about the province's growing list of unsolved crimes."

Apparently, the program was created in Canada, but it might be worth looking into.

On the other hand, maybe it was better to look for something closer to home, so he changed his search string to "unsolved crime reward in Washington DC" and received a staggering 739,000 entries. He was on to something here. The third entry in the list of pages started with:

"The MPD offers a reward of up to $25,000 to anyone who provides information that leads to the arrest and conviction of the person or persons responsible for any homicide committed in the District of Columbia. Individuals with information about unsolved homicides should call the MPDC at (202) 727-9099."

He got this far in his search when the computer beeped, indicating some movement at the harbour. He quickly turned his attention to the Scope and saw a small yacht looming into view and two people waiting on the dock. He instructed the computer to start filming the unfolding scene and watched with interest as the yacht stopped by the pier, moored, and dislodged two crew members onto the dock. After a brief discussion, one of the islanders talked into a cell phone and a few minutes later a van drove down the road and stopped next to the pier. Zack watched, and filmed, as the four men started unloading boxes and boxes from the yacht and transferred them into the van. Zack needed to know if the boxes contained weapons and he had a very hard time fine-tuning his Scope to look inside one of the boxes. He nearly gave up when one of the boat's crew did it for him by opening a few and displaying the contents. Zack had no doubt, one of them was full of what seemed to be land mines, another contained automatic rifles. He had it all filmed and was ready to call Petuccini with the news confirming his suspicion.

~

Petuccini was disappointed. He would have to restart his search for a suitable island soon but, at the moment, he was more interested in his fast-approaching wedding day. He never regretted proposing to Maria but knew that marriage would be a major change in his lifestyle. On one hand, he was relieved to leave behind all the headaches and worries that accompanied the task of running a casino. On the other hand, he was concerned about such a drastic change in his life. He had never done anything else and now wasn't sure if he would find enough purpose in his life. Retirement sounded fine, but then what? How would he spend his days? What would he do? Marital bliss would fill only so many hours, but he felt that he needed something, new challenges, new goals, new accomplishments, and he wasn't sure how to find those.

When he learned about Zack's momentous discovery of that ancient civilization, something clicked in his mind, an excitement that he had not felt for years. Here was a mystery and he was intrigued by the conundrum. What had happened? Were they forced to leave? Could it happen again, here on Earth? He determined to follow this up with Zack's Scope. He paid Zack the five grand he had promised for researching the use of that island and now offered him another five to find out what had happened such a long time ago. This time, however, he wanted to participate in the hunt and accompany Zack, to reveal the answers to this old mystery.

Zack told him that he had told Senator Hopkins about 'Atlantis' and was waiting for news of his decision regarding this secret. They just couldn't announce it publicly without revealing the existence of the Scope and, by mutual agreement, it was out of the question. They decided to call the Senator again and see if he was willing to interrupt his vacation and join them in a conference to decide how to proceed. As it turned out Senator Hopkins was thinking along the same line and was planning to hop on a plane and join them for a discussion before any more plans could be made.

ATLANTIS 2

Ivo received an answer almost immediately, asking him to meet a physicist called Judd, at his earliest convenience. After looking up the name he realized they were both teaching at the same University and Judd, indeed, was a physicist, a youngster, recently granted his degree in Information Theory. This looked promising. Further research, on the other hand, was worrisome: several complaints have been lodged against him for practical jokes and pranks, both from students and faculty. Ivo couldn't, for his life, imagine how one meeting could turn into a prank and the mere possibility of time travel was too good to risk losing. He decided to keep an open mind, but a cautious one. So, he replied to the request suggesting a meeting in the university cafeteria for lunch the next day.

Ivo got there first and was munching on his sandwich when a young man walked up to him and introduced himself as Judd. The first impression was favourable, Judd had a serious expression, unlike someone bent on a stupid joke.

"Ivo, thank you for meeting me, and my apologies for the way I contacted you, but I was anxious to let my request be seen by the entire history department. Mass mailing seemed to be the most efficient way to accomplish that."

"Efficient, I'll grant you that, even if a bit unorthodox."

"I'm well known for my unorthodox ways of doing things. I'm sure you have looked me up and found all the complaints about my pranks.

He said it with such a charmingly innocent expression that Ivo couldn't help laughing in response. The young man looked so earnest and sincere that he started liking him despite his reservation.

"OK. Judd, tell me what this is all about."

126

"As I mentioned in my invitation, I'm trying to track down a very old document that came to my attention while researching the possibility of retrieving visual information from the past."

"What has it got to do with 'limited time travel' as you hinted in your email? You can retrieve visual information from the past by viewing recorded events in visual form."

Judd's face acquired a mischievous expression.

"Ivo, the information I'm trying to view isn't recorded anywhere, on any medium. I intend to view events as they took place, in real-time. You could call it spying on the past."

Ivo was intrigued because he saw immediately how it could help him in his own research.

"Why do you think this would be possible?"

I'm following up on an ancient myth about a mysterious device that could look into the past. I found a reference to it in a Catalogue of archived documents but could not locate the actual manuscript. That catalog entry referred to it as possibly a personal diary. I don't have any experience in tracking down historical material, that's what I need help with."

Ivo considered this explanation and saw a glimmer of hope for this investigation.

"Well, if you show me what you have, especially the reference to that diary, I might be interested in looking into it. If such a device were possible, I must admit, it would be a great help in my own research."

Judd looked pleased with his interest and wasted no time giving him the links to the catalog and the keywords he had to search for.

"Please look into this and let me know if you want to research it any further."

Ivo promised to do that and, after they shook hands, they both returned to their offices.

~

Ivo was full of hope. The link to the archive Judd had given him looked familiar and he couldn't wait to see if his hunch was correct. When he had started his research into deep history of his planet, he collected all the relevant documents from the Archive and they were still in their boxes in his office, stacked up against the back wall. He had started going through them one by one two weeks ago, but there were still two boxes he had never opened. What if Judd's diary was in one of them? Wouldn't that be a lucky coincidence?

As soon as he was back in his office, he wasted no time taking the lid off the first of the two unopened boxes. It was full of very old records, neatly stacked and labeled and he carefully removed them one by one, reading the labels and then putting them aside. None of them looked like a diary. When the box was empty, he carefully put everything back and proceeded to examine the second one in similar fashion. He didn't have to go too far because the third package he examined did have the look of a personal diary. Its label read "Age unknown, found in the ruins of an old laboratory building."

He removed it and then put the first two packages back in the box, closed the lid, and moved it back to the wall where all the others were neatly stacked. He carried the package to his desk and carefully opened it. He had a slightly guilty feeling for doing it alone, without the young Physicist sharing in the excitement, but decided not to tell him about it until he was sure that this was the one with the right information. Why raise false hopes until he was certain?

The pages were very fragile, suggesting ancient origin and Ivo handled it carefully. The language was unfamiliar even though he could make out a few words here and there, so he scanned the pages with his universal translator that historians routinely used when dealing with very old documents. Once the translation was complete, he had no problem reading the contents on the translator's monitor. The first line read: "Personal Diary of Assoc. Schum."

He skipped over everything that was of a personal nature, even though the author had been long dead, he didn't feel good about spying on his private life. He was looking for two different kinds of entry: any reference to the ancient migration and to the time travel invention. He found them together, close to the end of the diary. The writer commented on how unfortunate he was in not being able to take his Viewer when they escaped from the island. They were forced to abandon everything before a deadly tsunami destroyed their settlement, barely leaving them time to take off in their spaceships. Ivo could hardly breathe; he was so excited to hold this first documentary confirmation of his theory.

The last entry in the diary was a description of his year-long neutrino experiment in a deep cave laboratory, in the Trident Karst mountains. The last words in this diary were "to be continued." Presumably, this referred to the next volume because this one was completely full. If true, then he must have started a new one and that may still be in the cave where the lab must have been such a long time ago. If that cave system was still there and accessible, he might want to go there to find more clues to both the ancient migration and the time travel device Judd was looking for.

He couldn't wait any longer, called Judd's number, and left a message to the young Physicist to visit him in his office at his earliest convenience.

~

Judd was beyond excited when Ivo showed him the diary. "I know that cave!" he exclaimed "I used to do some exploring there years ago."

His excitement rubbed off on Ivo, he was almost sure of the young man's answer before he asked:

"One of the things I learned about you is that you are an experienced cave explorer. Do you think you would like to take a look?

"Just try to keep me away from it Ivo," he grinned widely "I'll start getting all the gear together tonight. Do you want to come along? It can be quite tough physically, but you seem to be in good enough shape for some healthy exercise?"

"Well, I'm not as young as I used to be, but if you show me some tricks in spelunking I would like to tag along. I assume going down will be easier than coming back up and you may have to haul me up part of the way. If you think you are up to it, then I'm all for it."

Judd laughed good-naturedly at the joke.

"I won't have to do that because I have a power winch that can take care of pulling us back to the surface. Hopefully, the cable is long enough to reach the bottom of that shaft. If not, we can always extend it with the extra length cable I intend to bring along."

"When do you want to do it?" Ivo couldn't believe how excited he felt about the prospect of this new adventure.

"It will take a few days to get all the equipment together, so what do you say to early next week?"

"That will be perfect. I have to take care of a few errands before we go. How long do you think this expedition will take?"

"Shouldn't take longer than a day, sir. We'll take my flier to get there because it has an adequate cargo compartment for all the gear we'll need and the flight there won't take more than a couple of hours. Then we'll see what awaits us."

"Sounds great and I think if we're partners in this mad adventure, you may dispense with the honorific. Just call me Ivo, I have been calling you Judd already and I'm not that much older."

The young man grinned happily and shook his hand before hurrying off to make his preparations.

~

The flight to the mountains was smooth and uneventful. Judd was a competent pilot and the flier was well equipped for passenger comfort as well as adequate cargo space, filled with mysterious bundles. When they finally landed, they were in front of a vertical rock face, their flier resting on a level area that would have been used as a staging surface when the cave was in use. An opening in the rock face was the obvious entrance. A few boulders were lying on the ground, presumably from past rockslides that dislodged them from above. Ivo looked up at the rock face, trying to guess if anything else was loose to endanger them, but all he could see was solid rock with some sparse vegetation in the cracks. Judd started hauling out the bundles from the cargo space and suggested that Ivo help him sort them out on the ground. Coils of rope and a rolled-up steel cable were the first to emerge, followed by what looked like the power winch and then overalls, helmets with attached flashlights, a huge power pack, presumably the power source needed by the winch, and a few mysterious contraptions that Ivo couldn't identify.

"The vertical shaft is about five hundred units from the entrance," Judd explained, "and we have to carry all this gear to the edge of that deep well. The next task will be to determine the depth of that shaft and then set up the winch with enough cable to reach the bottom. When all this is done, then we'll have to lower all the gear that we'll need down there before lowering ourselves as well. We change into these overalls and don the helmets. It's going to be very dark a hundred or so units from the entrance, we'll have to turn on the lights."

"Judd, does anyone know we are here?" Ivo asked anxiously "just in case we need help?"

"Relax, Ivo, rule number one in spelunking: make sure that you have alerted the cave rescue people to let them know where you are and what you are up to. We'll have communicators with us down there and I'll set up relays both at the top and bottom of the shaft and the cave entrance, so our communication line will be assured."

"Looks like you thought of everything!" Ivo couldn't keep admiration out of his voice for the competence of his young guide.

"Well, I hope so, in my experience, the unexpected tends to jump on you when you least expect it," Judd had a reassuring grin on his face "let's get this show on the road."

They changed, donned the helmets, and started carrying all the gear inside the cave. The floor was smooth as if polished by eons of water and sand blown inside by the weather. The walls were also smooth, with a wavy pattern that also suggested torrential turbulent water cascading through it a long time ago. Everything was completely dry now, no sign of even condensation on the walls or the ceiling.

It took them several trips to get everything inside and place all items at the edge of the vertical shaft that Ivo noticed almost at the last minute. Judd walked cautiously to the edge of the well and shone a laser depth finder down into the hole. He jotted down the reading on a pad, then pulled a little rubberized sphere from his rucksack. He flipped a switch on it to activate an embedded light as well as a tiny protrusion suggesting an antenna. He had a small box with a matching light switch and antenna that he also activated. Then, unceremoniously he dropped the sphere into the hole, and they could hear it bouncing from wall to wall for a while until they could hear it no more. Judd kept looking at the electronic gizmo, watching a digital display that indicated the depth the ball had fallen. When the digits stopped increasing, he compared the value to the figures he had jotted down from his laser depth finder. They were in close agreement, indicating a depth of 1200 units.

Ivo watched him closely, reassured by his practiced movements. "Are we OK with that depth? Do we have enough cable?"

"We'll need the extension, but it will be enough to reach the bottom, with about 150 units to spare. We'll take the ropes with us. We have about 500 units, in case we need it further down there."

All that remained to do was to anchor the power winch a few units away from the lip of the well and a pulley at the very edge to let the cable unroll smoothly without friction with the rocks. From one of the bundles, Judd brought out a power drill and proceeded to drill the holes for both anchors. Once he judged the holes deep enough, he pulled another power tool from the same bundle and shot two anchor spikes into the holes, about a foot deep. The spikes were of a larger diameter than the holes and the power tool forced them so tightly into the holes that no amount of human force could dislodge them.

"Well, that's it, Ivo, are you ready to start lowering the gear?"

"I'm as ready as I'll ever be, just let me know how I can help."

"There is only one bundle that contains everything we'll need down there. That contains the rope coils, climbing hardware, communicators, lights, power packs, and everything else that might come in handy. Let's hook up the power pack and cables to the winch and attach the bundle to the carabiner at the end. I have positioned the winch on the side where the shaft wall curves away from the hole, so we should be able to lower everything, ourselves included, without rubbing against the side of the shaft."

"Which of us descends first?" Ivo asked anxiously "I'm a bit reluctant to be the first to go down into the unknown."

"Don't worry, I'll go first after the bundle is down safely. I have a remote controller for the carabiner to detach it from the bundle, so we'll pull the cable back up, then I'll lower myself, and then have the winch pull back the cable again. You'll have to attach yourself to it with the harness you'll be wearing and then I'll lower you by the remote controller. We'll have our communicators, so we can talk all the way down. Is that OK with you?"

"Sounds like you have everything under control. I'll trust you not to lower me too fast."

He said it with a grin, hiding his apprehension.

The news of an ancient civilization Zack had discovered was a bit of a shock to Gordon and Muriel. They had known all along that the Scope could produce unexpected results for historians, and the Senator did expect them to pop up once he started his research into American history. However, they had never anticipated news of an ancient civilization from 50,000 years in the past. They both agreed that it was important to follow it up more closely before deciding what to do. It was impossible to make the discovery public without revealing the secret of the Scope and they were extremely reluctant to do that. The potential abuse of a 'spying machine' by government, business, even organized crime was undeniable, and they could see powerful forces going to any length to get hold of it.

Muriel was supportive of his plan to visit Zack, even though she regretted interrupting the intimacy they enjoyed during the last weeks. She only cautioned Hopkins about Brady, who was still a present danger and might pick up his tail once he returned to the capital.

"Gordon, be extremely careful and return here as soon as you can. The dogs would really miss you if you didn't come back."

Gordon wasted no time to reassure her.

"I won't even go to my office or contact any of the people I work with, I'll go straight to Zack's place. I wish you could come with me; this might be a once-in-a-lifetime experience."

"You know I can't," Muriel sounded regretful "you know I can't leave my projects, never mind the dogs. I have a buyer for that turtle, and I promised to finish it for his wife's birthday."

Gordon held her hand and hugged her with his other arm to reassure her that he understood. During the last two weeks, they had been together signs of this kind of intimacy became more and more frequent and neither of them seemed to mind. After all, they were an old couple even if their relationship had been interrupted for decades. It was the here and now that mattered to both.

"I promise I'll call as soon as I have watched the scene Zack discovered and give you a full report."

Muriel smiled at Gordon and reminded him that they had better leave for the airport if he didn't want to miss his flight. The last thing she told him when they parted company at the Montpellier Airport was: "Please don't take any chances, the dogs aren't the only ones who would miss you."

The sound of her voice followed him onto the plane and replayed in his mind over and over during the flight to Washington.

~

Zack was ready when Hopkins arrived. The Senator had called him from the plane and advised him of the time of his arrival. He had the Scope turned on. He had replaced the built-in monitor with a 48" wide wall-mounted TV screen that he had recently acquired. This way they could see a lot more detail than from the small monitor built-in the Scope.

"Zack, what you told me about your discovery is so fantastic that I still have difficulty believing it. If it's a joke you'd better tell me now."

"Senator, why don't we watch it together and you tell me if you think I wasn't telling you the truth."

Zack already had the space and time coordinates set all he had to do was push the scan button.

They watched the laboratory that appeared on the screen. Half a dozen people were working at the benches. When Zack selected one of them and zoomed in for a closeup, Gordon gasped when he saw the face. It was 100%

human. "Are you sure, Zack, you are not showing me a science fiction movie?"

"Trust me, Senator, this is the real stuff. Just look at the time coordinates I set for the scene, 50,000 years in the past. The space coordinates are set to the place where Jack Bansky found the Time Scope."

"So, he didn't invent it himself? Found it in an alien lab?"

"Found it in the ruins of the lab. He seemed to be following a map into an underground corridor at an abandoned archeological site. I have no idea how he found that map, I'm just telling you what I saw."

"Where did they come from?" Gordon had a hard time keeping his eyes off the screen, but he turned to Zack with a lost expression on his face "and where are they now? What happened to them? How come no sign of their civilization was found anywhere on the planet? And, if they evolved somewhere else, how come they look 100% human?"

Zack turned on his tablet computer and showed it to Hopkins.

"Ever since I discovered these people, I couldn't think of anything else, so I started to investigate various theories about alien visitors. I'm a sci-fi fan and I have read a lot of stories that might explain, or at least suggest an explanation. I have summarized the three most likely scenarios here, take a look."

Hopkins saw three highlighted and underlined items, each followed by some text below. He had no intention of reading it now, so he asked Zack to summarize for him, while he turned his attention back to the people going about their business.

"The first thing that popped into my mind was the "Atlantis" legends that spoke of an ancient and advanced civilization that left Earth after their continent was destroyed by tectonic events. The second idea was suggested by an old Star Trek Next Generation episode. That was based on the idea that an extremely advanced alien civilization seeded all kinds of planets in the Galaxy with RNA to launch evolution, so they all evolved in a similar way. The third and most promising theory was suggested by a sci-fi author called James Hogan, in his novel "Inherit the Stars". It suggested that our solar system used to have another planet between Mars and Jupiter, with an advanced technological civilization of humanoids. Their planet exploded during an all-out nuclear war and became the Asteroid Belt. The few survivors on their moon were cast into space toward the sun, but gravitationally captured by Earth and became our own moon. The survivors on the Moon traveled to Earth in their remaining spaceships, wiped out the Neanderthals, and became our Homo Sapiens ancestors."

"Fascinating," Hopkins exclaimed, wiping sweat off his forehead "if any of these theories are anywhere near the truth. It still doesn't explain what happened to them. Where are they now? Why don't we have any archeological and historical records?"

"Senator, I can only speculate. 50,000 years ago, Earth wasn't a very hospitable place. Ice Age, super volcanoes, and tsunamis may have convinced them to seek another planet. Some of them must have stayed behind with limited resources and reverted to savagery when these resources ran out. We are their descendants."

"This is the craziest story I have ever heard," Gordon was shaking his head "and the only way you can convince me that this is for real is by scanning forward and showing me the scene where they take off in their space ships. Maybe we can even find out where they went?"

"I have already thought about that, but it might take a very long time. At the moment I need to start looking for some paying clients or Suzy will skin me alive. I only wanted to show you this and let you decide what to do with the information. Whatever you do, please don't reveal the existence of this Scope."

"Relax kid, I have no intention of doing that." Hopkins realized this was the first time he called Zack 'kid', must be Petuccini's bad influence. "By the way, how did Petuccini react?"

"You won't believe this, but Joe went completely bonkers and offered me five grand if I can solve this mystery. Not only that but he wants to come along for the hunt."

"I thought he was getting married?"

"He wants to start after his honeymoon and that gives me enough time to line up another client so I can keep both my girl and my skin."

Hopkins laughed at this sheepish confession, recognizing Zack's priorities were not too far from his own.

~

Brady came to a decision: it was time he stopped hiding in his house and faced the world. Ever since his humiliating defeat, he had refused to see anyone or even look at his email. Now he was ready to see who wanted to contact him, who were his real friends. He had no doubt about his convictions, and he shouldn't apologize to anyone, he should stand up proudly in front of the whole country and pursue his agenda with increased energy and determination. For the moment, the presidency was out of his reach but, knowing how many millions of Americans supported him enthusiastically, he might have a second chance next time. He sat down at his computer in his war room and looked at the hundreds of emails he had received since that debacle.

He read through all the encouraging messages from friends and supporters, looking for names he could use in his renewed quest for power. Each time he found a promising name he jotted it down on a notepad. He was almost at the end of the list when one email caught his attention. It was from his old friend from the regiment, Colonel Boxer. It suggested a meeting as soon as possible to make up some plan of action to, as it said, "save our country from the dangerous liberals who grabbed the power that should be rightfully yours."

Now this was definitely something worth pursuing, so he sent off a reply, suggesting lunch the next day at the officers' club they had frequented before they retired. This done, he spent the evening replying to all those emails he had neglected before. To the names on his list, he sent a thank you note and suggested that they keep in touch in the interest of their common goal.

~

Joe Petuccini and Maria Montrose were sitting on the balcony of their rented house in Puerto Vallarta. The wedding was set for the next day and, as Maria assured him, everything was organized and ready for the event. The beautiful flowers were everywhere, and the sound of the exotic birds could be heard chirping and crying throughout the house. The butterflies were still in cages, to be released when they were pronounced husband and wife. There was nothing else to do but to enjoy the beautiful evening, look out at the whitecaps rolling in from the sea, and sip their drinks, fully enjoying the tranquility of a Mexican evening. After the hustle of the last few weeks, this felt like heaven.

"Penny for your thoughts", Maria prompted in a dreamy voice that revealed total happiness.

"You might think that I would have more romantic thoughts, cara, but I am still thinking about the events on Brady's unmasking last month."

"You never talked about it since then, do you have any idea how it was possible? For me, it's still a mystery."

Joe came to a decision. If they were going to be married, he shouldn't keep secrets that big from his wife, especially since Muriel Hopkins already knew and he was sure Zack's girlfriend would be next to find out. He was going to tell Maria about the Time Scope. He was absolutely convinced that he could count on her discretion - her loyalty was beyond doubt.

Maria listened to him with a look of incredulity spreading over her face, in obvious doubt whether to believe Joe's account. When she finally believed that he was telling her the truth, suddenly everything fell into place. The Time Scope explained how it was possible to observe and record Brady in his war room without leaving any sign of intrusion. Once she got past this point, the full significance of this device hit her with the possible consequences.

"Joe, this is scary!" she exclaimed "this gadget is very dangerous and can be used for horrible ends in evil hands. Are you sure it's safe to have it around? What if someone like Brady gets hold of it?"

"It's safe for the moment; only six people know about it and they can be trusted. It's in Zack's house and both I and the Senator are keeping an eye on him, making sure that he uses it only for his detective business. It helped us a lot when he found out about Brady's plans and Trevor Smythe's murder. We may need it again to find out if Brady is still pursuing his plans of revenge.

"Joe, this is still scary, but I don't want to talk about it anymore while we are in Mexico. I don't want anything to spoil the mood for the next two weeks. I intend to get married only once in my life and everything must be perfect."

Joe couldn't argue with this and was happy to drop the subject, but he was relieved to have this secret off his chest. He believed that sharing this incredible knowledge brought them even closer and he resolved not to keep anything else from her in the future.

~

Unaware of being the subject of a discussion between Joe and Maria, Zack was busy Googling unsolved crimes that offered a reward. His first try brought up a list of murders. He started reading about the cases but soon got discouraged. Case after case looked either hopeless or gruesome and he didn't want to get involved with any of it. Then he tried "unsolved robbery with a reward in Washington DC" and got another long list. The first item on the list that caught his attention was "10 unsolved heists we won't soon forget".

Now that looked more interesting. However, looking at the cases he soon realized that these were mostly multi-million-dollar robberies, way out of his league. Next, he tried "missing person with a reward in Washington DC", hoping he wouldn't have to deal with gory murder cases or high-stake robberies. It would be nice to solve a case that could bring a family together. His first try didn't look promising: "Police are upping the reward for information about a missing 8-year-old girl". The article suggested that she was murdered, and Zack had no desire to find kidnapped and murdered little girls. Zack got more and more discouraged, wondering if his plans were viable.

Then he remembered a mystery novel he had read in which an armored car was robbed by masked women with antique rifles. As it turned out the women were the wives of the security guards on the truck. It was all an inside job and the case took a long time to crack by a very clever detective. Nobody got killed, kidnapped, or even hurt; it was a nice clean job. Now, something like that would be interesting to handle. So, the next search string he entered in Google was "armored car robbery with a reward in Washington DC".

The first entry in the list that appeared caught his attention: "FBI, Police Seek Men Involved in Brinks Armored Car Robbery". That looked interesting. The article stated the facts, and this was so far the most encouraging one he had seen:

"An armored Brinks truck was robbed by two men in October, according to the FBI and two Maryland police departments. FBI and Takoma Park police investigators said a Brinks armored truck was delivering money to a Suntrust Bank in the 6900 block of Laurel Avenue in Takoma Park, Maryland, just before noon on Oct. 25. The guard was approached by two men with assault rifles, who stole the money the guard was carrying. Officials said the men fled the scene, and the guard was not injured. Witnesses described the robbers as two black men, about 6 feet tall, thin, and wearing Tyvek or painter's style suits and gloves. The getaway vehicle was described as a maroon 4-door sedan, possibly a Lexus 350, with temporary tags. The armed robbery is being investigated jointly by the FBI, the Takoma Park Police Department, and the Montgomery County Police Department. The FBI is offering a reward of up to $10,000 for information leading to the arrest in this case."

This looked like a clean, simple case that he shouldn't have difficulty cracking. He had the location and the time, all he had to do was tune the Scope to the proper coordinates and wait for the robbers to show up. After that, it would be a simple case of tracking the escaping car and seeing where they would end up. He could earn $10,000 with very little effort. Zack got really excited; he could almost feel the money in his hands. However, the investigation had to wait till the next day. It was very late, and he was sleepy and tired. Better leave it for the morning after he had a good night's sleep. His last thought before drifting off was "Suzy will be thrilled if I pull this off!"

Ivo safely descended to the bottom of the shaft where
Judd was waiting for him with a powerful lantern
illuminating the whole area. He was standing about 8
units above Judd, on top of a huge pile of cables that
covered the entire surface around his feet.

"Ivo, in case you are wondering, you are standing on
top of the old elevator. When this site was abandoned,
obviously they wanted to make sure that nobody could use
the lift anymore, so they must have lowered it to the
bottom and then dropped its cable. If you step over the
edge, I'll lower you all the way to the floor."

Ivo did exactly that and, standing on solid ground
again, he looked around. All he could see was a horizontal
corridor with tracks embedded in it, leading off to the
darkness beyond the range of their lantern.

"This way, Ivo, I'm sure we'll find what we are looking
for."

They followed the corridor and soon they came upon a
door on the right side, labeled with some characters. About
thirty units farther another door with another label on it,
so hopefully this is where the individual scientists' offices
were located. The fifth door had the label they were
looking for: Ivo recognized the ancient writing
representing Assoc. Schum. The door was unlocked, and
they entered with high expectations.

The place was quite spartan, as you would expect in an
underground facility. A bed, desk, chair, bookshelves,
filing cabinets, and a large trash can was the entire
furnishing. Judd put the lantern on the desk and started
systematically opening drawers and examining the
shelves. While he was doing that, Ivo examined the
contents of the trash can, on the assumption that Assoc.
Schum would have removed everything important when
he left for good. However, he might have left something in
the trash that they could use for a clue. He turned out to
be right, his historian's instinct rewarded him with a large

stack of papers that he carefully placed on the desk and started going through them.

After he had found nothing important on the shelves and inside the drawers, Judd joined him in searching through the discarded papers. Neither man said anything for a while, absorbed in studying the pile. Suddenly Judd stopped riffling through the papers and held a few pages in his hand and studied them intently.

"Have you found something interesting?" Ivo asked anxiously, a bit discouraged after not seeing anything of interest in his own pile.

"Seems to be a circuit diagram that may have something to do with the Viewer. Keep looking for anything that looks like electronic specs of any kind."

A few minutes later, Ivo found a stapled sheaf of printed text that appeared to be what they were after. He handed it over to Judd who studied it in silence for a while. Finally, with a huge grin on his face, he announced success: "This is exactly what I was looking for. I can't read it until you translate it for me, but it could be a detailed description of the device. Ivo, we are in luck! Based on this, I should be able to replicate the device after I've had a chance to study it back in my own lab."

"You mean we are done here? We can go home? I'm getting a bit claustrophobic and wouldn't mind seeing daylight soon."

"Let's just walk to the end of the corridor and see if anything important is left in the lab. I assume it's located beyond the offices."

They found the lab exactly as Judd had assumed, but it was completely empty. So were the other offices they examined, and they had to go back to the surface with the only 'treasure' they found in the long-abandoned place.

The ascent to the surface was uneventful and, after they moved all their gear back to the flier, they took off for the University.

"Judd, thanks for the adventure. Give me a day to translate this document."

"I thank *you*, Ivo, I couldn't have done it without you. After you have translated this text, it will take me a few days to study it and I'll let you know if I can reproduce this invention."

"I hope you can, because if it works, it can revolutionize historical research in general, and my own quest in particular."

~

Jenna was busy in her kitchen. She decided to cook her own dinner: nothing special this time. She needed a break occasionally from all those restaurant meals she loved sampling. She was stirring a stew on the stove when her communicator beeped. Not wanting to interrupt her delicate task, she ordered her bot to answer it.

She heard the conversation taking place in her living room between Skippy and a male voice she recognized as Judd's, a young colleague who started in the department recently. She wondered what he wanted; they hadn't crossed paths before. She had heard of his practical jokes and was instantly suspicious. What's he up to now?

After a brief conversation, the call ended, and Skippy rolled into the kitchen to report.

"So, what was that about," she asked, curious despite her suspicion.

"Jenna, I have a message for you. Do you want to hear it now?"

"Yes, please, replay it."

The same male voice, now clearly audible.

"Jenna, you may remember me from department meetings: my name is Judd. I'd like to talk to you about a possible project you could be interested in. I have discovered an old invention that allows limited time travel by retrieving visual information from the past. I will attempt to recreate it and could use your help with the theory. Please let me know if you are interested." This was the end of the message and Skippy rolled out of her kitchen to attend to its household chores.

Jenna was intrigued by the idea of viewing events from the past. Not that she had any curiosity about historical events, nor did she want to spy on anyone, but the mere possibility of doing it at all fascinated her. On the other hand, if this was one of Judd's elaborate pranks, she would be really irate. He was practically a kid and she was a respected professor of Theoretical Physics; it would be highly inappropriate for the young man to try anything as disrespectful as a joke on her.

Musing about the past-viewer, as she called it in her head, suddenly she realized what a great help it would be to Ivo in hunting the elusive migration event. She wondered if he had ever thought about the possibility of time travel.

Jenna liked him very much. He was intelligent, funny, curious, everything she valued in a man. The 'what-if' idea popped into her head more than once, but Ivo showed no sign of similar interest, so she put the thought out of her mind each time she caught herself fantasizing about a romantic relationship. He was still a good friend and she enjoyed his company every time they met. Come to think of it, hadn't she promised him more invitations to culinary adventures? He seemed to enjoy it so much, maybe it was time to invite him to another outing?

She knew of another interesting place Ivo probably had never heard of. This was a restaurant with completely transparent walls, entirely underwater in the ocean, anchored over a most spectacular coral reef, surrounded by the most exotic marine flora and fauna. The entrance was from a surface vessel via a watertight elevator that entered the roof of the building through a spaceship-like airlock. She had not been there for some time herself, so maybe they could spend an enjoyable evening there? She might even ask him about Judd's idea of a past-viewing device. He would probably salivate at the prospect of such an opportunity. She decided to send him a message and ask if he was game for another adventure.

~

The restaurant was as spectacular as Jenna had promised and Ivo couldn't take his eyes off the swimming, swirling marine life inches from his face on the other side of the transparent wall. Fish of all sizes and shapes, in dazzling colours swam by their table. The coral reef under their feet seemed like a magic carpet. Jenna just sat there, watching his face with deep satisfaction. He certainly seemed an appreciative audience to her presentation. She felt she truly deserved the reputation of a culinary super-guide.

"So, what do you think of the place?" she prompted him, wanting more than the pleasure of watching his face.

"This is unbelievable! How do you find them?"

"I spend quite a bit of time away from differential equations. When my brain is too tired to think about gravitational waves, I get on the net and start looking for something different, usually in the culinary entertainment department. I'm pleased that you like it."

"*Like it* is an understatement. I don't know how I can return the favour. I am just a dry, dusty, boring historian who is madly in love with his own pet theories."

"Speaking of your 'pet theories', do you happen to know of a young Physicist by the name of Judd? He has some pet theory of his own that you might find interesting."

Ivo burst out laughing, not quite believing that Jenna brought up the name that had been occupying his mind non-stop, ever since their cave-exploring adventure. He hadn't heard from Judd since that day and he was wondering how Judd was doing with that time travel project. And now Jenna brought it up.

"Do you know him?" he asked.

"Barely. He contacted me about a mad idea that I thought might interest you. If it could be done, it would be a great help in your research. Why, do you know him?" She began to suspect that Judd had contacted others besides herself. Maybe he needed help in retrieving ancient documents and a historian would be a logical choice.

"Know him may be an understatement. We spent some terrifying time together cave exploring last week, hunting for more information relating to his mad idea. We did find something, too, and Judd said he was going to study it to see if he could recreate the device if it was a real possibility." He proceeded to tell her everything about their adventure.

"Now, this is quite interesting," Jenna laughed "he contacted me too about the possibility of cooperation on this project. He said he needed help with the theory, but I wasn't sure if I could take him seriously, He is famous for his pranks and practical jokes."

"I can assure you he is quite serious and, I have to admit, I could give his right arm for a device like that. Can you see how it would help me, or any historian if we could actually visit places in the past and finally resolve all those disputes?"

"*His* right arm?" Jenna laughed. Aren't you overly generous?"

"You wouldn't expect me to be generous with my own?"

"Why not, he is a lot younger and he would need both in his spelunking adventures. A historian needs only one to dust off ancient documents."

"Oh, I see the high regard you have for historians. However, you may be surprised how many other tasks a historian can perform with both arms. Like hugging you if you could help him make this happen?"

"Do you want me to look into it? See if there is even a remote possibility? I can see you have gone to some length to help him retrieve his documents." She felt herself blushing at the mention of a hug from Ivo, but he didn't seem to notice it.

"Would you, Jenna?" I would be eternally grateful and would even offer an adventure in return that only a historian could dream up."

"OK, Ivo, this is a deal. Now let's shut up for a while and eat our dinner before it gets cold. I like cold fish only when it's hot!"

Belatedly she realized that the last thing she said could be interpreted with a more personal meaning. He glanced anxiously at Ivo's face but saw no sign of suspicion. He wouldn't know that she was talking more about him than about their meal.

~

Judd could hardly wait for his girlfriend to leave. He had had a breakthrough idea and was eager to follow it when Shara showed up unexpectedly, to return the heating pad she had borrowed the last time they were together. Judd was very fond of her - she was funny, vivacious, great in bed, but she had one fault that bothered him occasionally. She would go on chatting non-stop about girl stuff that didn't even remotely interest him. Usually, he would wait patiently for a break to suggest a topic that they both liked to talk about, such as her acting career. Judd truly appreciated her talent and never missed an opportunity to see her on stage. However, at this moment, he needed to be alone to follow through with that hunch about the time travel device. He had been battling with it for days, going through the rescued documents with a mental magnifying glass, trying to understand the theory it was based on. His weakness was space-time mechanics and he badly needed help from an expert. That's why he contacted Jenna and was still waiting for her to respond. He was just about to ask Shara to give him an hour to finish his current task when the comm-signal came to his rescue. To his delight, it was Jenna on the other end of the line.

"Judd, I have thought about it and decided that I am interested enough to take a look at what you retrieved from that cave."

"So, you know about it?" Judd was surprised "how did you find out?"

"Ivo is an old friend of mine and I told him about your project. No surprise there, he practically begged me to help you or, at least, take a look and let him know if it was viable. I must admit, I am curious too. So, when do you want to get together?"

Judd was beyond excited at the prospect of working with Jenna, the top expert in the department in space-time mechanics, exactly what he needed.

"Any time you say, Jenna, even right now if you have the time."

He looked at Shara's face and saw that she wasn't thrilled by the prospect of being replaced by a boring physicist. He felt mildly guilty but decided to make up to her the next time they were together. He was very fond of her and didn't want to hurt her feelings, but this was important and an unexpected opportunity he didn't want to jeopardize by putting it off.

"Actually, I can come over now if you give me your address. I promised Ivo that I wouldn't wait to look into it, at least to determine if this mad idea was feasible at all. He can't talk or think about anything else and that turns him into a bit of a bore."

Judd gave her his address and looked sheepishly at Shara.

"Forgive me, love. This is such an opportunity for me, I just can't put it off. I hope you understand; I promise to make it up to you somehow."

She smiled at him reassuringly. "Don't worry about it, I'm sure you find a boring physicist preferable to your beautiful, sexy, alluring playmate any time. I know when I can't compete with a middle-aged woman. So, I'll see you after you begged me long enough to grace you with my presence."

She said it with her head cocked, slightly lowered eyelids, and a crooked smile that she knew he always responded to. She knew how to push his buttons.

Judd couldn't help responding, she was so beautiful, so much fun, that he almost regretted inviting Jenna over. He would have to get together with her again very soon, he promised himself. When he walked her to the door, she turned around to give him a pack on his cheeks and, avoiding his offered lips, she left without another word.

Judd's regret didn't last long. Once she was gone, he returned to the document he had been studying when she showed up. He almost had it, the breakthrough idea was on the edge of his mind, all it needed was coaxing out and Jenna was the right person for the job.

Brady went to the meeting with great anticipation. Colonel Boxer was a retired army officer, just like himself, and Brady did not doubt the man's ideological convictions. They had had many enjoyable discussions in the past and Boxer was one of the most devoted supporters of his campaign. The fact that he had contacted Brady, even after the revelation of his Nazi leanings, spoke volumes about his loyalty. The restaurant, the Blue Heron, was a place with tables far apart, so they could have privacy for their discussion, even if none of the booths happened to be free. Since their meeting was set for 11:30, chances were they would find one available. When Brady got there, Boxer was already sitting in one of the most remote booths and waved at him from the back of the room.

"Sir, over here" he bellowed to Brady's dismay. He was anxious to avoid the attention of the few patrons already there. He walked to the table and sat down without comment.

"I'm so pleased that you came," the other extended his hand over the table "I was very anxious to talk to you after that disgraceful election."

"It took me a while to get over the betrayal by my campaign manager," Brady explained "but now I'm ready to get back into the fight to, as you suggested in your email, save our country from that disastrous election result. You were the first one I contacted and want your opinion on how to proceed."

"I thought you already had a plan. I came to see what you wanted me to do."

"It's not exactly a plan, more like an idea. I was wondering what would happen if Sam Triden had an accident?"

"Are you thinking of assassination?" Boxer exclaimed louder than he intended. The idea shocked him to the core.

He thought Brady was an old-fashioned Republican, not a cold-blooded killer.

"Keep your voice down man, it was just a thought. I told you it wasn't a plan!"

" I was thinking more along the lines of starting your own party. You would have a lot of followers, even from the party that dumped you so ungracefully. Many would join you if you stated clearly what you stand for. You could amalgamate all the existing fringe white supremacist parties that already exist."

"A party? Hmm. It never occurred to me. I'm more of an action guy. I hate politics and left it all to Trevor Smythe. I see now that was a huge mistake. I don't know anything about starting a party."

"Sir, you already have a huge organization: your election committee and its support structure. All you need is to announce it and we could take care of the rest."

Brady, while still a bit reluctant, began to warm up to the idea. All he would need to do was continue the same campaign rallies and speeches. He liked that. He liked the crowd screaming and stomping and egging him on. This would certainly eliminate the danger involved in organizing an assassination. Even if it succeeded, the country would still be stuck with a Democratic VP who would take over.

And then, Brady remembered from his reading so many Hitler biographies: isn't this the way Adolf rose to power? After the failed Munich putsch, he spent some time in jail, wrote "Mein Kampf" and then got busy with the Nazi party that took him all the way to total power.

"Garry, you may have something there. I will seriously consider it. If you know the right people to spearhead this action, arrange a meeting with them for a strategy session."

"I know exactly whom to talk to, sir. It won't take more than a week to bring them all together. Believe me, they'll all be behind you."

~

Suzy was thrilled with the idea of solving the Brinks robbery but was more than a little bit dubious about his deal with Petuccini, concerning the aliens. It all sounded like science fiction and she had a hard time wrapping her mind around the whole thing. However, the five grand Joe had offered for the investigation was serious money, not to turn your nose up at, especially at the beginning of their budding business venture. Now that she had quit her job and was ready to move in with Zack, she had a real stake in making it a success.

"Zack, I am willing to go along with Petuccini's mad request if you promise you'll spend equal time on the Brinks robbery. That's where our future lies, not in chasing long-dead aliens."

"Actually, they are not aliens at all. I believe they are our true ancestors. At least they look 100% human. Aren't you at least a bit curious? I can show them to you on the Scope."

"I have a lot more practical concerns right now if you still want me to move in with you. We need to organize your house so I can have my private space. You also need office space, furniture, another phone line and I don't know yet what else? Let's leave the aliens or ancestors, or whatever you want to call them, for a later time."

Zack was excited to hear Suzy planning their life together. He forgot all about Petuccini and started seriously thinking about the arrangement. The house he had inherited from his parents was large enough to provide enough room both for their individual and common space, as well as for their office. The ground floor could stay the business part, while the top floor, with the four large bedrooms, could provide for their personal needs. They spent the rest of the day measuring floor spaces, drawing plans where their furniture would go.

~

Petuccini's honeymoon went so fast it was now a blur in his mind, as he was driving to Zack's place. Everything had been perfect, just as Maria promised and now he was married - a new and not a little bit scary experience. For the time being, they were still living in and running the casino until the ownership could be transferred to the Markos consortium. After that, he wasn't sure. He would have to resume his search for an island to retire on. At the moment he was burning with curiosity about those long-dead aliens Zack had discovered. Zack had only told him briefly about them and Petuccini was anxious to see for himself. Who were they? What happened to them? How come no one had ever found any trace of them? He had to know, and Zack was the key to finding out.

The young man was ready for him, with the Scope turned on and the coordinates set.

"OK kid, show me your little green men!" Petuccini leaned back in the comfortable armchair Zack had brought into his lab, gazing at the large wall-mounted screen with anticipation.

"Where do you want to start, Joe? By the way, they are not little, or green, but you already know that."

"Figure of speech, Zack, don't get excited. Just show me the scene where you first found them."

Zack had already set the coordinates, anticipating Joe's request. He pushed the Scan button and the monitor came alive, showing the same scene he had viewed a dozen times. Ha panned around in the lab, showing all the benches with the strange-looking instruments, then zoomed in on individual faces. Most of the aliens seemed to be in their mid-thirties, with a few gray-haired men and three younger women staring intently at what they were doing.

Petuccini sat quietly, seemingly mesmerized.

"If I weren't sure that you are not brave enough to show me a contemporary lab just to fool me, I wouldn't believe I'm really viewing something from 50,000 years ago."

Zack laughed, "You are right about that. Knowing your fearsome reputation, I wouldn't dream of pulling your leg."

"That reputation is well earned, kid, don't dismiss it too easily. So, tell me where do you want to go from here? How do we go about solving this mystery?"

"I have a theory, same as what I told the Senator and I want to follow it up. Now that I know they are here, or rather there, I have to keep jumping back in time to see where they had come from. I must warn you that it will be boring and tedious, I have no idea how long it will take. I wish the Scope could track backward but I haven't found a way to do that yet. So, I'll have to keep resetting the time coordinates further and further into the past until I see something changing. This lab was built in their past and that's the first event I need to find. Are you sure you want to sit in for the boring part?"

Petuccini considered and agreed that his time was more valuable than watching Zack fiddle with coordinates.

"You have my cell phone number, call me when you have something interesting to show. I'll be in Washington for a few more days to finalize the sale of my casino, so I can be here again in an hour or two if you have something new to look at. Don't get up, I'll let myself out."

Zack smiled at him in acknowledgment and turned back to the Scope to adjust the time coordinate."

~

Suzy was scared. For the first time in her adult life, she didn't have a job. No income, a few hundred dollars in the bank and she was completely dependent on Zack for everything she needed. She didn't like to depend on anyone, least of all Zack, and she was wondering if she had made the wrong decision to quit her job at the nursery. She liked it there, surrounded by flowers and pleasant company all day. Now she was by herself in her apartment, packing her things for the move to Zack's. This serious, responsible Zack was still very new, she didn't know how much she could trust it. She knew that he had money, both from his inheritance and from the investment the Senator and Petuccini put into his business, plus another five grand would be coming from Joe if they solved the mystery of the aliens.

She would have to come to some financial arrangement with Zack, so she would be a paid employee of the business. A regular income she could count on would go a long way to reassure her. She would have to discuss this with him before she did any more packing. Maybe it would still be possible to get her old job back or find a new one if they couldn't come to an agreement.

She picked up the phone and dialed Zack's number. He answered after the third ring with a curt 'hello', sounding impatient. He must have been watching his beloved Scope.

"Zack, I need to talk to you, the sooner the better. Can I come over now?"

"Hi Suzy" Zack's voice sounded genuinely happy to hear from her and that was reassuring. "Come on over. Joe just left and I'm up to my eyeballs with aliens, but it's just boring stuff. It can wait. I also want to talk to you about your move and the business arrangements."

Suzy felt her anxiety dissipating, hearing Zack's enthusiastic voice. Maybe it wasn't a mistake to team up with him. A big risk, with a potentially big reward. Yes, it was time to take a chance. Maybe she had been a bit too comfortable, maybe it was time for a change.

~

While waiting for Suzy, Zack kept jumping back in time with the Scope in varying increments. When he tried a few days at a time, he didn't see any significant change. Sometimes the lab was empty, full of activity, once he saw everybody gathered around the center, animatedly discussing something. He wished he could hear the sound, wondering if he could understand what they were saying. It was unreasonable to expect intelligible conversation unless the inventors had a 'universal translator' built into the Scope. He smiled ruefully when he realized how much Star Trek influenced his thinking.

Increasing the time jumps to weeks, months, even years didn't result in anything interestingly different. Jumping back 100 years brought a change: the lab wasn't there anymore. What he saw was an overgrown field without anyone or anything visible. Maybe he could track forward from that point and let the computer beep if anything changed. He would have to focus on something on the empty field to start the tracking, and it had to be likely to change over time. He noticed a small sapling and knew that it was going to grow over the next hundred years, so the Scope could latch onto it and follow its change. He gave this a try and, when the tracking started, he increased the speed to one year a minute. Then he started his program on the laptop to alert him when the scene changed significantly. Now he was ready to relax and wait for the Scope to do the job. He retrieved a can of beer from his fridge, put on some soft music, and waited for either Suzy or the computer, to require his attention.

As it turned out, it was Suzy who won the race: the doorbell rang before the computer alerted him to significant change. He rushed to the door to let her in and surprised her with a big hug and a passionate kiss that he had been saving up since the last time they had been together.

"Zack, thanks for the greeting but I really need to talk to you. Let's not let things get away from us. Time for everything and now it's definitely not sex."

Zack smiled an apology and led her back to his lab where the Scope was still tracking forward.

"Before you tell me what's on your mind, I have a present for you." Zack smiled mischievously, pulling a key out of his pocket. "This is your house key that lets you come and go any time from now on. You'll be living here any day now and you'll need this."

"Thanks, honey, I appreciate this, and it has to do with what I want to talk about."

"Shoot, I'm all ears. Actually, only one ear because the other one is waiting for the computer to tell me if it found aliens arriving at the lab scene."

"Zack, I need both of your ears, so please pause the tracking, and let's go to the living room. This is serious and it needs your full attention."

"You haven't changed your mind about moving in? Zack asked anxiously.

"Not if we can come to an agreement that I find acceptable."

"OK, I'll stop the tracking and we can go to the living room. I'll get you a beer unless you think it would be too indulgent under the circumstances."

Suzy laughed: "A beer is fine and please don't look so worried. All I'm after is an acceptable business arrangement. I understand that you set up a corporation with the Senator's help and all the money they have invested in the business was deposited into the corporate account?"

"Yes, that's correct, that's the way my investors wanted it and they are both silent partners in the business."

"That's what I thought, and, in that case, it would be appropriate if I was hired as an employee with a fixed monthly salary. I need to have a steady income that I can count on."

"I thought that we would be equal partners in this?"

"I'm not ready for this yet, for my peace of mind I need a steady income and, if you can't guarantee that, I can't participate in this venture."

"Of course, I can guarantee it, I have plenty of money in the bank to pay you a salary, just tell me how much you want?"

"Same as I made at the nursery, which wasn't that much, as you know."

"No problem, consider it done. So, when are you planning to move?"

"I have already started packing but stopped when I got scared of what I was getting into. I don't have a lot of furniture, most of it is junk from the Salvation Army, so I can move any time my room is ready for me. Have you decided yet which of the bedrooms will be mine?"

"Why don't you choose right now? Let's go upstairs and see which you like best."

They trooped up the stairs. The rooms were sparsely furnished except for one that looked lived in. Suzy had no trouble recognizing Zack's style. Discarded clothes were littered all over the floor, several plates with half-eaten snacks occupied most horizontal surfaces, a large TV screen set against a wall, across from the unmade bed was unmistakable as a man's cave.

"Not this one," she said, rolling her eyes "didn't anyone make you clean up your room when you were young?"

She instantly regretted saying that, remembering that his parents were killed in a car accident when he was only 10 and he was raised by an aunt until he was old enough to move back to the house.

Zack didn't seem to mind the reference to his childhood.

"That's me, Suzy, you should know it by now. You can pick any of the others. I suggest we keep the largest for our bedroom unless you don't want to sleep with me regularly."

"If you promise to live up to our agreement and take the business seriously, then I'll want to sleep with you. However, I need my own room for my privacy and, if you don't mind, I'd like this one that looks out on the backyard. I love to watch the birds and squirrels when I'm alone, and your backyard is really beautiful with the tall trees and the wildflowers. I'll have to do something about some tame flowers soon. Just because I'm not in the nursery anymore, it doesn't mean that I can live without them. By the way, can we have a cat?"

The three of them were together for the first time since the project started. Jenna called the meeting when it became obvious that the remote viewing device was a serious possibility. She and Judd spent the last two weeks examining the ancient manuscript Judd had found, analyzing both the theory and the electronics described in the documents. They couldn't doubt it: not only was it possible, but they could even enhance it further, enabling it to track backward in time as well as forward. Judd was naturally super excited and wanted to charge ahead and build it. Just as naturally, Ivo was all for it too, but Jenna, being more mature, cautioned them against proceeding headlong into development without examining all the implications.

"What's there to examine?" Ivo asked for the third time, getting exasperated. Here they were on the brink of the discovery he had been waiting for all his life and Jenna was being overly cautious.

"OK, Ivo, let's take this one step at a time. Assuming it worked, and then you discovered the original planet, then what?"

"Simple, my theory would be finally proven, and I could rub their stupid faces in their decades-long derision of my theory."

"Is that all you are after, Ivo? I am disappointed. Have you thought about what would happen if we found that our ancestors are still living on that planet?"

"I guess, we would say hello to them if you managed to establish some form of communication."

"And then what? How would we react if they were superior to us in technology and could pose a threat? Or, what would we do if they were way behind us in development and we could give them a hand? How would our interference affect an unknown civilization? Could we hurt them in unanticipated ways? We need to think of these implications before jumping into the unknown, facing these dilemmas unprepared."

Ivo was unsure how to respond to Jenna's rapid-fire questions. He had never thought about these aspects, but he could see that she had a point.

Judd on the other hand was still clutching for straws.

"Could we just build it, test it, make sure that it works, and then examine the implications?"

"Judd, I have been around for some time and experience shows me that any invention, when it is a working reality, will be used by someone somewhere, for some purpose or another. Our imagination always runs away with us and it's wiser to think things through first."

"But, wouldn't it be possible..." Judd still tried to wiggle out of his disappointing setback, but Jenna was relentless.

"There is no danger in waiting and, in the worst case, it will only delay the project for a few weeks at the most. I suggest we contact Trivas, chairman of the Planetary Advisory Council. The possible consequences are too great for us three to decide."

This was a fair suggestion and nothing else needed to be said. Nobody would ever argue with the Planetary Council - they knew too well how important it was to reach a consensus on issues that might involve the whole planet.

~

Trivas, chairman of the Planetary Council, had not been called with an unresolved issue for years. They had not had to face decisions that would affect the entire planet since moving all their heavy industry to the moons. Things usually worked out naturally among those who were involved and needed no overall guidance from him. All major planetary decisions had been made a long time ago and everybody was happy with the result: the population had a relaxed, productive lifestyle where everyone was free to pursue his or her interest, as long as it did not impinge on others doing the same. If there was a disagreement, they would just sit down and discuss it calmly and come to the best compromise that naturally suggested itself.

But, it seemed, now they faced a decision that could affect their whole planet with unforeseen consequences. The night before he had received a call from Central University, advising him of an invention that could potentially result in major disruption of their way of life. It also could have serious ethical implications. This device allowed visual information retrieval from the past, from any combination of space and time coordinates. If it were built, it would allow the user to visually roam the entire galaxy, search for other civilizations, maybe even find the mythical 'original planet', and find out if their remote ancestors still lived on it. Then decisions would need to be made about what, if any, relationship they would want to establish with them.

The call had come from a historian and two physicists who claimed to be close to building the device and had a disagreement they couldn't resolve among themselves. Ivo, the historian, was naturally anxious to use it in his research, so he could track their planetary history back to the remote past. Judd, one of the physicists, was gung-ho on pursuing his pet research idea, without worrying too much about the ethical implications. Jenna, the other physicist, while excited about the scientific breakthrough, nevertheless cautioned the other two about possible consequences. She wasn't dead set against it but suggested that they contact the Planetary Council so the issue could be properly examined, discussed, and a consensus reached before they would proceed any further.

That seemed like a wise precaution and Trivas agreed with her. He decided to call the Council into session, first time in years, to examine all the pros and cons of this exciting and potentially disruptive project.

~

Jenna was surprised and pleased to receive an invitation from Ivo to an archeological dig. Ivo made it clear that he was returning a favour for those two exotic restaurant visits she had lured him to and now he had something special for her that only a 'boring' historian could offer. Even though it wasn't going to be a 'date' but you could never tell: one thing might lead to another and Jenna wouldn't mind if it turned out that way. They met early in the morning in the University parking lot where Ivo was already waiting, standing next to his flyer with a mischievous smile on his face.

"So, what's this big adventure you promised me? You were so mysterious on the comm-link that I'm suspecting something dark and dangerous."

"Nothing like that, don't get your hopes up. It's exciting only to historians, but you might find it intriguing nevertheless."

"How far do we have to go?"

"Oh, it will take a couple of hours to get there, so you have to resign yourself to be locked into a small cabin with only me for company."

"If you promise you'll behave," she laughed, hoping that he wouldn't "I'm sure we'll find some safe topic to talk about. Maybe you can prepare me for the visit, tell me what it's all about?"

Ivo took her travel bag and stashed it away, next to his own in the baggage compartment. They both climbed aboard, and Ivo started the anti-gravity engine. It came to life with a soft hum and the flyer lifted off the ground, slowly accelerating while gaining altitude. For a while neither of them wanted to talk, watching the ground slide away under them, faster and faster, giving them the thrill they didn't want to miss. In a few minutes, they were high enough to see the whole town laid out below them as if they were looking at a map. For the capital city of 20,000 residents, it was on the small side, somewhat larger cities on both continents weren't rare, but their city was their scientific and intellectual center. They had only one University, simply called "Central University" but it was enormous, housing experts and specialists in every possible discipline.

Once past the town's limit, they were flying above a sparsely wooded landscape that gradually turned into a forest of evergreen trees, with small houses tucked away in good-sized clearings.

"I always wanted to live in one of those," Jenna pointed at a small bungalow "and I fully intend to retire in one when the time comes."

"That time shouldn't come yet, for a long, long time," Ivo smiled at her "You are still very young, I'd say in your prime."

"Ivo, you are not flirting with me?" she smiled back, trying not to show how much she hoped he was.

"Maybe I am, a little," he confessed "but I really meant it. So, forget about retiring soon. Besides, Judd would never forgive you if you abandoned his pet project."

"He is quite keen on making progress, isn't he?"

"You have to forgive him, he is very young, just starting out, and anxious to make a name for himself."

"How about you? Aren't you just as keen? After all, this might be the key to making progress in your own pet project."

"You are right about that, but I can wait a few weeks for you to build one. The possibility of proving my theory is exciting, of course, but I did see the points you raised about consequences."

"Tell me about your theory, Ivo. You never fully explained it to me. I know that it has to do with the myth of the 'original planet' but what makes you so sure there ever was one?"

"It's what is missing. We have followed our history back for thousands of years and have not seen significant changes in our technology, our sociology, or our way of life. More than that, we have never found any fossil records of biological and anthropological evolution anywhere. This doesn't seem possible, we had to originate sometime from somewhere and the only possible explanation I can come up with is that we showed up on this planet from somewhere else, already fully advanced to the point where we had space travel technology."

"Isn't it possible that you just haven't found the evidence of evolution yet? After all, most of our planet is still uninhabited wilderness and you may have looked at the wrong places?"

"We have had digs all over the planet, even in remote places randomly selected, it's not possible that we would end up with a net-zero."

"Tell me about this place we are going to now."

"This is the site of an old settlement, no more than a dozen buildings, including the ruins of a larger structure that resembles some kind of scientific or technological institution. It's in the middle of an old-growth forest."

"What makes it so interesting that you wanted to show me this particular site?"

"This is the first site we have found that suggests a darker side of our history. There are signs of past conflicts, even violence, and I want to find out what caused it, what they had to fight about. In our peaceful, consensus-based social system it's inconceivable that people would have to resort to violence to resolve their disagreements."

"What signs of violence?" Jenna was taken aback by the very idea of people purposefully hurting each other.

"We have found remnants of what appears to be weapons. There are inexplicable holes in the remaining walls. We have found skeletons that were badly broken, punctured, and twisted. We have found beds with straps attached to them suggesting people were restrained while lying on them. We have found a large room that suggests a chemical laboratory of some sort, but we couldn't identify the nature of the experiments. So far, it's a total mystery. I just wanted to show you something completely unusual that very few people are even aware of."

"I can certainly see why you find this fascinating, even disturbing. It definitely explains why you are so keen on proving your theory of ancient migration. I'm very pleased that you invited me to this exploration. It helps me understand something new and that's always welcome. I get bored talking only to physicists, you are like a breath of fresh air."

She said it in a semi-serious way, lightly touching his arm resting on the control panel.

Nothing was said for a while, both immersed in their own thoughts while watching the landscape fly by below them.

~

Judd and Shara were sailing on his catamaran, gliding over the smooth waters of the small lake at the edge of the city. Judd had to take a few days off until the Planetary Advisory Council had a chance to discuss the ethical and practical implications. He wasn't very happy about this; he felt ready to start building and could see no harm in at least testing the theory to know if it was viable at all.

He invited Shara who was usually free during the day until her evening performance or rehearsal, depending on what phase their current production was in.

"Hey, Judd, why the gloomy face?" Shara prompted him, trying to drag him back to the present from wherever he had disappeared.

"Sweetheart, I am pissed off with some colleagues who stopped me from working on what could be the greatest invention of our time. I'm not saying that they haven't valid reasons, but overdoing caution puts a brake on progress."

"I didn't know you were working on something that exciting, how come you never mentioned it before?"

"It was all very technical until recently, something you wouldn't be interested in."

"And now?"

"Now we have had a breakthrough and could build the device if only Jenna cooperated."

"Why did she stop you? Don't make me drag it out of you bit by bit, just tell me the whole story from beginning to end. While you are doing that, what if I steer your boat to that little island there, drop the anchor, and prepare to have some fun? It has a nice sandy beach and I feel like a swim. I haven't brought a swimsuit, but I'm sure you won't mind skinny dipping?"

Judd had no objection, actually, he welcomed the opportunity to use her for a sounding board, at least to sort out his own thinking. "…and now we have to wait for the mighty Planetary Advisory Council to finish their deliberations." He finished the tale and looked at Shara expectantly, hoping for sympathy.

"Sounds to me like a sensible precaution. What's wrong with waiting for a few days or weeks?"

"You don't understand! I'm on the verge of the biggest breakthrough any scientist can hope for at the start of his career and I'm stopped for no good reason. What harm can it do at least to try and see if it works? I just need to know, or I'll blow a few gaskets!"

Shara looked at him, carefully considering her response to his outburst. She was very fond of him and understood his impatience but, at the same time, she was aware of his young age and relative immaturity. She had been a victim of his practical jokes a few times. She was worried that his impatience would egg him on to try his experiment behind the others' backs and that thought really alarmed her. It was unthinkable in her world that someone would act unilaterally before a consensus was reached with everyone involved. She didn't remember it ever happening and wanted to make sure it wouldn't this time.

"So, what are you going to do?" she asked anxiously while looking at his face set in a rigid determination that didn't look good at all.

"I think I'll just fiddle with it a bit on my own, just to test out the key concept. That couldn't do any harm." Judd declared defiantly. I haven't decided yet, but that's the way I am leaning at the moment."

"Judd, I seriously advise you to discuss it further with your friends before going behind their backs. It would be a major betrayal of their trust and it might have serious consequences."

Judd smiled at her reassuringly, determined to close this subject. If he was going to decide on this issue, he would do it by himself, without undue interference from uppity girlfriends.

"OK, Shara, I'll sleep on it. Don't worry about me doing anything stupid. You should know me better by now."

"I hope so," Shara wasn't convinced that he would come to the right decision, but he obviously didn't want to talk about it anymore.

In the meantime, they had arrived at the small island, dropped anchor, and stripped for their much-anticipated swim. Her body was breathtakingly beautiful, and his well-muscled physique made them a perfectly matched pair. They spent the next few hours exploring these bodies to their hearts' content, basking in the glorious sunshine, the mild silky water, and their uninhibited youth.

All was well for the moment.

The meeting was held in Brady's house to avoid public scrutiny. For maximum security, they met in his living room, instead of the war room that had already been bugged once. Even though no trace of the cameras was ever found, he didn't want to take any chances.

The three visitors, handpicked by Garry Boxer, were seated on the two long sides of the dining table. The head of the table was occupied by Brady, with Boxer on the opposite side facing him. Brady opened the meeting:

"Gentlemen, acting on Colonel Boxer's advice I decided to form a new party: The White National Party or WNP, to represent the real Americans, those of us who don't want to let rapists and murderers overrun the country. Since I'm a soldier and I know nothing about starting a party, I must rely on your experience and expertise to set it up and organize it properly. The best way to start is by introducing ourselves to each other. We may start with Garry. Some of you already know him but let's do this properly so no one feels left out. Please state your full name, rank, if any, your expertise and experience, and, most of all, your motivation for joining this party."

Garry raised his 6'2" frame from his chair and looked around the table. "Since I know all of you, I don't need to say much. My name is Colonel Garry Boxer, regular army, retired. That covers my name, rank, and expertise, so all I have to state is my motivation. We must secure the existence of our people and a future for white children. The beauty of the White Aryan woman must not perish from the earth. Call me sentimental, but I have two children and a beautiful wife, and I owe it to them to stand up for their rights." He sat down, surrounded by smiling faces and polite applause.

Next to stand up was Herb Gibber, a middle-aged man with graying hair and a startlingly square head on broad shoulders.

"Some of you know me, but I'll state for the record. My name is Herb Gibber, CEO of the Gibber Consortium. It's an international trading company with contacts and assets all around the world. My experience is in organizing large-scale enterprises. My motivation is almost identical to what Garry stated, with one important addition. As General Brady said, I don't want to let riffraff run our country into the ground. It took me a long time to build up my business empire, I don't want it taxed out of business for the benefit of black junkies and Mexican welfare mothers."

Joshua Gromley was a man in his mid-forties with jet-black hair and a slightly bent posture. When he stood up, he looked around the table with a quizzical smile, hiding his overwhelming feeling of contempt for the idealists. He was a realist and knew that all that prattle about white supremacy was self-delusional bullshit. It was about one thing and one thing only: power. This group allowed him to acquire it on his own terms: manipulation of the masses with targeted propaganda.

"My name is Joshua Gromley and I am a retired Fox News host. My expertise is in mass communication. The citizenry has been sufficiently dumbed down to be steered in the right direction. General Brady, your new party's success depends on one thing: powerful propaganda. You need to be able to push the right buttons, in the right sequence, to motivate people to behave exactly as you want them to behave. My motivation is simple. I want to pull the strings of the idiots who have no idea what they want. I'll tell them what they want and make them believe it. I'm your man." He sat down, accompanied by muted applause. Not everybody liked cynically explicit speeches, they wanted to hang on to their illusions and excuses as long as possible.

Horace Handerson was a balding, middle-aged man with intense blue eyes, a fixed stare, and prominently protruding ears. His small 5'6" frame bent over the edge of the table, supported by two rigid arms, resting on the surface with splayed fingers.

"My name is Horace Handerson, I am a retired federal judge. I worked in the previous Republican administration, reforming federal prisons. My expertise is organizing correctional institutions on the principles of discipline and a policy of zero tolerance for any activity that could be interpreted as subversive or disobedient. In any party, to guarantee success, we must assure the loyalty of everyone involved. It can be done with a scientifically proportioned mixture of bribes and punishment. My purpose is very simple: I want to guarantee that the lofty ideals of white supremacy are carried to victory by pragmatic and time-proven methods. My motivation is unapologetic hate for the permissive, degenerate climate created by the liberal morons who allow almost total anarchy in our fine country. I want to live in an America that, if necessary, brutally enforces discipline and obedience."

The same polite, but slightly muted, applause followed his speech. It was a bit too candid for more delicate ears.

Brady was the last to address the group and conclude the meeting.

"Gentlemen, thank you for your frank and powerful statements. I suggest that we ask Herb to start the administrative activity necessary to register our party and I'll ask Joshua to summarize our thoughts in a publicly consumable manifesto. Horace, you'll be required to set up party disciplinary protocols and to make sure that all new members know their expected roles and sign a rules-and-regulations document. Once we have taken these initial steps, we must expand our core group to include some experts in fundraising, as well as someone experienced in recruiting membership. For now, we have a good start, I suggest we meet here once a week to report on progress. That's all for today, gentlemen, thank you for volunteering for this historical event: the birth of our party that stands, without apology, for what so many Americans have been waiting for, for so many years." This concluded the meeting and they all shook hands and left energized, ready to start on their assigned roles.

~

Zack was in an unusual territory. His carefree lifestyle belonged to the past. He had commitments and responsibilities piling upon his shoulders. He had never had a schedule before, he had just tinkered with his hobbies and had the occasional fun with Suzy. Now he owed people in various ways and he wasn't sure he liked it very much. On the other hand, he liked the new respect he received from both Petuccini and the Senator. He also liked the trust Suzy awarded him, if still somewhat on the cautious side. Most of all he liked the idea of them living and working together. In addition to all that, now he had a sort of income that he knew he badly needed. So, probably it balanced out and, maybe, he was a little bit ahead on the balance sheet.

He had three things on his plate right now: solving the Brinks robbery, finding out more about the aliens - both potentially paying jobs. For his own peace of mind: keep an eye on Brady, just in case he was on the warpath again, bent on revenge. He decided to make the third task into a brief daily routine and look in on him at varying times each day to see what he was up to. That's how he happened to witness Brady's meeting with four people Zack had never seen before. He recorded the meeting for later analysis and decided to consult his mentors about it, just in case they knew who these people were. He only wished that the Scope could provide sound but knew enough Physics to realize that voice was probably beyond the Scope's abilities.

Wanting to be on Suzy's continued good side he wanted to tackle the Brinks robbery next. He expected Suzy to arrive with her moving van later in the afternoon and he wanted to surprise her with some progress on real detective work. However, before spying on the robbers, he sent off a quick message to both Hopkins and Petuccini: "Brady is up to something. He had a meeting with four men in his house. You may want to see for yourselves."

Having done that, he was ready to catch the robbers red-handed. According to the article: "just before noon on Oct. 25. The guard was approached by two men with assault rifles, who stole the money the guard was carrying. Officials said the men fled the scene, and the guard was not injured. Witnesses described the robbers as two black men, about 6 feet tall, thin, and wearing Tyvek or painter's style suits and gloves. The getaway vehicle was described as a maroon 4-door sedan, possibly a Lexus 350".

Zack obtained the GPS coordinates for the location and set the space dial to that value. He set the time coordinates to 11:00 AM on the critical day and pressed the scan button. The big TV screen came alive and Zack observed the scene. There was light traffic on the street, a few pedestrians walking, and occasionally someone entering or exiting the bank but no sign yet of the Brinks truck. As always, Zack was impressed by the details the Scope gave him. He could see doves sitting on wires, a squirrel running across the road, narrowly missed by a red Toyota, awnings flapping in the wind. He zoomed in on some faces and the image was sharp and clear, he would have no problem filming the robbers when they showed up.

After about 35 minutes, the Brinks truck arrived, stopped in front of the bank and a security guard opened the door, ready to pull two canvas bags out of the back. At that point, a maroon Lexus screeched around the corner from a side street and stopped two feet away from the guard. It happened exactly as the article stated: two men jumped out of the Lexus, lined up their weapons on the guard, and grabbed the canvas bags the guard was holding. It was like watching a crime movie on TV. Zack couldn't see the robbers' faces, covered in masks, but he filmed the whole scene.

His main task would start when they jumped into their getaway car. Zack had already zoomed in on it and pushed the Track button. The Scope followed the car through the Takoma Park streets, zigzagging from street to street to evade pursuers if any followed. No one seemed to follow their car so, after a while, they slowed down and started driving normally like law-abiding citizens.

They drove to a suburban house and stopped the car. Both robbers got out and, by this time, their masks were gone, so Zack had a good chance to zoom in on the face of one of them before they turned away from the 'camera' and walked into the house, carrying their loot. Zack zoomed onto the house number and the street sign, then the license plate of the Lexus. Now he had everything he needed to claim the reward. The big question was how to claim it without revealing the Scope's existence. He decided on a story of driving through town when he observed the robbery. He 'followed' them to their house and filmed as much as he could with his dash camera before driving home. He had no intention of approaching the robbers as they were both heavily armed.

He looked up "Crime Stoppers Anonymous USA" on Google and received the following information:

"Crime Stoppers USA 1-800-222-TIPS How do I report a crime? Your local Crime Stoppers program will forward the information you have concerning unsolved felony crimes and fugitives wanted for felony charges to the appropriate law enforcement agency. Before calling a local program listed below, please be prepared to give as much detail about the crime or fugitive including but not limited to the following:

- What type of crime was committed or what the fugitive is wanted for.
- When the crime occurred or when the fugitive will be at a specific location.
- Where the crime occurred, where items from the crime can be found, or where the fugitive can be located at a specific time.

- Who is involved: name, nickname, age, date of birth, address, height, weight, tattoos, clothing, vehicle description, and people they associate or live with.
- Any other details you think will help law enforcement solve the case or capture the fugitive?

Also, have a pen and paper ready to write down your "secret number". Most Crime Stoppers programs will provide you with this secret number and that will become your identity and your means of staying anonymous. Never share your secret code number with anyone and never give your name or any information that could identify you to Crime Stoppers."

This was exactly what he had been hoping for and he wasted no time in calling the number. After he was directed to make a local call, he submitted all the information relevant to the case and received his 'secret number'. He was told to call again for information on the progressing investigation. He would have to identify himself only with the secret number each time he called and, if the criminals were successfully prosecuted, he would have to use the same number to claim his reward at any financial institution. Now he had to wait patiently for the case to proceed through the police investigation and the courts. It would be a while before he received the reward, but he had no doubt that this was his first earning of his detective agency. Come to think of it, he would have to call it something. He decided to wait for Suzy to help him dream up a good name for their joint venture.

~

Senator Hopkins was still in Washington when he received Zack's notification on Brady's meeting and decided to take a quick look before returning to Vermont. He called Zack from his car, announcing his visit, and was pleased with the young man's eagerness to consult him. As it turned out, he arrived only minutes after Petuccini, who also wasted no time in checking out this new development. The three of them watched the big screen of the Scope, just like old times. Petuccini only recognized Brady and Gibber who often appeared on TV news, but the Senator knew everyone present. He was scratching his head with some alarm.

"What on earth are they up to? I would have expected Brady to lie low for a lot longer but now he seems to be on the move. The good news is that this time he isn't after revenge, judging by the composition of the group, it's more like he intends to organize something big that he needs expert help with."

"Maybe his own party?" Petuccini ventured "I wouldn't put it past him."

"Hmm, that's not impossible" Hopkins agreed "being a Hitler disciple himself, that would be like following in the master's footsteps."

Zack just stood back, silently watching his two mentors, fully aware that this level of conspiracy, if it was that, was way beyond his experience and even, let's be honest, his interest. As long as Brady wasn't after them anymore, he couldn't care less what he was up to. Let the old men deal with it. When they were finished speculating, he promised to keep an eye on Brady, but he was more eager to talk about aliens from the past.

"By the way, I saw my little green men arrive at the site of the lab, in case you want to know. Do you want to watch them start building it?"

"Actually, I'm more interested in finding out where they came from." Petuccini sounded eager to continue going back in time, but Zack was reluctant to do that now. To keep jumping back after readjusting the time coordinate every time, was a tedious job, he preferred to let the Scope do the work and start tracking forward automatically and find out where they had gone. If his theory was right, sooner or later they would leave Earth and he was eager to watch them get into their spaceships and take off. He could program the scope to increase the tracking speed to a year a minute and program his computer to alert him if it noticed a major change in the view.

He explained his thinking to Hopkins and Petuccini and both were just as eager to find out where the aliens had disappeared to.

"By the way, I have solved my first crime case" Zack announced proudly, to let his silent partners know that he was actually starting their business and making progress. He explained what he had found and how his reward was on the way.

"Wow kid, that's great news!" Petuccini slapped him on the back, "now I'll have some return on my investment. Good job!"

The Senator just smiled and congratulated him on his success.

"Zack, you may still justify an old man's faith in youth. Keep up the good work and keep us informed."

There was no trace in the room of the tension, fear, and animosity of a mere month before.

Judd didn't have to fight with his conscience for too long. Before he could be tempted into progressing with the device on his own, the Planetary Advisory Council made their recommendation: proceed with the invention, test it, but do not initiate first contact with alien species, should you find any. Especially not the inhabitants of their original planet, if one indeed did exist, and if anyone was still living on it. The only restriction they recommended was to use it only for historical research at least 1000 years in the past. That restriction seemed superfluous - nobody would consider violating each other's privacy.

Judd could live with that restriction; he was anxious to know if it could be built and if it could function as predicted by the theory. Ivo was just as eager to start using it to verify his theory about the original planet. Jenna had no more objection and the two of them started assembling the components in the University's main electronics lab. They had improved the design to allow the Viewer to track continuously backward in time and drastically increased its range to follow a tracked object practically anywhere in the Galaxy. It didn't take them too long to put it together and the long-awaited moment to turn it on arrived. They had invited Ivo for the occasion and Jenna watched his face with mild amusement. She had never seen him so excited before.

"Ivo, are you ready for a disappointment?" she asked anxiously, trying to prepare him for the possible failure of his quest.

"I'm not going to be disappointed," he answered somewhat testily "even if the original planet turns out to be only a myth, this device will be an invaluable asset to all historians, not just myself. But I'm sure that we'll find our planet of origin, all the facts I know point to its existence."

"OK, Judd, turn it on and see what happens!" they both said at the same time and Judd didn't need further encouragement. The first thing Ivo was anxious to observe was what happened at the archeological site he and Jenna had visited. They found clues to their dark and violent past and they were mystified as to what happened and why. Ivo had the space coordinates and from carbon dating, they knew the approximate time those events had taken place. So, Judd entered all the data into the Viewer and pushed the Scan button.

The screen lit up but all they could see was some meadow with wildflowers and a few bushes scattered around. They could see a barely visible settlement on the horizon and Judd adjusted the controls, zooming in on the distant buildings until they had a close-up view. Ivo realized that he had been holding his breath all this time and made a conscious effort to relax. This was unbelievable, they were watching a long-gone settlement, from 45,000 years ago, with people moving about, vehicles driving on the roads. It appeared to be a small town with mostly one-story houses, a few with signs, several flat roofs with fliers parked on them. One larger building came into view and Ivo recognized it as the ruins they had visited.

"Please Judd, zoom in on that building and see if we can get a better view."

Judd did that without a word, and the familiar shape came into focus. It was a two-story structure, with windows on both floors and a flat roof. A parking lot surrounded it on three sides, with about a dozen vehicles clustered around a side door. The front entrance had a double glass door, with five steps leading up to it from the road.

"Is there any way to look inside?" Ivo asked anxiously.

"Very simple, Ivo, all we need to do is wait for someone to enter the building and then we can activate the tracking function and let the 'camera' follow him or her inside."

"Can't you just adjust the space coordinates by a few units to move to the other side of the door?"

"No, I can't adjust the space setting with such a fine increment. Best wait for someone to enter."

As if on cue, they noticed a young man in a lab coat walking briskly toward the door. Judd quickly zoomed in on him and pressed the track button. It was like magic as if they were sitting on the man's shoulders and walking through the door with him. They were gliding along over the floor of a long corridor with doors on both sides until they arrived at another double door. Their 'guide' walked through it and they were inside a large laboratory with workbenches around, each covered with strange-looking instruments. Some were occupied by people in lab coats, busily adjusting controls on whatever they were working with.

They spent an hour exploring the building with different 'guides' walking to various parts. The only other place that didn't look like someone's office was a large open space on the second floor that looked like a hospital ward with single beds arranged in a grid pattern. Some were occupied by people lying down, seemingly asleep, with unidentified equipment fixed to brackets over their heads. This was a total mystery; they didn't have any idea what was happening.

The last place they visited was found by following a young man walking into an elevator. They 'joined' him going down to a basement that seemed to be storage for equipment and documents. At least that was their impression seeing one wall covered by filing cabinets and bookshelves.

"Can you jump forward in time, Judd, I'd like to see how this place changed over time. I can't imagine what could have caused those holes and signs of destruction we observed in the ruins."

"Before I do that, I suggest we have a break. I'll need to make some adjustments to the resolution matrix so we can have a sharper image. We could also have lunch and maybe discuss a strategy for further research. We know that the Viewer works, now we must decide who can have access to it for what purpose. Once the news is announced, I'm sure we'll have tons of requests for viewing time."

They all agreed to pause for lunch and digest this incredible event. Watching long-dead people from their planet's history wasn't an everyday experience.

~

It took Judd longer than he had expected to make the adjustment to the Viewer, so they postponed further investigation until he had it ready. Ivo didn't mind because he had to think over his strategy for the research he had just started. The first thing he had to do was contact the chief archeologist at the site and tell him about the basement below the level they had already explored. As far as he knew, nobody was aware of it. If it was a repository of old documents, no time should be wasted in trying to get into it. Finding these documents could fill the gap in the visual knowledge obtained from the Viewer and maybe explain what their ancestors were up against on this planet. It could contain references to the migration from the original planet and that would be a major breakthrough in his research.

As it turned out, he was a step behind his colleague at the site. Rong, the chief archeologist at the site laughed aloud hearing his suggestion.

"Ivo, you are way behind the times. We unearthed it a week ago and found it to be a treasure trove of practically intact artifacts. There are machines of unknown design, extra beds stacked against a wall, and, most of all, bookshelves with actual books and videotapes on them and five filing cabinets full of old documents. It's going to take us years to catalog all that, let alone understand the contents."

Ivo found it hard to breathe. This was exactly what he had been hoping for and he knew that he had to be there in person, searching for clues. He just couldn't wait years it would take for systematic and painstaking processing that archeologists would insist on.

"Rong, would it be all right with you if I joined your team? I'm very anxious to find something relating to my own research?"

"Still hunting for your 'original planet'?" Rong chuckled with amusement "come on down here and have at it, the more the merrier!"

"Thank you so much, my friend, I should be there tomorrow by noon."

Ivo rang off and made a few more calls, notifying his friends and colleagues that he would be absent for an indeterminate period.

Judd welcomed the news because he was still having trouble with the adjustments and realized that he would need at least a few more days to work out the wrinkles. Jenna wished him luck and promised another exciting restaurant visit after he returned. The last thing she said stayed in his mind for the long flight: "I wish I could go with you, Ivo, I'm somewhat used to your company now and would enjoy sharing an adventure with you, but I guess flirting is the last thing on your mind at the moment. So, go and find the evidence for your theory. You deserve a breakthrough."

Ivo had never realized before how much he too enjoyed Jenna's company and this was the second time she used the word 'flirting'. Maybe there was more to it than mere jesting between two colleagues. Thinking about it gave him a pleasant daydream of him and Jenna being perhaps more than friends one day.

~

Judd finally finished the adjustment to the Viewer and was pondering what to do next. His theory about information dispersal was proven and he could spend weeks writing it up in a scientific paper, but the excitement of the hunt was gone. It would be smooth sailing from here on. Judd wasn't much interested in smooth sailing. It was only work and he detested work.

However, he was intrigued by the discovery of the old hospital and research lab and knew from Ivo that it had come to some kind of crisis later in time. He wanted to know what happened and, Ivo being away for who knows how long, he decided to investigate on his own. He didn't think he would be cheating the historian, more like doing the grunt work for him, so he could study the events when he returned. Jenna was busy with her own research and wasn't interested in further archeological investigation, so he decided to invite Shara to join him. She was astonished when he had told her about the Viewer and had been pestering him for days to let her see it. This seemed like a good opportunity to show off and have an enjoyable companion for the long and tedious investigation.

Shara arrived a bit out of breath, apparently, she took the stairs two at a time, bypassing the elevator up to his floor.

"OK, hotshot, show me this magical contraption that can spy on people long dead!" she smiled at him with real admiration and Judd was more than pleased that he had invited her.

"You are looking at it, right here on my bench." He pointed at the Viewer that didn't look very impressive; just a testbed with all circuit boards visible, connected by wires and cables of different thicknesses, a weird-looking metal mesh hanging off standard lab support, and a control panel with buttons and dials. Finally, a screen hanging from above the bench was connected to one of the circuit boards.

"You mean this exploded microwave with the guts hanging out? Is that what you want to impress me with?"

"It's not how it looks, it's what it can do, sweetheart. Do you want to see it in action?"

"By all means, show me something that I haven't seen before."

"Unless you are a mortician or a grave robber, you haven't seen too many dead people and I bet, even then you wouldn't have seen them walking and talking."

With that, he turned on the Viewer and pointed at the screen above it. The last scene they had watched before breaking for lunch showed up in a much higher resolution than they experienced the first time around.

Shara was watching the monitor intently, occasionally rubbing her forehead as if she wasn't sure she could believe she was seeing people from the remote past.

"OK, here we go." Judd made the first-time jump 10 years ahead. Nothing changed as far as he could tell, the same busy lab and hospital scene as before. He wanted to make the next jump, but Shara wanted to look around a bit, so he spent some time walking around, following different people, zooming in on faces, all seen by him before, all new to Shara.

"Are you sure you are showing me people from the past? They don't look any different from people I can see today."

"Look at the time dial, you'll see that it is set to -45,124 which means that you are watching events, as they happened, roughly 45,000 years ago."

"I guess I'll have to take your word for it. Why would you make it up just for me?"

Judd made several more jumps ahead until, after the third ten-year jump, he saw something different. The building seemed somewhat damaged. Pockmarks that hadn't been there before appeared on the walls and several windows were broken. He had to go back in slower increments until he found the cause. He did that, kept narrowing down the time window until finally, he saw something quite different and not a little bit alarming.

He came upon a pitched battle between two groups of people outside the hospital. One group was wearing uniforms, helmets, and protective shielding while the other was dressed in regular clothes and carried some sort of weapons. He could see flames erupting from the muzzles and could see chunks of masonry breaking off the side of the building. The projectiles were flying around the protective shields of the first group, not hitting them but passing harmlessly. The people in the uniforms weren't firing any weapons but seemed to be aiming miniature parabolical mirrors at the people in the other group. Whenever the parabola lined up with a person, he crumpled to the ground unconscious. Shara was clutching Judd's hand so hard that it started to hurt.

"What's going on? What's happening? Why are they hurting each other? I have never seen anything like that, I couldn't imagine that people were capable of doing that to each other!"

"I have no idea, sweetheart, but this sure explains the damage we saw earlier on the building."

In the meantime, the battle came to an end. All the attackers were lying motionless on the ground. More people came out of the hospital with stretchers. They picked up the fallen attackers one by one and carried them inside. Judd wanted to know what would happen to them, so he zoomed in on one of the stretcher-bearers and tracked him inside. They walked to the hospital area and gently moved the motionless body onto a bed. Then they attached restraining straps to the torso and positioned a strange device over the prostrate body to point directly at the forehead. Some dials were adjusted, switches were thrown, and several lights were turned on from a small control panel at the foot of the bed.

"I have no idea what they are doing and why" Judd admitted in response to Shara questioning look "we need to wait for Ivo to make some sense of this. He is the historian, after all, it's his job to figure it all out. I think we have seen enough for a day."

Shara was still shaken by the scene they had witnessed. Nothing like this was ever seen or done in their world, as far as anyone could remember.

"Never mind a day, I'll never want to see this, or anything like this again, as long as I live. It seems that our people have a dark and frightening past I'd like to forget about."

"I'm sure Ivo would vehemently disagree with you - it's his job to find out what happened and why and maybe alert us to the possibility of something like this coming our way again. Who knows what unimaginable combination of circumstances made this possible? We can't form an opinion until we know more. Maybe Ivo will find a clue, or explanation, in all those archives he went to study at the archeological site. We saw filing cabinets and books in the basement and I'm sure he is busy paging through them right now. I can hardly wait to show him this sequence of events when he gets back, although he might be pissed off with me for not waiting for his return."

"Judd, I strongly suggest we leave this place now. I want you to take me to a nice restaurant and then a nightclub and, after we are properly loaded, to bed. I need some serious cheering up."

Judd had no objection to this plan, so he shut down the Viewer and walked Shara out of the building, with his arm reassuringly around her waist.

Retired Senator Gordon Hopkins and his wife Muriel
Hopkins were sitting in their favourite chairs, in front of
the big Franklin stove, looking out through the floor-to-
ceiling windows in their living room, watching Daisy and
Bearcub chase each other in the snow. Since Gordon had
not been running for reelection his term was over and he
permanently retired from politics, moving back to
Vermont. After weeks of living together in their old home,
they remarried in a quiet ceremony, attended only by a
few of their closest friends, who weren't surprised at all by
this turn of events and were very happy for them.

They didn't need another honeymoon, the domestic
bliss of being together again, leaving his turbulent life in
politics behind for good was enough, all they needed was
the tranquility of their beautiful forest and their faithful
canine companions. The excitement of the last few months
had taken a lot out of them; in their late sixties, they
didn't need to add to that. Their total happiness was only
clouded over by disturbing news from the outside world.
The country was in an ugly mood, divided as it had never
been before.

The millions of Norman Brady's supporters felt bitter
and cheated by their party withdrawing Brady's
nomination, after the unmasking of his Nazi leanings.
They had been on the verge of victory, ready to celebrate
the election of the first proudly white president and that
victory was snatched away in the last minute by their
party's cowardly leaders.

Instead, they were saddled with another Democrat who
was wishy-washy about the real issues facing the
beleaguered white population. The economy was in
shambles; jobs were disappearing faster than anyone had
ever seen before. Brady had not minced words about their
situation. The nation that used to be white had become
darker and darker over the decades. He blamed the

immigrants, especially people of colour from the Middle East, Africa, and South America, for all their miseries, and his followers believed him.

Most of his supporters were unaware of how the march of automation killed jobs faster than any other factor. They just believed that Brady was telling them the truth, exactly as it was, and they trusted him as they had never trusted a politician before. And now he had been betrayed, cheated, cast aside by the very people who had embraced him before. This couldn't be accepted, couldn't be tolerated. Following the election, an upsurge of racially motivated violence erupted all over the nation. Random attacks on all segments of people of colour became a daily event.

And then came the bombshell: Brady resurfaced after a long absence, with the announcement of his new political party: the WNP or White Nationalist Party. It had published its platform, describing its basic principles which were openly and proudly racist. It called on the white population to support the party's aims in reestablishing the supremacy of the descendants of the original settlers. The response was overwhelming. Within days, all the until then fringe white supremacist parties and organizations scattered all over the nation announced their support for Brady. The recently established membership recruitment offices were swamped by the crowds lining up outside their doors, ready to join and pay their membership fees. Within a week they had enough members to qualify for official federal party status and the party was duly registered with the FEC.

Gordon and Muriel were horrified by this turn of events. After their struggle to stop Brady from becoming president and threatening to drag the country into potentially disastrous adventurism on the world stage, now they were threatened again by a new party that aimed to stoke the fires of fear and hatred that a large misguided segment of the population suffered from. They should have known better; they shouldn't have imagined that Brady would just fade away and disappear forever.

And, this time there was nothing they could do, nothing anyone could do. The racial resentment that had been simmering and brewing for decades finally found a focal point and they just had to wait to see how it would play out. It all depended on the sanity of the overall population. The question on both their minds was the same: are there enough decent, intelligent people left in the country to counter this new outbreak of insanity?

The rest of the world, outside America's borders, was busy with its own problems. It had never looked crazier than it did now. More and more countries were struggling with economic and racial problems, Venezuela was on the brink of civil war, most of Africa was in turmoil and starving. China clamped down on its population with high-tech surveillance, monitoring every move, making Orwell's Big Brother look like a friendly uncle. India and Pakistan were in a direct confrontation over Kashmir as well as the shared rivers directly affected by climate change. Japan was on its way to developing its nuclear weapons to counter a perceived Chinese threat. The European Union was beginning to fall apart after Britain finally left, the resurgence of nationalistic and populist leaders in almost every country in the Union made advances daily in the polls. Hungary's far-right ruling party spread anti-immigrant propaganda to justify its dictatorial suppression of all dissent, even France, Spain, Germany, and most other members had their growing anti-immigrant movements, that threatened to gain real power in the next elections.

Gordon and Muriel watched these terrible events unfold. Day after day, they watched the news with more and more reluctance, bracing themselves for a new disaster: political, military or environmental catastrophes threatening to tear the planet apart.

~

Zack was mostly unaware of these threats, he was busy following his aliens with the Scope, waiting for the computer to signal a major change in the scenery. Tracking for change in the lab was automated with time increments of a year a minute and Zack wondered how long it would take for something to change. He had to wait a long time: by dinner time there was still no beep from the computer and Zack wasn't sure if anything would happen before he went to bed. It had been 5 hours since the scan started and that would be the equivalent of 300 years for the aliens.

When the computer finally beeped, he rushed to the Scope, stopped the tracking, and looked for the change that he was alerted to. The first thing he noticed was the near darkness in the lab and then the empty workbenches. Nobody was around anymore, the place looked deserted. Maybe it was the middle of the night, Zack thought, so he started jumping ahead by one-hour increments, waiting for the day shift to arrive, but it never happened. The lab remained deserted. What was even more surprising was that it also remained dark. The time stamp on the scope showed noon hour next day and it was still in almost total darkness, illuminated only by a few emergency lights.

Zack thought that maybe an experiment requiring total darkness was underway and maybe it was dangerous enough to require the evacuation of the premises for the duration. He decided to check his theory and verify that it was indeed daylight outside, so he adjusted the vertical space coordinate to raise the 'camera' above the roof. That's when he got his second big surprise: he had to go up way higher than where the roof should have been, but finally, he emerged in bright sunlight as he had expected. However, when he looked down, he couldn't see the building at all. Everything was gone, the building, the cars in the parking lot, the parking lot itself, all were buried under what appeared to be a mudslide.

Zack was horrified to witness that much destruction. However, this explained why the site had never been found until archeologists unearthed it 45,000 years later. His plan of following the aliens to the point where they completely left Earth was thwarted, with nobody to follow from where he was now. He had to go back and find the moment just before the disaster and see where the people escaped to. They must have escaped because he had not seen any corpses inside the buried lab, so they must have had ample warning to evade being buried alive.

Zack needed a break. He also needed to call Petuccini to let him know about this new development. He was anxious to earn the five grand Joe had promised him for solving the mystery and he didn't want to leave him out of the hunt for the final piece of the puzzle. He looked at the clock and it was time for dinner. To save time he decided to order pizza and spend the last hour before Suzy's arrival with the moving van to clean out the room she had selected. Zack had already removed everything that Suzy didn't want, so all it needed was a quick vacuuming, removing cobwebs, and washing some old stains off the wall.

Petuccini didn't answer his mobile so Zack left a message hinting at a breakthrough in his research. By the time the pizza arrived Suzy's room was ready, and he settled down to a relaxed quiet dinner, undisturbed by buried and disappearing aliens. He had just finished his pizza when he heard the key in the front door and Suzy walked in, for the first time she used her own key to enter the house, like someone who actually lived there. Zack savored the moment while running to the front door, picking her up and twirling her around in a joyful embrace.

"Welcome home honey!" he greeted her, putting her down after a quick kiss on the struggling girl's cheek, missing the mouth of Suzy's shaking head.

"No time for it, Romeo, I'm paying for the van by the hour and you better start helping me unload, or you'll have to pay for the extra time."

Zack couldn't care less about the extra hour the van would cost, but he respected Suzy's concern and, without further delay, he accompanied her to the driveway to open the back and side doors and start removing her meagre possessions. A few pieces of furniture, lots of boxes and plastic bags, and a huge number of plants in containers of various sizes were the lot. The biggest piece they had to tackle was an upright piano that surprised Zack - he had never seen it, never heard of it, and didn't even know that Suzy played the instrument. There was no time for explanations because the driver kept looking at his watch that suggested one more hour would have to be paid for if they didn't remove the last few pieces in time, so Zack jumped into the van and started handing bags and boxes to Suzy. It looked like they had made it in time because the driver looked disappointed when both doors were slammed shut.

"Well, that's it, Suzy announced to the driver, three hours, $150 as agreed. Here is the cheque."

"Thank you and good luck!" the driver hopped into the van and drove off. Now all they had to do was carry all the boxes, bags, and furniture into the house and move them up to her room.

"Zack, can we leave the piano downstairs in the living room, please?"

"No problem, we'll make room for it somehow and I'm really looking forward to hearing you play it."

"Not much to hear, I'm afraid, it was my parents who made me take lessons while growing up, but I have never been very good at it. I can play simple pieces like Fur Elise, but that's about it."

"So how come you kept it?"

"You can call it sentimental reasons. I always imagined myself playing soft music to my baby, once I had one and, besides, that was the only serious piece of furniture I ever owned. I decided to hang on to it and, maybe, sell it if I badly needed money."

The piano looked almost new and very heavy. Zack was scratching his head trying to figure out how to wrestle it over the curb and the front step when he heard the phone ringing inside the house. He rushed to answer and was greeted by Petuccini's loud voice:

"Hey, kid, real progress at last? I'll be there in half an hour. I was just leaving for Ocean City when I got your message. I have a couple of hours before leaving for the airport, so show me what you got!"

"Joe, would it be possible that your driver gave me a hand here? I have Suzy's piano sitting on the sidewalk and it's too heavy for me."

"No problem Zack, my driver is a real weightlifter and I don't mind lending him to you for a few minutes. No charge!"

There was nothing else to do but wait. Everything else was already inside and up in Suzy's room, so they sat down to wait for Petuccini and his weightlifter driver. Zack used the time to tell her about his success with the Brinks robbery. He had kept it a secret, a surprise 'welcome home Suzy' present.

"Zack, that's great!" she seemed impressed by his progress "How long do you figure before you get the reward?"

"Oh, it will be a while, they have to follow up the information I gave them, arrest and prosecute the perps and then it has to go to court, so I assume it will be months before we see any green. But, once I solve a few more cases, there should be a steady flow of money coming in."

"Have you got your next case lined up yet?"

"No, but I have made real progress on Petuccini's assignment and that will bring in five grand that we don't have to wait for. Joe is very prompt with his payment, that's one thing I really like about him."

As if on cue they heard a car arriving in the driveway and went outside to see Petuccini and a big burly figure emerge from inside. It took the three of them no more than a few minutes to get the piano inside. Petuccini sent the driver away, instructing him to pick him up later for the drive to the airport. "I'll call you when I'm ready, so don't go very far."

When he was gone, he turned back to Zack with eager anticipation clearly visible on his face.

"OK, Zack, show me what you got!"

"Suzy, you'll have to excuse us for a while," Zack apologized "but I think you'll be busy unpacking your things upstairs."

"See you guys later. Let me know if you find anything interesting." Suzy smiled at the two men looking like little children who anticipated catching Santa Claus on Christmas night.

~

The Scope was already set to the coordinates at which the computer announced the strange events in the lab and Zack explained what was happening. He followed the same path he had taken before, leading Joe up through the roof, the thick layer of mud covering the building, all the way to sunlight where they could look down and see the desolation.

"Wow! What a mess! This must have been a tsunami of some size," Petuccini exclaimed "but it also buried your chance of finding out where they went. Nothing left to track, so what are you going to do now?"

"I'm going back in time again, to find out the exact moment when the disaster happened and see the people escape. Then I can track them again."

Petuccini was rubbing his temples with both hands, still looking bewildered by this unexpected turn of events.

"I'll never get used to what this damn contraption of yours can do. Jumping back and forth in time, at will, needs some time to get used to."

"Well, here we go, but it might be tedious again for a while because I have to keep jumping back and forth until I pinpoint when the event happened. Are you sure you want to watch me do that?"

Petuccini, never a very patient man, declined.

"Just let me know when you find something, I'll be back in town tomorrow to sign some legal papers. You have my number, if I'm busy, just leave a message."

Suzy came downstairs when she heard Petuccini's driver honking outside and said a friendly goodbye to the man they had so much feared and hated just a few months before. It's weird how time can change your perceptions and feelings toward each other, she mused, as Petuccini left.

The rest of the evening was spent in a domestic arrangement of their new life together, moving things around in the living room to make room for the piano that finally got pushed against a wall, surrounded on three sides by the couch and the two armchairs.

"I don't know about you, Mr. Time, but I'm tired to the bone and want to sit down, enjoy some quiet rest before you bury yourself again in your Scope. Do you think you could put on some music and get me a beer? And don't think that this is an invitation for you know what. I'm too tired even to think about that now."

Zack smiled at her reassuringly and did as he was told.

"Looks like I'm already properly trained to become an ex-bachelor."

They both laughed at that because they knew that which of them became the master of this house still remained to be seen.

ATLANTIS 6

Ivo arrived at the archeological site with high hopes. In his briefcase, he carried the same universal translator he had used to translate the diary he and Judd had retrieved from the cave laboratory last month. This device had been invented and developed for historians a hundred and sixty years before when they started discovering ancient manuscripts. It included a scanner, a high-resolution camera, and an extremely high-speed processor running the program with a pattern recognition algorithm specially designed to recognize and analyze language-resembling visual and audio data patterns. Ivo was prepared to spend the next few days selecting likely subjects from the archive documents and scanning them in, page by page, video by video.

Rong greeted him at the front door of the geodesic dome that the archeologists used for meetings. He had a huge smile on his face and, when they shook hands, he led Ivo to the conference table which was covered with about a dozen ancient-looking books and video cassettes.

"I took the liberty of selecting some of the most likely volumes for your research. This will get you started in comfort and keep you from under our feet at the site. After your visit down there, you may study these in detail. I assume you brought your translator - we have only one and are using it full time, so we can't lend it even for an hour."

"No problem, Rong, I wouldn't go near ancient documents without it. But I must see the place first, you can't talk me out of that, so don't even try."

"I've expected that, so let's go."

"Do I need to change my shoes or clothes?"

"Don't need to do anything, the new dig is quite passable, you can come as you are."

Ivo parked his travel bag on one of the chairs and followed Rong out to the other side of the parking space, to the building he remembered from his last visit. Once inside, they proceeded to the southwest corner where Ivo had seen the elevator on the Viewer. There had been nothing there on his last visit to the site. Now he found the elevator shaft with a temporarily installed hoist hanging over a hole in the floor. Ivo looked at it with thinly disguised suspicion, not quite trusting the flimsy-looking contraption, and Rong laughed at his hesitation.

"It's a lot stronger than it looks. We use it all the time."

Just as he said that a worker walked by them, placed his feet into the sling attached to the hoist's cable, and put his weight on it. Activated by the pressure, the hoist started lowering the man who soon disappeared below the floor. A few minutes later the hoist reappeared, ready for the next 'passenger'.

"See? Nothing to it. I'll go down first and then you follow me."

Ivo did that and soon he was standing on the floor of the basement archive he remembered from the virtual tour. The place was now fully illuminated by evenly spaced lanterns, connected by a thick cable that led to a small generator in one corner. He walked straight to the filing cabinets and the bookshelves and stood there for a while as if in a dream, looking at books over 45,000 years old.

"Don't touch them yet, we have to prepare them for viewing with specialized preservatives before they can be scanned. They are quite fragile and require careful handling. You are an academic historian, not familiar with the techniques archeologists have to use."

"I assume the documents in the dome are already prepared."

"Yes, they are, ready for you whenever you are. If you tell me what you are after, I'll select further likely volumes and have them prepared for you."

"Thanks, Rong, you are very helpful. I'm after anything that looks like a personal diary, executive summary, or reference notations. At the moment I'm not interested in the details of anything, I am trying to see the big picture.

Where did these people come from, what were they doing here, what was this laboratory for?"

"That's what I thought you were after when I selected the samples that I prepared for you. Now that you have confirmed my assumption, I can select and prepare further volumes for your research."

"Rong, you don't know how grateful I am for your help."

"I have to admit I have always been fascinated by your theory of the original planet. I want to know myself if there ever was one. If I weren't so busy with the technical details of this project, I would join you in the hunt, but there are a lot of people depending on me and waiting for instructions, so I'll let you go back to the dome and start your work. Let me know if you need anything else."

With that last comment, Rong patted him on the back and walked off to the other end of the basement to a group of people in dusty overalls who were obviously waiting for their boss.

Ivo glanced lovingly at the shelves one more time before walking back to the hoist and stepping into the sling. He would soon hold those prepared books and documents in his hand and start the long and tedious process of scanning them into his translator one by one, page by page. This was going to be a long day.

It took him three days of painstaking work to find what he was looking for. It appeared to be the personal diary of the chief scientist running the lab. He had a partial translation with many of the words followed by a question mark in brackets, placed there by the translator whenever it encountered a word with multiple possible meanings. Ivo had his translator print out the documents, so he could make notes on them as he progressed. The diary started on the day of the author's arrival at what he called "the landing site". Ivo could hardly breathe as he turned the pages, hoping to find the confirmation he needed.

This was the longest stretch we have had to cover in our journey. Our capsule (landing craft?) was almost out of fuel, barely enough to break to a safe landing speed before the chutes opened. We made it down in one piece and finally rested on solid ground. We took the necessary measurements before opening the main hatch and everything seemed safe, exactly as the original survey promised us from orbit. We disembarked and our captain gathered us around him, standing on the new world. There were a hundred and twenty-seven of us, soon to be joined by the crew from the five other ships currently in orbit, once we certified the orb (planet?) safe. We looked around and everything was lush green with unfamiliar vegetation, predicting a tolerable climate. The air felt a bit chilly but fresh and clean, not what we were used to on the island we had to abandon. The sulphuric fumes that had enveloped our settlement were still stinging my eyes and nostrils with an unpleasant memory. We knew we had to leave in a hurry, our instruments registered a deep underwater earthquake that followed the volcanic eruption, to be followed by a tsunami of devastating power. We sent off a hasty message to the southern continent, advising our main settlement of our escape, and took off with our ships. Once in orbit, we had a long conversation with the others and tried to persuade them that they join us in a new search for a more hospitable planet. We didn't want to go back to that hellhole or join the others who were busy daily fighting the savages. We had enough of that planet. We had tried long enough; it was time to leave. Not waiting for a decision by the others we left orbit and took off searching for a new orb (planet?).

Ivo had to stop reading at this point because his hands were shaking so hard, he couldn't hold his scanner steady enough to continue reading. Here was the confirmation he had been searching for all these years, not quite hoping that he would ever find it. Now he was sure: his people had come from another planet. They had to abandon it because of geological upheavals that threatened their survival. He resumed reading, once his nerves calmed down. The next several pages were filled with scattered and sporadic entries describing the arrival of the five other ships from orbit and the feverish activities that followed. The next long entry was made several years later after they had established their settlement. It seemed they had come to another crisis.

We have a serious problem. The settlement has split into two groups that want different rules. Most of us are happy to continue sharing both the work and the resources equally, but the small faction, led by Zormat wants to establish a merit-based reward system that we used to have before we embarked on our long journey from our homeworld after its destruction by that asteroid. We couldn't come to an agreement, so Zormat and his followers left with a substantial part of our resources and started their own settlement a few days from our own location. There was nothing we could do to stop them, but I am really worried. This is the first time that our people split into rival groups and it doesn't bode well for the future. What if they come back and try to force us to adopt their lifestyle? We must be prepared.

It was at this point that Ivo realized: his species had gone through all this once before when their survivors arrived at that unfriendly planet after their homeworld had been destroyed. So, his species had two original planets, not one. Planet #1 was their homeworld where they evolved, Planet #2 was the one they first escaped to, but some of them had to abandon later, and Planet #3 was where they finally settled down. Ivo was born there 50,000 years later.

Ivo had a very bad feeling about this, already knowing about the signs of battle and violence he had observed on the building at the archeological site. Still unaware of Judd's finding the actual battle scene, he continued reading the diary with growing anxiety. The entry appeared to be made five cycles (years?) later.

We had a big meeting last night in the large conference room. Our chief biogenetic scientist, Mazer, made an analysis and proposal regarding the threat we are facing from the splinter group who moved away five cycles (years?) ago. They want to come back and unite the two groups under Zormat's leadership. Mazer announced a breakthrough in his research in finding a neurological cure for antisocial behaviour, which is a combination of chemical and radiation treatment. He proposed that if they attack us, we could use his method to treat as many of them as we can capture and cure them of their aggressive and self-serving attitude. His proposal was accepted, and the decision was made to build a hospital facility with a biogenetic lab attached, so the necessary radiation facility could be installed as well as the required medicine developed.

The last entry in the diary was made three cycles later. Apparently, they successfully established the hospital and, after a horrendous battle with Zormat's followers, they managed to capture and treat all the survivors. The diary entry described the harmonious consensus they had managed to establish within the united group and the continued expansion and thriving of their settlement.

Ivo wiped his forehead that was covered, he had just realized, with sweat. There were more documents to scan and read, but he had what he had come for. It was time to go back to the University and continue his research there. Now he knew what he was going to search for with the Viewer, he could hardly wait to share this exciting news with Jenna and looked forward to the enjoyable restaurant visit she had promised.

~

Ivo wasn't even a little bit pleased with Judd for going ahead without him. He hated missing out on the excitement and, also, it stole his thunder of discovery at the site. How could ancient manuscripts compete with witnessing the events described in the diary? Nevertheless, after he calmed down, he viewed the scene Judd had found with unspoiled fascination. Now he could watch the events with the full knowledge of what had happened and why. At least he had the opportunity to explain the background to Jenna who was also watching the scene for the first time.

He had called her last night, after talking to Judd and invited her to join them the next morning to see it for herself, if her schedule allowed. Jenna was more than eager to rearrange her schedule; she wouldn't miss the exciting new developments for anything. Besides, she had a surprise she wanted to spring on him and could hardly wait to see his reaction.

When they finished watching the scene in the Viewer, Ivo read from the transcript of the diary and was satisfied with the rapt attention both his colleagues paid to the narrative. Finally, all three were on the same page in the history of these mysterious ancestors. Judd was satisfied that he had managed to prove his theory with a working prototype of the Viewer, Ivo finally saw the proof of his own long-debated theory about the original planet, and Jenna was pleased that Ivo was in a jubilant mood, the best she could hope for before she made her suggestion to him.

She thought that it was time to test the waters with Ivo and find out if there was any chance of a more intimate relationship between the two of them. So, she invited him for another dinner at one of her special places, carefully selected to surround them with a romantic atmosphere.

~

The place was both a restaurant and a nightclub, with a live band playing soft, melodious pieces. The decoration was stunning: all walls and the ceiling were covered with crystal formations, suggesting the inside of a cave. The millions of tiny surfaces reflected the candle lights on every table and ghostly holographic bats were flying in the air, all over the place. Ivo's and Jenna's table was inside a booth by the wall, well away from the other tables to give them a feeling of privacy. All the tables were clustered around a dance floor where several couples were swaying with the rhythm, most of the dancers' eyes closed in a dreamy expression.

"Wow!" Ivo exclaimed "if the food is half as good as the decor, I'll go home bloated, I can see that. What do you call this place?"

"They call it the "Matchmaker" and, honestly, I had no hidden agenda when I brought you here. I only wanted a nice private place where we can discuss the implications of this new discovery you made. You are aware of them, aren't you?"

"I'm not quite sure what you are referring to, I can think of several implications, mostly historical, but I didn't expect you to notice them."

"No, it's not the historical connection I'm thinking of. Ivo, we are facing a potentially serious ethical dilemma here."

"What do you mean ethical? I don't see it."

"Think, Ivo, what would happen if we found your original planet and our cousins were still living there?"

"We have discussed this before, that's why we had to consult the Planetary Advisory Council."

"And they told us not to initiate first contact. Have you thought about why?"

"No, I have to admit, I was more interested in proving my theory than speculating about first contact issues."

"Well, now that you have proven your theory and, not only that but from that diary, we also know a large number of facts that we can't ignore."

"I still don't see how the information we received from the diary would have any ethical significance."

"OK, let's take it one step at a time. We know that our ancestors came from another planet where conditions were unfavourable. They had to leave their island and come here. However, there was another larger settlement on the southern continent and those people didn't leave. If they had, there would have been a mention of it in the diary. There wasn't any. So, let's assume that they stayed there and evolved into the current inhabitants. There was mention of fighting the 'savages' so we can assume that with their superior technology, they wiped out the natives and took control of the planet."

"Yes, that sounds like a reasonable assumption, but I still don't see where you are taking this."

"We also know that their species, our ancestors, still had the aggressive disease and there was no hospital yet to cure them. Whatever happened on that planet is partially our responsibility. So, what will we do if that planet had evolved in the wrong direction and ends up if it hasn't yet, like our home planet?"

"Oh, my word, Jenna, I see where you are going with this. Our ancestors destroyed one world to the point where they had to abandon it and, maybe even now, they are doing it to another world!"

"I see you have got my point. So, what do you think about it?"

"Well, on the other hand, your reasoning rests on a large number of unproven assumptions. We may not ever find that planet again and, if we do, we may find that they had evolved out of the aggressive disease and are completely fine now."

"That's all possible, Ivo, but we have to be aware and be prepared for unpleasant discoveries if you pursue your quest. I just wanted you to be aware of potential dangers."

"Thanks, Jenna, you certainly put the bug in my ear, but there is nothing we can do about it tonight. So, forget about it for now and let's enjoy the place. Do you want to dance?"

"I didn't dare to hope that you would ever ask, but miracles do happen, I guess. Lead on Ivo, show me that even historians know how to treat a lady."

Zack was super frustrated with his lack of progress in learning more about the aliens. He had found the scene in which they evacuated the lab, presumably to escape the approaching tsunami. He had tracked them to spaceships that he had not seen before. There were six large silvery disks on the ground, supported by launch pads. He observed the people loading cargo and, when everything was safely aboard, embarking themselves, leaving the parking area empty. He tracked a man inside and found the interior fascinatingly simple, devoid of the high-tech accoutrements he was used to seeing on the ISS. He observed the aliens strapping themselves onto padded hammocks, ready for takeoff. When they were all lying on their backs, he waited for signs of acceleration, but the only sign of movement he observed was through one of the portholes that showed the buildings quickly receding as the ship gained altitude. Soon they were above the cloud cover and nothing else could be seen for a while. The sky became darker and darker and, finally, everything looked dark with all the stars of the Milky Way burning brightly.

"Now I'll find out where they went," Zack thought, settling in to watch the exciting voyage in space. However, his joyful anticipation didn't last long. After a few more minutes the Time Scope screen went blank and he couldn't see anything.

"That's no time for a breakdown!" he cursed aloud "I have no idea what went wrong and how to fix it." He glanced at the space coordinate and saw the vertical value rapidly increasing, but every attempt he made to regain visual contact failed.

"Maybe if I go back to the beginning of the ascent and try again, the glitch will disappear," he thought, unless it's permanently damaged.

He was in luck, resetting the time and space coordinates to the starting point did the trick and he could start tracking their ascent as he had done before. He was holding his breath, waiting to reach the point where the screen went blank, hoping to safely pass beyond that coordinate, but his hopes were dashed when the exact same thing happened, at the same point.

"Well, the Scope isn't broken," he assured himself, "chances are that it cannot track beyond the limit of its range. If that's the case, I'm totally screwed. I have no way to find out where these people went. What's even worse, even though I can find the time when they arrived on Earth by jumping back and forth in time, I have no way to track them backwards in time. The Scope can only track forward. This means I can kiss Joe's five grand goodbye; I can't deliver what he wanted to know."

Zack was super frustrated, but there was nothing he could do about this situation, so he resigned himself to start looking for a new paying client, as he had promised Suzy he would. Before starting his search, he reluctantly made the call to Petuccini, leaving a message about his failure to solve the mystery. As he finished leaving the message, Suzy came downstairs, and, seeing his gloomy face, she hugged him from behind the chair and suggested they break for dinner.

"Good idea, Suzy, I was just about ready to start a Google search for our next client, but I sure can use a break. The last two hours were very intensive, and it all ended in total failure to solve the mystery of the aliens. That means we won't get the five grand from Joe either, so the sooner we find another paying client the better."

He explained the problem he ran into and, surprisingly, Suzy didn't seem too upset about the loss of that big chunk of money.

"Actually, I'm happy that the wild alien chase is over, because our future is here on Earth, not in outer space. It was fun watching them for a while and, I admit, quite an intriguing mystery, but it didn't have a future in making a living."

Zack's disappointment was somewhat mollified by Suzy's positive attitude and he resolved to forget about the aliens and start looking for work they could do together. *"Joe just has to lump it and live with the disappointment."*

~

Norman Brady was bored. His party was taking off beyond anyone's expectation, but it required careful planning and organization and neither of those was his strength, or even interest. He was a soldier; a man of action and he didn't see any immediate opportunity for his kind of battle. He left the organization part to Herb Gibber and the propaganda campaign to Joshua Gromley, both highly competent in their expertise and doing a great job. Brady needed something he could do well, and he chose to join Horace Handerson in organizing and arming their security militia. He knew from Hitler's biographies that having a well-disciplined and trained paramilitary force, such as Hitler's SA, was key to his success. There were countless ways he could use a private army to intimidate his opposition, even swing elections in the future. So, he threw himself fully into planning the composition and training of his future 'troops'.

There was no shortage of volunteers from the ranks of the newly recruited party members, his only problem was financing the whole thing. The membership fees collected to date amounted to a substantial sum, but weapons and uniforms did not come cheap and he needed serious funds. Luckily, his good friend Hugo Schermer was an absolute wizard at soliciting a financial contribution from rich industrialists and corporations who embraced Brady's white supremacist platform so, in a short time, he was able to start arming and training his new recruits. Brady was in his element. To underline his agenda, he ordered uniforms in all white, resembling the French foreign legion's mercenaries. He recruited several career military officers from his old regiment - it appears there was no shortage of racist sentiment among the ranks. In a few months, his private 'security force' swelled to 4000 'bodyguards' all over the country, and their uniforms and sidearms were worn with pride.

Brady spent almost all his time at rallies, spreading his message to those who were eager to hear unapologetic pride in being the white descendants of the original settlers. These rallies almost always ended in near riots with the crowd enthusiastically chanting racist and anti-immigrant slogans. Bonfires, candlelight marches, militaristic brass bands, and colourful banners were popular - all out of Hitler's playbook.

While all this was going on, the rest of America stood by in silence, refusing to believe that history might be repeating itself, intimidated by the sheer size and ferocity of Brady's movement. It was all completely lawful, Brady made sure that he gave no excuse to any government agency to crack down on his activities and he was particularly respectful of the standing military forces of the USA. In all his rallies he repeatedly emphasized that his party was seeking a legitimate and democratic share of the political scene and, beyond the psychologically intimidating effect of his large paramilitary force, he did not authorize any overt acts of violence against his enemies.

Brady was content. Things were humming the way he preferred them to hum and he spent the morning hours daydreaming about the inevitable ultimate victory. He was going to show the fucking assholes that a Norman Brady can't just be wiped off the map. Once he had real power, he would look after those bastards who helped Trevor Smythe to unmask his intentions and humiliate him in front of the whole country.

His reverie was interrupted by Horace Handerson who walked into his office, looking determined.

"Norman, I have a question for you."

"Shoot!" Brady chuckled over the unintentionally chosen word.

"What are we waiting for?" the other sounded aggrieved, jutting out his chin and assuming a combative posture, slightly leaning forward in Brady's direction.

"What do you mean, Horace?" Brady really didn't have a clue as to what was bothering him.

"We've been ready for weeks, your troops are trained, armed, in uniform and they are just sitting there, costing a lot of money and not doing anything."

"What should they be doing?" Brady was perplexed now, without an idea where Handerson was going with all this.

"There will be a demonstration this afternoon in front of the White House, demanding that the administration sign the amnesty law for illegal immigrants, passed by Congress last week. I think we should show our hand and hold a counter-demonstration with our troops, it's time they took notice that we are here, and we are strong."

"Hmmm, not a bad idea." Brady was rubbing his chin thoughtfully, then added a note of caution. "Make sure they are not carrying their arms for the occasion. I don't want things to get out of hand, we are not ready yet to risk a crackdown by the government." Brady was painfully aware of what had happened to Hitler when he acted prematurely.

"I'm happy you approve," Handerson looked pleased and energized "I was hoping you would, so everything is ready. It's set for 3 PM this afternoon. You may come and watch or just see the TV coverage."

"Oh, I'll be here all day, I have meetings all afternoon with Hugo and his bankers, but I'll leave the TV on, so I won't miss it. Just make sure things don't get out of hand. Shouts and taunting are OK, but no violence. Not yet."

~

Gordon and Muriel were watching the TV when the news started, showing the demonstration at the White House. It seemed perfectly peaceful, a small crowd of about 50 protesters marched on the sidewalk, carrying placards with signs like "Immigrants are human too", "Help the helpless!" and "They deserve a home" - nothing Gordon and Muriel could disagree with. When the law was passed by Congress they had cheered, hoping the new Democrat president, Sam Triden, would have no problem signing it into law. The demonstration was organized by the "American Immigration Council" and the news briefly displayed the Council's mission statement: "Promotes laws, policies, and attitudes that honour our proud history as a nation of immigrants. Through research and policy analysis, litigation and communications, and international exchange, the Council seeks to shape a twenty-first-century vision of the American immigrant experience." Gordon was particularly pleased to see both sexes and all ages represented among the protesters.

"Looks like there is still some conscience alive in this country" he commented to Muriel. "Imagine what the scene would be like if Brady was president?"

"I'd rather not imagine such a horrible thing," Muriel shook her head as if trying to dislodge the unpleasant thought. "It's scary enough to see him shouting to the idiots at his rallies."

"I don't know how those morons can still believe in him after they saw that video we published. They don't seem to mind that they are cheering for another potential Hitler."

As if an answer to Gordon's rhetorical question, the TV camera swung sharply toward the other sidewalk where a new procession had just arrived. About a hundred people appeared, marching in formation, in identical white uniforms, carrying placards with well-remembered slogans, like "America for Americans" and "No criminals and rapists!" and "Protect your heritage!" They came to a dead stop, facing the other protesters across the street and lit torches, holding them high.

"Oh, my God!" Muriel exclaimed, "now they have troops, straight out of Hitler's playbook."

"I'm sure they thought that the white uniforms were a clever idea, being a white supremacist party, but they buried any hope they may have had for votes from the black American community. The stink of Ku-Klux-Clan is too strong to ignore for any person of colour."

The two groups were staring each other down and the tension on the street was easy to see. Finally, one of the pro-immigrant demonstrators, a young woman, crossed the street and started talking to a middle-aged man who seemed to be the leader of the counter-demonstrators. She didn't have a chance to say too much because the man standing next to the leader spat in her face and knocked her down to the pavement. Gordon and Muriel gasped in unison at this unexpected display of violence. The woman painfully got on her feet, a thin trickle of blood oozing out of the cut on her forehead where it had hit the stone. That was the end of any hope for a peaceful, orderly demonstration. As if obeying a command, the two groups charged at each other hitting, kicking, and wrestling. Before the police could intervene, dozens of bodies were lying on the pavement and the few policemen present wasted no time in calling for backup to help subdue the crowd.

In a few minutes, the sound of sirens was fast approaching the scene. Dozens of more policemen in riot gear spilled out of the vans and attacked the fighters, pushing them to the ground and cuffing their hands behind their backs. It took almost half an hour for the last demonstrator to be subdued and loaded into the vans, it seemed indiscriminately from both groups.

Muriel was shaken to her core; she had not seen anything like this since the Vietnam War and this was even more frightening than that.

"Gordon, we have to do something." She looked at him with pleading eyes. "We can't just sit idle while this is going on. I don't know what we can do, but we have to try. Could you use Zack's Scope somehow to spy on them and discover their plans before they can put them into action? Maybe if we know what they intend, we could somehow forestall it. There must be others as horrified by all this as we are, and we should organize an anti-Brady resistance group. You are the politician, what do you think?"

"I've been thinking along the same line, Muriel, and that means I'll have to go back to Washington and visit Zack, as well as talk to my friends on the hill to see what's going on. This must be stopped."

They looked at each other sadly, knowing that their tranquil 'honeymoon' in their beautiful Vermont forest came to a sudden end and they were back in the trenches again.

~

Zack was spending his day searching for the next likely client. He got over his disappointment at being unable to solve the mystery of the aliens, but he wasn't looking forward to telling Petuccini that he had given up the search. He hated to admit defeat. Up to this point, he had thought that the Scope had unlimited range and could solve any mystery. Now he realized that it had a built-in maximum in space coordinates, and he was permanently confined to planet Earth. He had fantasies of roaming the Galaxy, at least visually, and finding out what's out there.

"Oh well," he thought "as Suzy said, our living is here on Earth and not going on 'wild alien chase'. But it would have been nice to earn another five grand."

As if on cue, thinking about Petuccini, his phone rang, and it was Joe on the other end.

"Hey, kid, how's it going? I'm in your neighbourhood and can drop in for a few minutes if you aren't too busy?"

Zack was just about to tell him about his failure but decided it would be better to break the disappointing news in person. Besides, maybe Joe would want to compensate him for the partial result he had obtained, so he said it was fine, come and visit any time.

He barely had time to go back to his search when his phone rang again.

"Never rains but pours!" he mused, picking up the phone again. It was the Senator to say that he wanted to talk to him, the sooner the better.

"If you want to come over this morning, Senator, I'll be here, and you also have the chance to meet an old friend. Joe will be dropping in too and we can have an anti-Brady reunion."

"If you think you are kidding, Zack, think again. Have you seen Brady's army on the news?"

"Yes, I have, and it made me sick. I can't believe that people can be so stupid, but I don't see what we can do about it."

"That's what I want to talk to you about and it's just as well that Petuccini will be there because I wanted to talk to him too."

They agreed to meet in an hour and Zack said goodbye with an uneasy feeling about the whole thing. The last time they were all together, he was roped into a conspiracy that consumed all of his free time.

"Suzy won't be pleased about this," he thought morosely "but I don't know how I can say 'no' to the Senator. He is my silent partner and provided a lot of the cash I needed to get started. At least Joe will be here too, so I won't be alone with the Senator."

As it turned out, Suzy wasn't angry at him for agreeing to hear the Senator out. She had seen the violent clash between the demonstrators on the news and was very much alarmed by it.

"See what they have in mind and if you can help without jeopardizing our future business. I hate that bastard Brady as much as you do and if we can give him a black eye again, I'm all for it."

Ivo and Jenna didn't spend any more time talking about the ethical implications of their discovery. They were having too good a time to waste it on distant cousins on the other planet. As it turned out Ivo was a fairly good dancer for a historian and, besides, he was good company. Jenna was quite pleased with the way the evening turned out. They discovered a few things they had in common and Jenna was surprised that Ivo had artistic talents. Apparently, he wrote poetry, played several musical instruments, and was dabbling at woodcarving. She was amazed at what you could find out about someone whom you had known for years. She was particularly interested in his musical talent because she herself had played music since she was a child and thought that maybe they could play duets someday.

Ivo also had a good time and found dancing with Jenna a stirring experience. He had been married once, a long time ago, but it ended in a painful divorce, after which he stayed away from women and immersed himself in historical studies, archeological excavations, conferences, and publishing books. Holding an attractive woman on the dance floor, swaying to the rhythm of soft music, brought back old memories of being in love and enjoying physical intimacy. So, when it was time to leave, he screwed up his courage and asked her to join him for a nightcap in his house.

"Jenna, I know that you had no ulterior motive when you brought me to a place called "The Matchmaker" but, I have to admit, it did have an effect on me. I find you very attractive and, in case you feel the same way, we might want to explore this further and see where it leads."

Jenna looked at him with an amused look and held out her hand for him to hold. "Let's find out, Ivo, we are both scientists and experimenting is in our blood. I'm also curious to see where this might lead and, if we insist on honesty, I find you attractive too, and not just in the intellectual sense."

Ivo's place was not far from the 'Matchmaker', so they decided to walk the short distance. The air was warm and heavy with the fragrance of blooming spring flowers, so they walked slowly, holding hands, enjoying the mood with happy anticipation of the night ahead.

~

Judd's effort to cheer Shara up was rewarded with a more intensely emotional night than they were used to. Apparently, witnessing the violence in their remote past was a traumatic experience for both, more for Shara than for Judd who tried to look at it with a detached, scientific curiosity. After Ivo had explained the reason for that confrontation, he was satisfied that this could never happen again due to the biogenetic treatment their ancestors had all received. The peaceful, intelligent cooperation they had grown up with was proof enough that their species was beyond its barbaric past.

However, the ethical implications Jenna brought to their attention couldn't be ignored. It became imperative to make every effort to find the original planet their ancestors had migrated from. If the group that stayed there still existed and evolved without genetic treatment, that place could be in very bad shape. They were responsible and owed it to whoever lived on that planet to help them overcome their mental affliction.

So, Judd settled down to the long and tedious task of tracking their ancestors back in time. The first task: verify that the diary Ivo found described the actual events that had taken place.

The Viewer he and Jenna built had the ability to track backwards in time, so he could automate the whole process. He set up criteria on the controlling computer to alert him to specific changes he was looking for. He had already seen the battle scene, but he wanted to find the exact time when their ancestors arrived in their spaceships. If he found that, then he could track forward again in appropriate time increments to record a cross-section of their entire history. He could also track backwards in time and find the other planet they had come from. Once the location of that planet was determined, then he could jump ahead with the time coordinate, while keeping the planet in focus and see what its condition was in his own time. Then the Council could decide if they needed to do anything about the current state of affairs.

The plan was simple enough, but even with computer-controlled automation, it proved to be a long and tedious process. Judd didn't like long and tedious processes: he was a theoretician, and he preferred to deal with the big picture, not the minute details. Luckily, he had a few graduate students he could rope in for the task and, once he explained what this was about, he had an enthusiastic volunteer for the job.

Magra was a very attractive young woman, a bit of a tomboy with her hair cut short and wearing the most casual clothes Judd has ever seen on campus. She looked as if she had just come from the gym after an hour of strenuous exercise. Still, Judd found her very sexy in a cute, unpretentious way and didn't mind working closely with her. He had to make sure that Shara didn't find them sitting close to each other, in front of the computer in animated conversation. Shara was the jealous type and Judd had been in trouble with her before for noticing sexy young students. So, he explained to Magra what he wanted, showed her how to control the Viewer, and left her at it.

After that, he felt free to indulge in another sailing adventure with Shara. He expected her to be free as she usually was during the day before rehearsal started at the theater. He wasn't disappointed and left the lab with

Magra at the Viewer. He walked toward the elevator, whistling a happy little tune.

~

Jenna received a call from Trivas, inquiring about their progress with the Viewer device. He hadn't heard from them for weeks and wanted to make sure that no hasty action was taken once the Viewer was functional. He knew that he could only advise; he had no authority to tell others what to do, or what not to do. That wasn't the way his society worked. Still, he knew that the potential for doing harm was great with this invention and the more responsible and emotionally unattached people looked at it from every possible angle, the better chance they had of avoiding problems later.

Jenna too was pleased to receive the call and let Trivas know about new developments. She wanted to be reassured that her instinct regarding the ethical implications was correct.

"Trivas, good timing. I meant to call you and report on our progress. The Viewer is working, and we have already learned a great deal about our remote past, some of which you'll find very disturbing. I think we should get together and discuss it in person, if you have the time to meet, maybe this afternoon?"

"As it turns out, I have nothing scheduled for the rest of the day. What if I visit you at the University and you show me this fantastic invention and some of the results of your research?"

"Let me check with Judd, the young Physicist who is controlling the Viewer, to see if he is available today?"

"That's fine, Jenna, call me when you have done that."

As it turned out Jenna couldn't reach Judd, but found his young assistant instead, busy with the Viewer. She explained to Jenna what she was doing, and Jenna thought they were getting dangerously close to locating the original planet. High time the Planetary Advisory Council was involved. She called Trivas again and asked him to meet her after lunch in her office. She asked Magra to suspend research and join them. The young woman was thrilled with the invitation from the department's most senior Physicist and didn't hesitate to tell her everything she knew about Judd's plans regarding the search with the Viewer.

"And what do you think about it yourself?" Jenna asked the eager young woman "Don't you find it too fantastic?"

"I have to admit I was a bit surprised to find out that our species may have migrated from another planet, but once I got used to the idea, I think it's a very exciting possibility."

Jenna explained to her that the gentleman they were going to meet was the head of the Planetary Advisory Council who wanted to know where they were with their research and Jenna needed her to show him the Viewer and some of the scenes they had witnessed before.

"Why do we need the Advisory Council?" Magra was surprised, and not a little bit excited, to find herself in the middle of a project with Planet-wide implications.

"If you pay attention to the discussion that I'm going to have with Trivas, you'll find out."

As if on cue, Trivas arrived, and, after the introductions, they proceeded upstairs to Judd's laboratory.

Trivas wasn't much impressed by the looks of the Viewer but understood that it was still a work in progress and not a finished product. He was much more interested in what it could do and watched in silence as Magra showed him the battle scene from their past. He was just as shocked by this revelation as everyone who had seen it before. Nothing like that had ever happened on their peaceful planet, as far as anyone could remember. Once Jenna explained the content of the ancient diary that Ivo had found at the archeological site, he was even more convinced about the dangerous implications of this line of research. "What if it can happen again? How reliable was that biogenetic cure the ancients discovered and applied to themselves? What if we find the original planet and the inhabitants are still afflicted?"

This needed to be discussed in Council at the earliest opportunity. They would need to set up a research team to investigate the science and technology related to the treatment technology that he had never heard of till today.

He said his thanks to Jenna and told her to expect a call from him once the issue was discussed in a full Planetary Council meeting.

"Jenna, I'm very pleased that you consulted me. You were right, this newfound evidence about our violent past needs to be evaluated as a top priority."

"Do you want us to stop further search for the original planet?"

"No, you can proceed and collect as much data as possible but, as we advised before, do not initiate any kind of contact until we have a full consensus on what to do."

"I agree, Trivas, I'll let you know when anything new is discovered."

Magra, who until now listened with rapt attention, seemed alarmed.

"Are you sure you want me to continue? This is the scariest thing I have ever encountered and I'm not sure I want to have anything to do with it."

"Yes, Magra, I want you to continue because we need as much information as possible. Continuing this research will help us make the right decisions."

Magra felt reassured by the request, realizing that she would be doing the responsible thing.

~

Magra was watching the Viewer with renewed interest. She felt better now, after both Jenna and Trivas had encouraged her to continue the research and, once she got over the shock of witnessing their planet's violent past, she was becoming increasingly curious about the distant cousins if, indeed, they did exist and were out there somewhere in the Galaxy. The search was slow and tedious, following the plan Judd had outlined and she wondered if she could speed it up by jumping back in larger time increments than Judd had suggested. The biggest risk with larger time jumps back to the past lay in their planet's movement along its orbit around their sun. If she jumped back too far, there is no telling what the planet's new space coordinates would be. She somehow had to find a way for the Viewer to track the planet through space while jumping back in time.

She had access to the theoretical specs Jenna and Judd wrote before building the Scope, but it was way over her head. Reluctantly she dialled Jenna's number, hoping that she wouldn't be slapped down for the interruption. As it turned out, Jenna was intrigued by her idea and promised to look into it. In the meantime, she advised Magra to follow Judd's plans with the small incremental jumps.

Magra didn't have to wait long. Barely an hour later she was visited by an excited Jenna, with a huge grin on her face.

"Kid, I just had an idea and I can't wait to try it out."

"Wow, that was quick! Please tell me."

"All we need to do is adjust the tracking algorithm to keep the focus on the planet even through time jumps. It's a simple software change, we don't have to touch the hardware. I came down to try it out, so if you kindly move over…"

The next hour was spent in intensive reprogramming of their controlling software and compiling, testing, and applying it to the real Viewer, after they created a backup, just to be on the safe side.

They fired it up and instructed it to start tracking back in 100-year time increments while focusing on the ancient lab building. When, after the fifth jump the building disappeared, they knew that they were close, so reversed the last jump and shifted the focus from the building to one of the scientists working there and started tracking him back in smaller, ten-year increments. They kept it up, always tracking the same person, and, after another hour of tedious adjustments, finally, they saw him disembarking from a silvery space vehicle, one of six that were clustered around an empty field. Apart from these ships and the people milling around them, they could not detect any sign of life or human habitation. They had found the time when their ancestors arrived.

"Judd will be pissed off if he finds that we beat him to the discovery," Magra said anxiously, but Jenna just laughed.

"Serves him right, being too lazy to do the boring work himself. He tried to dump it on you while he went sailing with his girlfriend. This will teach him that science is not all grand ideas, but an awful lot of tedious experiments. So, let's see where they came from."

They restarted the tracking, focusing on one of the spaceships, and followed its flight back through the galaxy in one-year time increments. After about the thirtieth jump, they found the ship on solid ground again, presumably on the planet they had travelled from. At that point they couldn't wait anymore, they had to know where they were. The space coordinates displayed on the Viewer pointed to a solar system 27 light-years distant.

Jenna adjusted the space coordinates to move the 'camera' high above the surface to have a better view. When they looked 'down' they could see an island a small distance off the shore of a larger landmass. The island looked desolate, completely covered by mud.

This place didn't look at all like their own planet and they could have no more doubt: they had found the place their ancestors had migrated from.

The time coordinate told them that they were 54,798 years in the past. Looking at the planet from an even higher altitude they saw large oceans, irregularly shaped continents, but no sign of civilization: no large population centers, no sign of industrial activity, no roads, and no other sign of human life. Moving around the equator, they did find another larger settlement on a heart-shaped southern continent, but that was all. The planet was covered with lush, green vegetation, apart from the ice caps at the two poles and the occasional deserts here and there. It seemed uninhabited apart from the small colony near the equator. They both knew what they had to find out: is anyone still living on that planet in their own time? Ivo's diary described leaving the groups on the southern continent behind, there is no telling if they also packed up and left at a later date.

Finding out was a simple adjustment: they focused on the planet with the space coordinates and adjusted the time coordinates to their current time. Their question was answered immediately. The view of the planet changed drastically. Most of the lush vegetation was gone, replaced by sprawling cities, huge industrial plants, and massive development projects going on everywhere. The view from their altitude was much hazier than it was in the past, suggesting massive pollution of the atmosphere. The ice caps were considerably smaller than last time; the sea level seemed a lot higher because many small islands they had seen before vanished. They could see huge new islands floating on the ocean where they had not seen them before. When they descended to a lower altitude and could actually see the surface more clearly, they were shocked to find that these new islands were made up of floating garbage, the detritus of a dying civilization. As they circled the globe, they could see ongoing battles taking place almost everywhere they looked. They could see missiles flying through the air, huge explosions where they landed, massed vehicles with turrets protruding forward, ejecting shells of various sizes, causing further destruction where they landed.

Jenna and Magra stared at each other in shocked disbelief.

"We found them, kid, and they are in trouble. Huge trouble."

It was the first time the three of them were together since they successfully defeated Brady's presidential aspirations. That was almost a year ago and they were busy with lives that had nothing to do with politics. However, the dragon didn't stay slain and looked more threatening than ever. They all saw Brady's army in action and knew that something had to be done. Their only weapon was Zack's Scope and he agreed to use it to spy on Brady and his cronies, to try to find out what their plans were. If he saw something that posed a real danger to the country, or even to individuals, they should warn the appropriate authorities or persons to be prepared. Senator Hopkins would be their conduit to the right person in the political establishment.

Zack had only one caveat.

"I can't spend more than an hour or two a day on this task, because I promised Suzy to put my priorities on our mutual business. She gave up her job, her place, and moved in with me. She trusts me and I must live up to that trust. Unless it's an emergency, I want it understood that my commitment to this cause is a limited one."

"Zack, we understand and respect that restriction." Hopkins was smiling indulgently at the young man's earnest demeanor. He mused over how much growing up Zack had accomplished in a short time. "I will find out the exact coordinates for WNP's headquarters and will let you know."

"He recruited a large number of criminals for his army," Petuccini was rubbing his chin thoughtfully "I'll get in touch with some of my contacts and set up some new information channels. You never know who will let you know about important developments. Beyond that, there's nothing much I can do to help."

"That's a great idea," Hopkins fully approved the suggestion "and I'll do the same in my circles. How about that? Criminals and politicians united in a common cause. Wonders never end."

"Now that we are in agreement," Petuccini changed the topic: "What's happening with the aliens? Have you found out where they had come from or where they went to?"

Zack had expected the question and reluctantly explained how he had failed to track the aliens into the future and how he had no way to find out where they had come from. "Joe, I regret letting you down, but I most of all regret being unable to earn the generous fee you offered."

"Kid, it's all right and, since you have done a lot of work already and secured some partial results, I'm willing to pay you half of the agreed amount. You think it's fair?"

"Joe, it's more than fair and I sure appreciate it. Suzy will be happy that I didn't entirely waste my time."

"It would be nice to know more about the aliens," Hopkins mused "but maybe we'll still hear from them. The way you found them makes me think that they may find us yet in the future. Obviously, they are way ahead of us in technology since they had space travel so many years ago. At the moment, there is nothing more we can do about that. So, let's just deal with our domestic aliens: Brady and his party."

With that last comment, the meeting was over and both Hopkins and Petuccini left Zack to carry on with his life.

~

Senator Hopkins had been gone from Washington for almost a year and wasn't sure which of his old friends were still in Congress or in the White House, where to start his inquiry. When he moved to Vermont permanently, he had sold his house, so he had to check into a hotel for the few days he intended to stay in the city. Once he was in his room, he pulled out the address book that he had kept all these years despite the smartphone craze everyone subscribed to, and started looking through the names, trying to decide whom to contact first. He concentrated on his Democrat friends and finally settled on the name Tim Harvey. They had had a good working relationship and Hopkins respected Tim as an honest and principled politician. He was sure that the Democrats were as alarmed about the Brady menace as he was and, if anyone knew about any movement to defeat and discredit this growing menace, it would be Tim. He was in luck; Tim was in his office and he answered Hopkins's call on the second ring.

"Hey, Gordon, that's a surprise!" he greeted his old friend "I heard you moved to Vermont and got married again. Congratulations, how is retirement?"

"Tim, thanks and everything is fine in Vermont, but I'm a lot more worried about what's going on in Washington right now."

"You mean Brady and his thugs? And we thought that we had finished him a year ago."

"Do you know of some action to counter this new threat?"

"The problem is that he is so careful to keep everything legitimate, we have no excuse to crack down on him. Our biggest obstacle is lack of information about his plans, so we don't know what to prepare for."

"That's what I am calling about. I and a few friends have a spy in Brady's party organization and could gather intelligence about his plans and activities, but we are in no position to do anything with that information. Do you have any suggestion whom to contact if we find out anything dangerous?"

"Wow! A spy in the hornet's nest? Do I know him or is it top secret?"

"Let's just say that he is 100% reliable and I trust any information from him without reservation."

"Well, if that's true, let me talk to a few people and pass on your suggestion. Where can I contact you?"

"I'll be in town for a couple of days and then back to Vermont. Here is the hotel's number where you can reach me. My Vermont number is 555-2123."

"OK, Gordon, thanks for contacting me, this is the first glimmer of hope I have seen so far for countering Brady's party and I'll see what I can do."

~

Petuccini sighed into his morning coffee: it was time to call Domingo again. He had contacted him a while ago about an island he wanted to purchase for his retirement. Even though they had a pleasant conversation, Joe didn't like to contact his family. They had a history of coming after him with the family business that he didn't want to know anything about. He had made it clear, years ago, that he wasn't going to be involved in anything illegal, or even attend family gatherings, so they had left him mostly alone. However, there was the danger that if he contacted them, they would renew their interest, and he was dead set against that. He was finished with his past and didn't want it to come back to haunt him. However, this time he needed information and Domingo was the only member of his family he trusted enough.

When his cousin answered the call, he sounded his customary jovial self and greeted Petuccini warmly.

"Hey Joe, twice in the same year! That's something special, must be important!"

"Dom, I need information again," Joe admitted reluctantly "not for me but for a friend of mine and, for that matter, for our country as well."

"Now I am really shocked, Joe, when did you become a patriot, wanting to do something for your country?"

"This is not a laughing matter, I'm sure you have seen Brady's thugs on TV?"

"Yes, so what? Everybody needs a hobby and building a private army seems to be his. Nothing to do with me."

"Dom, I need to know what's the word on the street. What's he planning to do? Do you know anyone who joined his army?"

"I know lots of idiots who joined up to play soldier. He pays well and they like the fancy new uniforms, the sidearms, and all the other trappings. Some people like to live in a fantasy world."

"Is there any way you can find out what he is training them for?"

Domingo felt reluctant to get involved, but then he had a bright idea.

"Let's make a deal, Joe. You attend my wedding reception next week and then I'll find out what I can."

Now it was Petuccini's turn to feel reluctant. He felt that if he agreed, he would be stepping on the proverbial slippery slope. No telling who would accost him with more family obligations or business proposals. Before he could make up his mind, Domingo reassured him.

"Joe, you don't have to worry about the family trying to rope you in again. Frankly, they don't trust you anymore, you are pegged as the black sheep of the family. This would be only a social event and I'd like you to be there for old time's sake. I always liked you."

"Very well, Dom, give me the date, time, and address, and I'll be there." Petuccini resigned himself to spending a few hours with the typical Italian family wedding circus. He was reassured by Domingo's guarantee that he would be left alone by the rest of them, but he was not going to take Maria with him to be gawked at.

"OK, Dom, we have a deal. Please let me know what you can find out about Brady and his plans."

"I'll do that and let you know once I gather some info. Make sure you wear a tux for my wedding, I don't want you to show up in your usual outfit."

They both laughed at that because Joe had a habit of wearing casual clothes, as a protest, to the formal family events he used to attend before he stopped going altogether. When he hung up the phone, Petuccini muttered to himself: "I hope the Senator appreciates the sacrifice I just agreed to on behalf of his crusade."

~

Sam Triden, President of the USA had a dilemma. The dilemma was represented by three documents on his desk that he had been staring at for the past hour. One was the Congressional Bill sent to him earlier today for his signature: the bill, after months of debate and wrangling, proposed a path to citizenship for all illegal immigrants who had not been indicted for criminal activities. He was leaning toward signing it, but the second document gave him pause. According to a secret CIA intelligence report a huge migrant caravan was being assembled in Guatemala, ready to start marching north. The estimated size of this caravan was over 20,000 migrants. Triden knew that as soon as this became public knowledge, if he signed the blanket amnesty into law he would be crucified. The third document had the title: "A Century of U.S. Intervention Created the Immigration Crisis." This document didn't contain news for him, he had known for a long time that the US used South America as its backyard property, promoting military coups, corporate plundering, and sapping of resources which resulted in the poverty, instability, and violence that now drove people from Guatemala, El Salvador, and Honduras toward Mexico and the United States. He asked himself if he had the duty to acknowledge his country's responsibility and do everything that he could to mitigate this humanitarian disaster.

The document was factual and didn't advocate anything he could or should do. The list of American subversive and military activities was sickening to look at.

Military/CIA activity that changed governments

Cuba   1898-1902   Spanish-American War
      1906-09   Ousts elected Pres. Palma; occupation regime
      1917-23   U.S. reoccupation, gradual withdrawal
Dominican Rep   1916-24   U.S. occupation
      1961   Assassination of Pres. Trujillo
      1965   U.S. Armed Forces occupy Sto Domingo
Grenada   1983   U.S. Armed Forces occupy island; oust government
Guatemala   1954   C.I.A.-organized armed force ousts Pres. Arbenz
Haiti   1915-34   U.S. occupation
      1994   U.S. troops restore constitutional government
Mexico   1914   Veracuz occupied; US allows rebels to buy arms
Nicaragua 1910   Troops to Corinto, Bluefields during revolt
      1912-25   U.S. occupation
      1926-33   U.S. occupation
      1981-90   Contra war; then support for opposition in election
Panama   1903-14   U.S. Troops secure protectorate, canal
      1989   U.S. Armed Forces occupy nation

U.S. INDIRECT INTERVENTION
Government/regime changes in which U.S. is decisive

Bolivia   1944   Coup uprising overthrow Pres. Villaroel
      1963   Military coup ousts elected Pres. Paz Estenssoro
      1971   Military coup ousts Gen. Torres
Brazil   1964   Military coup ousts elected Pres. Goulart
Chile   1973   Coup ousts elected Pres. Allende.
      1989-90   Aid to anti-Pinochet opposition
Cuba   1933   U.S. abandons support for Pres. Machado
      1934   U.S. sponsors coup by Col. Batista to oust Pres. Grau

Dominican Rep.   1914   U.S. secures ouster of Gen. José Bordas

    1963   Coup ousts elected Pres. Bosch

El Salvador   1961   Coup ousts reformist civil-military junta

    1979   Coup ousts Gen. Humberto Romero

    1980   U.S. creates and aids new Christian Demo junta

Guatemala   1963   U.S. supports coup vs elected Pres. Ydígoras

    1982   U.S. supports coup vs Gen. Lucas García

    1983   U.S. supports coup vs Gen. Rios Montt

Guyana   1953   CIA aids strikes; Govt. is ousted

Honduras   1963   Military coups ousts elected Pres. Morales

Mexico   1913   U.S. Amb. H. L. Wilson organizes coup v Madero

Nicaragua   1909   Support for rebels vs Zelaya govt

    1979   U.S. pressures Pres. Somoza to leave

Panama   1941   U.S supports coup ousting elected Pres. Arias

    1949   U.S. supports coup ousting constitutional govt of VP Chanís

    1969   U.S. supports coup by Gen. Torrijos

Most US citizens were blissfully unaware of these atrocities or swallowed the administration's justification that was nothing more than transparent propaganda: full of lies, false interpretations, sanctimonious platitudes about freedom and democracy. Triden was disgusted by the mainstream media that refused to inform the citizenry about the stark reality of his country's role in propping up dictatorships and subverting any local attempt to create a meaningful democracy and national ownership of the country's rich mineral resources.

The result of this intervention was the current state of lawlessness with drug lords and criminal gangs terrorizing whole populations, driving them out of their homes, forcing them to leave everything behind and run for their lives toward the US, in their desperate hope that they might find some level of safety for their families.

So how could he refuse to take them in?

Triden was a decent, honourable man and he felt he didn't have a choice. This act wouldn't be only a humanitarian duty, but also amounted to reparation for past crimes committed by his country. He signed the law and braced himself for the coming firestorm from his enemies.

~

Norman Brady was enjoying his favourite activity of the day: inspecting new recruits to his paramilitary force. They were lined up on the training ground he had leased from a now-defunct gravel company. It was ideal for all kinds of battle simulations with its uneven terrain due to the extensive excavation that had taken place before the business shut down. It was about a hundred acres, partly covered with dense bush, a marshy swamp, and a small lake, but mostly it was just gravel dunes, pits, and winding trails where the local youth had held ATV races until Brady had the whole area fenced around. He put up big yellow and red signs warning of potential danger due to military exercises. There was a good-sized cement-block building where the old offices and storage place used to be.

The hundred or so recruits were lined up in a crooked line, still in civilian clothes and various degrees of unkemptness. Well, he was going to shape them up, make them ready and worthy to wear the WNP uniform. He had just started his inspirational address to the would-be soldiers when his cell phone alerted him to an incoming message. He hated to be interrupted in the middle of his 'sermon' but glanced at it briefly to see who it was from. It could be important; he had a crucial meeting with some bankers this afternoon. The call was from Horace Handerson, his security chief and that was unusual - Handerson had never called him before, as he knew better than to interrupt Brady's troop inspections. Had to be important. He answered the call and was startled by the urgency of Horace's voice.

"Norman, we need you here right now. Please delegate to your second in command and come back to HQ Asap. There's a big development on the immigration front, and we need to make immediate decisions."

Brady was alarmed by the mysterious message and turned to Grady Smith, his drilling sergeant standing behind him.

"Grady, I must go, something urgent came up. Take over."

Without waiting for the "Yes Sir!," he spun around and walked briskly to his car just inside the main gate.

When he arrived at HQ, he found most of the party brass already waiting in the conference room. The big wall-mounted TV set was turned on and they were watching the morning news with rapt attention. The commentator was analyzing the significance of the two breaking news items of the day: Sam Triden signed the amnesty bill for illegal immigrants into law and the news of a large migrant caravan heading north from Guatemala. The speculation predicted huge opposition from the anti-immigrant factions in the government.

Brady was livid. He looked at his followers who were watching his face attentively, expecting an explosion from their leader. Someone turned down the volume of the television and now the room was eerily quiet, like the calm before a storm. Brady sat down heavily in his padded leather chair at the head of the conference table and took a few deep breaths.

"We'll have to do something about this. This time he's gone too far. We must stop those migrants. I have been expecting something like this to happen and I had contingency plans that I discussed with the governors of Arizona, New Mexico, and Texas. I'll get in touch with them immediately to coordinate our strategies. I want to put our troops on high alert, ready to mobilize at a moment's notice. All leaves are cancelled effective immediately and I want to prepare a public announcement for the press with our response to this outrageous betrayal of our national interest."

Trivas didn't expect a call back from Jenna so quickly. When he heard what she had to say, he didn't waste any time calling an emergency meeting of the Planetary Advisory Council. The new developments Jenna had reported required immediate action. Trivas had been planning to schedule a Council meeting for the near future, but Jenna's account of finding the original planet and the conditions it was in required some serious soul-searching. Were they responsible? Was there anything they could do to help? Should they interfere? These were all difficult questions and they needed more data, so he asked Jenna to study the planet extensively and contact the historians at the archeological site to find out as much as possible about their own violent history and how they managed to overcome the affliction that caused them to be aggressive and destructive. They might need to recover the science and technology that now was lost in the remote past. Trivas wasn't surprised that their current level of neuroscience was way behind what their ancestors possessed. Simply, there was no need for it in their recent history because sanity, cooperation, and consensus-driven decision-making had been taken for granted by their citizenry. Why research an area no one had a need for? However, now that they were aware of the possibility of a mental disease that could destroy their way of life, they needed to learn everything they could about this dangerous possibility. Jenna fully agreed with Trivas and called Ivo for a meeting as soon as possible.

Ivo was still a bit groggy after their last night together and was just waking up when his communicator beeped, indicating an incoming call.

"Hey, Ivo, don't tell me you just woke up!"

"Why, have I missed something? I thought after last night you too would laze around for a while. I am lying here, savoring my memories. What are you doing up and chipper?"

"You'll be up and chipper too if I tell you what you have missed this morning!"

"All I missed this morning is waking up next to you."

"Well, that would have been nice, but the world wasn't going to wait for us with its stupendous news."

"What news? Stop torturing me woman, and just tell me what happened." Ivo was getting exasperated with Jenna's teasing.

"Judd's young student, Magra, called me this morning about a problem she had with the Viewer and I decided to give her a hand."

"Why not Judd? Where is he this time?"

"Oh, he went sailing with his girlfriend. Too lazy to do the boring work, he figured that's what students are for."

"So, what problem did she have and why was that such a big deal?"

"Ok, if you don't interrupt me anymore, I'll tell you everything that happened this morning and then you'll see why you have to get up and get moving. We have no time to waste."

And Ivo did see why he had to get up and get moving. The story Jenna told him about finding the original planet shot him out of bed as if it was on fire. He hated to have missed the discovery and was intrigued, almost beyond endurance, enough to want to see everything for himself. So, he told Jenna to wait for him, he should be in the lab in half an hour.

"Wrong, Ivo, you need to call the archeological site and arrange a meeting with them at the earliest possible moment. Trivas wants to send a science team there to study all the available documents in the basement archive that relate to the biogenetic theory and treatment that they used to cure all those crazy people. We need to be prepared for anything that might have caused that aberration and find a cure, just in case the same symptoms show up here. He has called a full emergency Council meeting and he needs all the data we can give him."

Ivo agreed, reluctantly, to arrange the meeting before rushing to the lab to see the images of the original planet. "It's not fair," he thought "that two people have seen it already. It's my baby and I want to see the confirmation of my long-suffering theories that have been ridiculed for so long by my esteemed colleagues."

Judd was equally miffed when he returned from his sailing trip with Shara and found Jenna, Ivo, and Magra clustered around the Viewer, studying something intensely, hardly noticing his arrival.

"What's going on guys? What are you all doing here? I thought it would take Magra days to follow my instructions?"

"Brace yourself, Judd. With a little help from me, she managed to actually find that original planet and you have arrived just in time to see it for yourself. Ivo will see it too for the first time, so pull up a chair and watch the show."

Judd could think of several complaints to get off his chest, but curiosity beat his desire to nurse his bruised ego. He did what he was told and pulled up a chair to comfortably see the viewing screen.

After they spent a long time exploring the found planet, observing all the disturbing scenes that Magra and Jenna witnessed, they sat in silence, for a long time, each immersed in their own unhappy thoughts.

~

It took over a week for Trivas's science team to find, scan, translate, and study all the documents and videos that related to the theory and technology of biogenetic treatment that their ancestors had applied to their antisocial elements. The theory was over the heads of all of the experts, who only understood that it had to do with stimulating the mirror neuron activity in the brain's prefrontal cortex, or PFC, resulting in increased levels of empathy and, at the same time affecting the amygdala in the temporal lobe, as well as the hypothalamus at the base of the brain to inhibit antisocial impulses. The treatment was a combination of radiation therapy and specially tailored psychotropic drugs. The two treatments together were supposed to pacify violent impulses and modify the brain's reward circuitry to motivate the treated patients to seek peaceful cooperation instead of aggressively competitive behaviour. Soon afterward the patients displayed dramatic improvement in their personal and social interactions. Once the process started, it entered a positive feedback loop in which the rewards associated with increased cooperation reinforced the physiological and psychological process, and the effect became permanently locked into the brain.

Trivas's experts didn't know how the actual process worked because nobody had studied these brain centers and activities in recent memory. They had no antisocial elements anymore, a testimony to the effectiveness of the treatment their ancestors had invented and applied so many millennia ago.

They had found a detailed description of the radiation process, as well as the exact formulas for the composition of the psychotropic drugs, so they could try it at any time themselves. The big problem facing them was the lack of subjects to try it on. They didn't have any antisocial elements in their society, so there was no way to verify the effectiveness of the treatment. Yet, they needed to make sure, so they would have an antidote to the madness, should it manifest any time in their future.

Ivo, Judd, and Jenna attended the Council meeting by special invitation, as witnesses to the horrible effect that mental disease had on their distant ancestors. The three of them sat quietly, following the discussion and testimony of all the top experts, and waited for an opportunity to make the suggestion they had agreed to present at the conference. When the discussion stalled for lack of new ideas on how to test the treatment, Jenna, as the most senior of the trio asked to be recognized and allowed to make their suggestion.

"Very well, Jenna, we seem to have run out of ideas, so why don't you tell us what you think?" Trivas looked around the conference table and, since no one had any objection, he signaled Jenna to go ahead.

"Ladies and gentlemen, the only place where we'll find antisocial elements, suffering from that genetic brain disorder we witnessed in our distant ancestors, is the newly discovered original planet. There are millions of people right now, destroying each other and their planet. We suggest that we select a large enough center of the population currently embroiled in violent activities and try the treatment on it. If it proves successful, we can apply it to the entire planet."

She couldn't continue because of the uproar of indignation from almost everybody around the room.

"We have no right to experiment on another sentient species, regardless of how they are related to us!"

This was the main objection she could glean from the hubbub that followed her suggestion.

When the noise died down, Jenna continued her presentation.

"I believe we have two compelling reasons why we should. First, they are on the verge of extinction anyway, destroying their planet and each other with more and more violent wars and deadly weapons. Second, we are responsible for their predicament. We know from the diaries discovered at the archeological site that our ancestors who migrated from there to our planet left another group behind who became the ancestors of the people who live there now. Nobody had the means to treat them and their entire history is a result of the same mental affliction that plagued our forefathers. Like it or not, we are the same species and we are the lucky ones who survived the biological heritage that these people are suffering from. I submit that we have no choice: for both theirs and our sake we must try to help them. We have to try the treatment on a selected group on one of their continents."

This time she wasn't interrupted by indignant objections, everybody sat quietly, considering her arguments.

Finally, Trivas broke the silence.

"Jenna, thank you for this valuable insight and we will consider and discuss it within the Council. When we have come to a consensus, we'll let you know how we want to proceed. This is the biggest crisis our planet has encountered in recent memory and we'll have to consider all the implications very carefully."

This was a polite dismissal and the University trio took their leave, confident that their suggestions would be seriously considered.

~

A week later Jenna received another call from Trivas, telling her that the Council had come to a consensus regarding the action they would propose to all concerned. They accepted Jenna's, Ivo's, and Judd's suggestion of trying the treatment out on the original planet, in a limited way, focusing on one population center. They would send one spaceship that would take up geosynchronous orbit over the selected location and start the radiation process with a tightly focused beam, aimed at the city. They would also inject the psychotropic drug into the low atmosphere. They would require input from the University to pinpoint the location where they should aim the experiment.

They had contacted all the relevant production centers, asking for an estimate of resources and a timeline required to produce all the components for the project. Once everything was ready, one of their intergalactic space vessels would be equipped with stealth technology and dispatched with the necessary crew and equipment. Once everything was in progress around the planet, they would return and monitor the treatment's effect via the Viewer. Undertaking this massive technological task was the biggest challenge their planet had faced since moving all their heavy industry to the moons.

Jenna passed all this on to her two colleagues and they thought it was a well-conceived plan. Ivo surprised everyone by announcing that he wanted to be on the spaceship. He was a historian, and this was a once-in-a-lifetime opportunity to observe their ancestors from a near vantage point.

So, the only task remaining for the Viewer crew, as they started calling themselves, was to find the right target. It had to be a city with a sizable population so they would have a statistically significant database to analyze the effectiveness of the treatment. They needed a city where an observable level of violence was in evidence, but not the major battles they had observed from space because the combatants in the war were dispersed over too large an area to make focusing difficult. Ivo and Judd volunteered to study the planet in more detail and come up with a recommendation.

As they let the Viewer scan the planet's surface, they instructed the computer to look for large buildings that might be an administrative centers where they were most likely to find decision-making bodies that they would want to treat for maximum effect. According to theory once these centers were treated, they should be able to observe a gradual drop in the level of violence as combatants stopped their irrational behaviour.

So, Ivo and Judd spent long hours scanning the big city they had found close to the island their ancestors had taken off from, looking for signs of violent and irrational behaviour. They didn't have to wait too long. On an empty field that looked like an abandoned excavation site, they could observe a large number of people in white uniforms, carrying weapons, driving vehicles with protruding turrets, and occasionally ejecting shells toward a target that always erupted in flames when the shells landed. This seemed an ideal place for the focal point of their radiation treatment. Localized, easily observable, and a large enough sample for a measurable level of violence but small enough to be used as a focal point.

Judd had a hunch he wanted to follow up. He modified his Viewer to detect unusually high levels of neutrino emission anywhere on the planet. He knew from the first diary he had found in the underground lab that the originally built Viewer was left on the planet when their ancestors abandoned it. On the off chance that it was somehow found and put into use by someone there, it would be easy to spot by its characteristic emission. If the original Viewer survived, was found, and is now in operation, then his Viewer would have no problem locating it. Judd thought that it was an extremely remote possibility but, since it was easy to modify the Viewer to scan for neutrino emissions, he decided to let it do that, just in case. He decided to include it in the expedition's equipment and tell them to test his theory.

Petuccini had his first fight with Maria. Reluctantly, he told her about his cousin's wedding invitation and about his plan to go there without her to minimize their exposure to his family.

"Maria, you don't know them. They are awful, sickening sometimes, with their syrupy kindness within the family and often brutal treatment of outsiders who stand in their way. I broke contact with them many years ago and have no desire to renew any kind of relationship again."

"So why are you going at all then?"

"I promised the Senator that I'd try to find out about Brady's plans, at least what I can from street gossip. My cousin promised to let me know but his price was my attendance at his wedding. I intend to make it as brief as possible. If you were there, it would be almost impossible to leave early because you would be the main sensation and they wouldn't let go of you."

"Joe, I understand all that, but there is one thing you don't."

"What's that that I don't understand?"

"We are married now, and I want to know everything about you, good and bad. That includes your family. I need to meet them so I can see for myself where you come from. I love you and I want to love you with open eyes. We'll just put up with the syrup and the hoopla and, what did you call it? The Italian circus."

"I can't change your mind, cara?"

"Not a chance, Joe, I'm going, and I want you to show me off proudly. I promise I'll look spectacular."

"I have no doubt about that and, actually, I wouldn't mind rubbing their noses into my success and happiness. I only hope that Domingo's information will make it worth my while to put up with them for a few hours."

As it turned out, it wasn't very bad. True, Maria was whisked away from his side the moment they entered and from time to time he could see her in the middle of a throng of admiring men, young and old but, as Domingo had promised, he was mostly left alone, to sip his drink in the comfortable chair next to the fireplace. That's where Domingo found him and wasted no time congratulating him on his beautiful wife.

"You lucky dog," he said "Where did you find her? I can see why you don't need anyone else; she is the kind that can fill a man's life, leaving no place for others."

"Never mind the compliments, Dom. Besides, you have nothing to complain about. Your wife looks pretty impressive herself. Congratulations and I wish you both a long and happy marriage."

"Thanks, Joe. I'm sure you want to get on with the main reason you are here."

"You know me so well, I can't lie to you. So, what did you find out?"

"All I know is street gossip and a few solid facts. Brady seems to be on the move. All leaves for his troops are canceled. Unusual activity at the main warehouse where they store their gear. They have leased a large number of trucks. They are planning something big."

"How do you know this if all leaves are canceled?"

"They had a few desertions by some punks who got scared when they realized that the future might hold more than street skirmishes and parades."

"That sounds ominous, I must inform my contacts immediately. May I use your phone?"

"There is one in the library and you'll be private there. Nobody goes there during a wedding reception, so you'll be undisturbed."

"Thanks, Dom, I appreciate it. Please show me to the library, I have never been to this mansion before and I don't want to get lost. And please tell Maria that I'll be ready to leave in a short while."

Senator Hopkins received the disturbing news from Petuccini and felt sorry to have his worst fears confirmed. Brady wasn't going to wait for the next election. Sam Triden's signing of the immigration bill pushed him over the edge. Anything was possible from that madman. Gordon needed to get in touch with Zack immediately and alert the kid to start monitoring Brady's HQ. Once he had a solid piece of intelligence, he would alert his contact in the White House and ask him to relay the information to the President.

~

Zack was in the middle of a Google search for their next client when he received the Senator's call. Hopkins wanted to meet with him as soon as possible. He sounded unusually solemn, but he wouldn't say what it was about. Zack immediately assumed that it had to do with Brady and was alarmed that he would be needed for another conspiracy. However, it was impossible to say no to Hopkins, so he agreed to see him in a few hours at his house. Suzy was even more worried and demanded to be present when the Senator arrived. She didn't want Zack to make any promises without her consent. They had a right to live their own life and the Senator needed some overwhelming reasons to get them involved again.

The Senator had never met Suzy before. He was surprised to see her with Zack, showing no indication of wanting to leave them alone. Zack cleared it up for him immediately after they were introduced.

"Senator, this is Suzy Turnbull, my partner in crime and she will sit in with us this time. Just as you have no secrets from your wife, we also share everything. If this is OK with you, go right ahead and tell us what you have in mind."

Hopkins considered this unexpected complication in their relationship but, seeing Zack's determined face, he realized that he had no choice. He had to trust her if he wanted to use the Scope. Suzy's open, honest face reassured him that he had nothing to worry about.

"Very well, I appreciate your commitment to each other and I'm sure that I can count on both of you to keep things in this room. What I'm going to tell you might be frightening. Believe me, it was scary for me as well when I first heard it. Apparently, Brady is planning something big with his private army. I don't want to sound dramatic, but it might lead to civil war."

Now he had their attention, judging by the sudden intake of breath and their instinctive reaching for each other's hands.

"You had better tell us what happened and why you think it could lead to that kind of shit!" Zack blurted out, forgetting to mind his words with his distinguished visitor.

"Petuccini warned me of unusual activities. Brady's militia seems to be mobilizing in a big way for some unknown purpose. All leaves are canceled, transport trucks lined up, equipment getting prepared. What we don't know is what he is planning, and we urgently need to find out and warn the President so he can neutralize this threat before it gets out of hand. We need you more than ever to use your Scope to gather solid evidence about Brady's intentions."

"Senator, that's the scariest thing I have ever heard, but you know I can't hear with the Scope, so how am I going to find out anything?"

"I know that you can only look but I want you to look very closely at his HQ, try to find some open documents, pamphlets, calendars, or anything that might contain visible clues as to what he is planning. As before, the future of our country might be at stake. I'm sure you'll do the right thing."

Zack and Suzy looked at each other and their faces said it all. They had no choice. This was way over their heads, out of their league. They had to trust this elderly gentleman who had spent a lifetime dealing with issues of

this size. There was just no way to say 'no', so they both
nodded their heads reluctantly and promised to start
looking immediately.

~

Brady's call to the governors ended with the desired
result. When he told them his plans, all three promised
their support for their common cause. They had to stop
that new migrant caravan from crossing the border. They
had had enough. No more illegal immigrants. If the
president wasn't going to stop the migrants, they had to do
it themselves. Brady volunteered to do the dirty work of
physically stopping the horde, even if his troops had to
shoot them down. Disarming the approximately 9,000
Border Patrol agents stationed at the unfenced section of
the border would be no problem for Brady's heavily armed
troops of close to 12,000. He only wanted the governors to
defend his troops from the army that the President was
likely to dispatch to disarm them. If Sam Triden had to
face three states' National Guards, he would have to back
down, unless he wanted to trigger a civil war. It was time
for a major confrontation over the immigration crisis.
Bold, decisive action was the only way to end the
politicians' useless wrangling over this thorny issue. Brady
was ready for bold, decisive action.

He held the final strategy meeting in Party HQ, with
the aid of maps and a huge calendar covering an entire
wall. He intended to conduct this operation with military
precision where every phase was meticulously planned.
The hour-to-hour timeline was displayed in a multicolour
chart. He stood next to it, facing his commanders who sat
at the big conference table and took notes as Brady spoke.

Unbeknownst to him, an uninvited and invisible
presence in the room was busy studying these maps and
the timetable on the wall and filming the entire scene for

later analysis. Even though he could not hear a single word spoken, Zack was terrified by the display of Brady's plan, realizing that the Senator had not exaggerated the danger they were all in. He kept the computer recording the meeting automatically, while he dialed Hopkins's cell phone number.

"Senator, I have what you asked me for. I have just witnessed and recorded Brady's war council, or whatever it was, and have a clear image of the maps and timetable displayed on the wall. He was standing there, with a laser pointer, explaining what he intended to do, when and where, and in what precise sequence. By the looks of it he intends to move his troops down to the Mexican border and replace the border guards."

There was an ominous silence at the other end of the line as Hopkins digested this information. It only took a few seconds and then he was his old decisive self again.

"Zack, I'll be there in an hour to pick up the memory card with the video recording. Continue to keep an eye on them and record anything else you think might be useful. I particularly need to know the size of his troops and the kind of equipment they intend to take with them. If you find any indication of those, make sure you record it as well. "

"What are you going to do with this information?" asked Zack, immediately realizing that Hopkins had no choice. He had to inform the President.

"I'll call my contact in the White House and, as soon as I have the memory card, I'll have to pass it on to the President. As you have done before, you may have helped save our country again. I wouldn't be surprised if they wanted to erect a statue someday."

A statue of him was the very last thing in the world that Zack wanted. He just hoped to be left alone to live his life with Suzy. If he hadn't needed the Scope for their business, he would regret ever finding it. That thing was very dangerous, and he feared a future when he might be asked to use it over and over, to avert one disaster after another.

He kept these thoughts to himself, of course, and to the Senator he only said that he would be ready, waiting for his arrival. Then he went back to the Scope to see if anything useful showed up in the conference room. The meeting was over, the room was empty, and he moved the camera around the room to study and film any piece of paper lying around. When it was all on film, he shut down the Scope and helped himself to a beer from the fridge.

~

As soon as the meeting was over, Brady's commanders each went to their trucks to carry out their assigned roles in the operation. The trucks were all loaded up, ready to roll. According to the plan, the timing was of utmost importance, they had to get down to the border before the President found out what was happening and tried to stop them. Once they arrived at their designated locations, they would waste no time taking control away from the Border Patrol. There would be a lot of confusion among these agents. They were not trained or prepared to face an enemy from inside the country. They would be underequipped, most of them carrying only a pistol or, at the most, a shotgun - no match for Brady's troops carrying submachine guns. Brady didn't expect any firefight with these agents but was prepared to respond in kind if needed. No more pussyfooting! Anyone opposing him would be treated as traitors, enemies of the people of the United States.

Brady didn't expect swift action from the government to stop his troops from reaching the border. They would, of course, notice the convoys of trucks heading south but they would need the President's authorization to stop them. This would take some considerable time because Brady timed his operation to coincide with the President's official state visit to China. The news would take some time to reach the President and some more time before he could make any decision about what to do. He would have to wait until the scheduled event for the day was over because he wouldn't risk offending the Chinese by walking out of a ceremonial meeting. Even after he was free to talk to his advisers, collect information, and make a decision, it would be hours too late to stop Brady's troops, they would already be at their destination and there was nothing the President could do to prevent him from taking control at the border. He expected drawn-out negotiations, threats even, but possession is 90% of the law and he would own the border. In the unlikely event that the President ordered the army to remove them, he had the trump card of three southern Governors to stand between his troops and the army. He felt confident that he had it all covered. He wouldn't have to wait for the next election, he had real power in his hands, and he would not let go of it.

One more task that needed to be accomplished was the public announcement he had been planning as soon as his troops were in position. Joshua Gromley, his propaganda expert had been working on it for weeks and was ready to release it to the media as soon as Brady gave him the green light. Brady was misty-eyed when he heard it for the first time. It was a defiant declaration of civil disobedience, calling on the people to support this heroic act, so desperately needed by their country, to prevent the continued invasion by the hordes coming to march through their border and threaten their way of life, stretch their humanitarian compassion and resources beyond the breaking point. Brady was sure that he would have the public's support because, according to recent polling, 59% of the population was against Triden's amnesty bill and 74% wanted to stop further migrant convoys crossing the American border. He saw no other outcome but Triden backing down and offering some form of compromise. That would make him look weak and ineffective, without public support. At that point, anything could happen and he would be there to take advantage of any opportunity that presented itself. One thing was clear: he would be at the border and he would not let it slip out of his control.

~

As it turned out, unbeknownst to Brady, President Triden was still in the country. His trip to China was postponed at the last minute because of security concerns, so he was still in the White House when Hopkins's message reached him. The video memory card was studied in the Situation Room and, after he and his advisers got over the shock of this unexpected threat to their authority, they realized that time was of the essence. They had to stop Brady's troops before they got underway. The president mobilized the 74th Troop Command unit, a brigade-level command of the District of Columbia Army National Guard, closest to Brady's compound. He ordered it to surround, disarm and arrest Brady's people. Their instruction was to avoid armed conflict but defend themselves if fired on.

They managed to surround the compound before Brady's trucks could move out. A tense stalemate ensued, Brady refusing to surrender, and his troops dug in around the perimeter behind their armored vehicles and razor wire fencing. In the meantime, the news media alerted to the confrontation, had arrived with their usual helicopters and cameras and all the news channels in the country started broadcasting the tense situation.

Brady decided to use this opportunity to have his prepared speech broadcast to the nation. He wore his full American military uniform and spoke proudly into the cameras trained on him.

"Fellow Americans, descendants of our brave forefathers who built this great country and left it to us to

256

protect from internal traitors and external invaders. I appeal to you in this moment of crisis to rise up and come to our aid in our sacred mission of protecting our southern border. Your President committed an impeachable, treasonous act by giving away our shared treasure, American citizenship, to all those millions who snuck into our country illegally and demand a share of our national treasure that you worked so hard to build. Encouraged by that treasonous act, many tens of thousands of migrants are heading toward the Mexican border and will soon be in a position to overwhelm our border patrol and sweep onto our land for more free and unearned hospitality offered by our deranged leaders. We were ready to move our militia south, in order to prevent this disaster, when the president ordered, again illegally, army units to stop and arrest us. We will not surrender! If they try to disarm and arrest us, we will respond with force. Our cause is just! We ask you to stand by us in our existential crisis."

This speech was televised and reported on every communication channel both domestic and foreign.

President Triden knew that he had no time to waste. If he let this crisis drag out, the outcome was unpredictable. Brady's act was clearly treasonous, but he had millions of followers and the risk of sustained confrontation could lead to civil war. The intelligence he obtained about the southern Governors' pledged support for Brady was an alarming indication of the danger he faced. Without wasting any time after Brady's proclamation, he ordered the army units to move in and arrest Brady's militia. He hoped that seeing the overwhelming firepower from the army, Brady would come to his senses and surrender peacefully.

He underestimated the fanaticism of Brady and his followers. At the exact moment, the first army vehicles crossed Brady's perimeter, the shooting started. Brady's people fired first, and then the army returned fire. All hell was loose and there was nothing he could do but wait for the inevitable end.

It had taken about three months to get everything
ready for the "Rescue Cousins Mission" or RCM as it was
officially called. The spaceship was loaded with all the
equipment they would need for the mission. It was
equipped with a radiation projector and psychotropic
aerial drug injectors: containers filled with the liquified
drug under high pressure that would be dispersed in the
low atmosphere over the selected city. The crew was
standing by with the addition of Ivo who had insisted on
going along.

Jenna tried to talk him out of it, but Ivo was adamant.

"I'll be back before you know it. You wouldn't want me
to miss the opportunity of a lifetime?"

"Have you ever been in space? That planet is 27 light-
years away, it will take the ship a month to get there.
What can you do for a whole month in a metal can,
surrounded by the blackness of space? You'll be bored to
death."

"No, I won't because I'll be busy deciphering their
language with my translator. There are hundreds of
languages in use on their planet, but we identified the two
most widely used, they call English and Spanish. Once we
found the planet, we were able to receive electromagnetic
transmissions from it. Both audio and visual. These are 27
years old by the time the waves reached us, but I don't
think much has changed as far as language is concerned."

"Why can't you do it here, in the comfort of your own
office?"

"I need to be there when the ship arrives to update my
language database with current data, as well as monitor
the status of the selected city for a few days before we
start the operation. And, we never know when, or if, the
need for actual communication comes up, in which case I
am the only one who knows how."

Jenna couldn't object to his arguments because they made perfect sense. And, she wasn't going to tell him her real reason for objecting to his trip. During the last months, their relationship had developed into a very close bond, both physical and emotional, that she knew she was going to miss sorely during his absence. So, she only said: "Make sure you come back in one piece and don't bring a young and sexy native damsel with you. I haven't told you yet, but I am the jealous type."

They both chuckled at the idea of kidnapping a princess from that dying planet.

When he was finally in space, Ivo got busy analyzing the accumulated transmissions from their target planet. The first thing he learned was that some natives called it 'Earth', so finally he had something other than 'the planet' to call it. Information was slowly accumulating about Earth and much of it was shockingly unlike his own home. The population of Earth was organized into hundreds of independent units that the natives called 'countries' and many of them were in a constant state of violence with each other, over resources, and also some totally incomprehensible differences that they called 'religion'. Ivo had no idea what that word meant, except that it meant different things to different countries. They seemed to have an irrational fantasy about some kind of supernatural entity that watched them every minute of their lives and rewarded and punished them according to their adherence to a code of conduct. Ivo put this 'religion' thing aside for later study, once he had more information.

The other shocking concept he gleaned from the transmissions was what they called 'money'. This seemed to refer to an artificial medium that controlled every aspect of their production and distribution process. This resulted in a huge concentration of wealth in the hands of some and totally inadequate access to even basic resources for others. Ivo couldn't understand why it was done since it seemed to involve a lot of wasted time fighting over and administering this medium, in addition to the inefficient distribution. So, he put this aside as well, in the same box with religion, to be studied later when he knew more.

A third thing he learned about them was their poor health and shockingly short life expectancy. They seemed to die at a very young age of 50-80 planetary cycles, depending on where on the planet they lived. Converting these cycles to his own time units, they died at less than half the age at which his own people usually retired. Maybe this was somehow connected to the insanely large overall planetary population, currently pushing ten billion. Earth was overpopulated to a density 20 times that of their own.

From the visual transmissions, he viewed many fictional episodes they called 'movies' featuring various forms of violence against each other, liberally sprinkled with sexual scenes. He decided that this is what they created and watched for entertainment. Ivo wasn't surprised at the sorry state of the planet. He finally realized how incredibly lucky they were to have avoided the same fate due to their ancestors discovering and treating that genetic brain disorder.

The one month of interstellar travel time went quicker than he had feared. By the time they arrived in Earth's solar system, he had a clear picture of its political/cultural situation and he had acquired fluency in one of their languages that the natives called 'English'. The selected city they were aiming for was called 'Washington', on the North American continent, in a country called the 'United States of America'.

The crew activated the stealth mode for their spaceship because, judging by the hundreds of artificial satellites orbiting their planet, as well as the huge arrays of radio-telescope dishes and optical telescopes they knew that the natives had some observational capability. The plan was to stay over the city in a geosynchronous orbit and start the radiation when everything was ready.

Ivo had only one decision that he had been struggling with. The more he learned about these 'humans' as they called themselves, the more he felt sorry for them. He didn't quite feel that he and his people had the moral right to force the treatment on the natives, without even a consultation to find out if they wanted to be treated. He knew that it was impossible to expect a planetary consensus, as was the most natural thing to do at home, but there had to be some individual human he could have an intelligent dialogue with about their situation and the possibility of outside help.

When Judd had told him about locating another Viewer in operation on the planet, he thought that it might be possible to send a message onto its screen and start a conversation with the operator. Whoever was using it had to have a higher level of scientific and technological awareness than the average population, so it might be possible to gauge one human's reaction to the possibility of a permanent cure to what some of them referred to as the 'human condition'. Ivo could read and write fluently in their language by the time they got there. All he needed to do was to acquire the space coordinates of the other Viewer if one did exist and was being used. If it was built by their common ancestors, as he assumed, it would have the capability of receiving electromagnetic transmission and displaying it on the screen. After a sleepless night agonizing about his decision, he just couldn't resist at least an attempt to communicate with a single human.

~

Zack stared at his screen in disbelief. He was monitoring the ongoing battle at Brady's compound, tracking Brady's movements inside the perimeter when the images were replaced by a text message from an unknown source. The message was in English and advised him to activate his manual input function to have a conversation about their predicament. Zack didn't even know if the Scope had a manual input function but was shown in the following message how to do that. It was as simple as pressing the 'Track' and 'Scan' buttons together, after which a visual keyboard would appear on the Scope's screen and he could just type his responses as he would do in any chat forum. He tried it and it worked as he was told it would. He had a weird feeling about this. The only source he could think of where this fantastic message could have come from was the aliens who had invented the Scope in the first place. The aliens he had tried to track through space when they left Earth 54,000 years ago. Nobody on Earth knew about the Scope.

The most obvious first question he typed in was just to make sure. He already knew the answer.

"Who are you?"

The reply came with a little delay.

"We are the people who invented your Viewer."

"Where are you?"

"We live on a planet 27 light-years away."

"Why did you contact me?"

"We are aware of your human condition and we can help."

"How?"

"Your problems are caused by a genetic brain disorder that we can cure. We used to have it a very long time ago and now we are cured."

"How can you cure our brains? I'm not sure I'd want anyone to mess around with my head."

"You have to take my word for it. We will do it anyway. I wanted to know how you would react."

"I can't make a decision of this size, I'm just a techno-guy, but I know someone who could."

"How soon can you get him in touch with me?"

"Give me a day. I'll have him here at the same time tomorrow."

"Very well, be ready at the same time after one planetary rotation."

No more text showed up on the screen, so Zack assumed that the communication was over. He sat there, mopping sweat off his forehead, afraid to look in the wall mirror, half expecting his hair to have turned white during this exchange. This was the most fantastic, the most unexpected event in his life and he wasn't sure whether it actually happened, or he was being delusional. He knew what he had to do. Senator Hopkins was the only person who had the intelligence and experience to deal with state-wide problems of some magnitude, but he was sure nothing even close to this size had ever come his way. However, that was the only person he knew to trust with this hot potato in his lap.

Gordon Hopkins was still in Washington, monitoring the news of the battle between Brady's militia and the army unit when he got an urgent call from Zack.

"Senator, you need to visit me tomorrow, because I have an unbelievable piece of information that you have to hear immediately."

"What is it, Zack, why don't you just tell me?"

"I can't sir, I have to show you in person, otherwise you might not believe it."

"Very well, Zack, I can drop in for an hour today. I hope you are not exaggerating the importance of whatever you have to show me."

"If anything, Senator, I am underestimating. When can you get here?"

"I'll be there in an hour, be ready!"

Zack knew that once the Senator heard his news, he would be there the next day as well, at the required time to carry on the dialogue with his alien visitor. He was ready to show Hopkins the automatically recorded exchange with this unexpected intruder.

~

The Senator sat motionless for a very long time, staring at the screen that displayed the 'conversation'.

"Zack, if this is a joke, tell me now and we'll pretend it never happened."

"Senator, you should know me better by now. I don't pull pranks of this size on anyone, least of all you."

"This is fantastic and almost unbelievable, but who else could have sent that message? Nobody else knows about the Scope, as far as I know."

"You can be sure of that, sir, and even if anyone else knew, they wouldn't know how to communicate with it. Even I had not known it was possible until about an hour ago."

"I guess, I don't have a choice, I'll be here tomorrow at the same time, or rather an hour earlier, to make sure we don't miss his next broadcast. And, please don't tell anyone, not even Petuccini or even Suzy. This is the most frightening thing that ever happened in human history. Or the most hopeful, if it is for real."

The next day they sat in front of the Scope's monitor, turned on, waiting in tense silence for the promised communication. Exactly at the same time as on the previous day, the screen went blank and a new message appeared.

"Are you ready to receive transmission?"

Zack typed a reply:

"Yes, ready and Senator Hopkins is with me. He is the person you need to talk to."

"Greetings to you Senator. My name is Ivo and I am a descendant of our common ancestors who left your planet 50,000 years ago, leaving parts of their group behind who became your Homo Sapiens."

"My name is Gordon Hopkins and I am aware of your message yesterday. I understand that you want to cure our heads?"

"Not all of you, not all at once. That will have to be your decision. However, I am going to show you a small demonstration of what we can do. There is a violent confrontation taking place not too far from your location. I will activate the process to fix the confused and aggressive brains of the combatants in the next hour. If you see the result of their coming to their senses, then you will know that I can do that for your entire planet."

"You said it will be our decision."

"That is correct. If you want, after the demonstration, I'll broadcast to this device the specifications of the technology required to accomplish it on your own. Your scientific and technological level will be able to duplicate it. After that, it will be up to you, we won't interfere further."

"If you can do anything to stop the ongoing violence you observed, I'm all for it. Depending on how it goes, I'm sure we would welcome any scientific and technological assistance that could help our species. But it will have to be our decision. Do I have your word on it?"

"You have my word on it, Senator Hopkins. We'll start the process immediately. It will take a few of your hours to notice the change. I'll contact you at the same time tomorrow to hear your decision on whether you want the technology."

The screen went back to visually monitoring the battle at Brady's compound.

~

Senator Hopkin's original idea was to pass all this information on to Sam Triden, should the promised demonstration prove the possibility of a cure for the human condition. It didn't take him long, based on his decades-long experience with the power structures in Washington, to realize that it was a bad idea. The president would demand to know the source of this information and immediately confiscate the Time Scope. He would start using it for spying on his party's political opponents. That was ingrained in the very fabric of every politician. No, there had to be another way.

If the demonstration worked, he would have to ask Ivo to apply it at least to the ruling circles in Washington. The President, the Congress, and the Pentagon at least, so their leaders would be sane enough to make the right decision regarding the alien offer. Better yet, ask them to apply it to the whole city, so at least there would be one center of sanity in the country from where it could spread to other parts of the USA first, and then the rest of the world. If they went about it intelligently, the US had the resources and the power to carry it out.

He knew that it would be an unimaginably great responsibility to make this decision on his own, without consulting anyone else. What if the treatment had side effects? Unforeseen consequences? He would have to trust the alien's word on that. What if it was a Trojan Horse, a prelude to enslaving their planet? On the other hand, a civilization that was that far ahead would have to be a rational, intelligent species to have survived this long. The background information he had already gleaned from their own Scope seemed to corroborate Ivo's story. At least he knew that the inventors of the Scope had lived on Earth 50,000 years ago and then migrated to another planet in the Galaxy. He knew this for a fact, having witnessed the exodus on the Scope.

Gordon Hopkins was a man of integrity and he was used to making important decisions based on his own sense of reality. Every fiber in his being told him that this was a once-in-a-lifetime opportunity to solve humanity's age-old problems. He couldn't waste it by indecision. If he was wrong, humanity could be badly hurt, but they were already doing it to themselves anyway without any chance of reprieve.

Senator Gordon Hopkins made his decision about the fate of his entire species and all he needed to do now was to wait for the promised demonstration.

The battle wasn't going well for Brady. His troops were squeezed farther and farther back toward his main building as the soldiers steadily advanced with their armored personnel carriers. He knew he could hole up in his compound building for a long time unless the army used heavy artillery to destroy his building, but he doubted that very much. Maybe if he held out long enough, the southern governors would intervene, and the public would be riled up enough to halt the assault and Brady could negotiate some kind of compromise.

As he watched the field through his binoculars, suddenly a thick fog enveloped the entire area, obscuring his vision. Where the hell did that come from? He could barely see his soldiers lying on the ground behind their protective embankment. He tried to wipe the condensation off the lenses, but that didn't help; the fog was thick and sticky. For an unknown reason, he felt a dread spreading through his entire body. Something was wrong here, something foreboding and spooky, like in one of those nightmares he used to have as a child when he tried to escape an evil pursuer and couldn't run fast enough. He found it hard to breathe, his eyes watered, and his stomach contracted in dry heaves, but nothing came up as he retched, trying to pull himself together. Did the bastards use chemical weapons on him? It was inconceivable that they would go that far.

As the fog started to disperse, he could see his soldiers again and was surprised to see them all stand up from the protection of their covers. They looked around in a dazed stupor that he started to feel himself. *"What are we doing here?"* Looking toward the enemy vehicles he couldn't believe his eyes: they stopped advancing and the soldiers were climbing out, looking as confused and dazed as his own people. Some stared at the weapons they were holding as if not quite sure what they were supposed to do with them. Others threw them on the ground as if they were red hot and backed away from their vehicles and one another, started walking toward the perimeter and away from the compound. Some of Brady's soldiers started to follow, not holding their weapons anymore either.

He suddenly felt an inexplicable urge to laugh and he doubled over as the waves of hysterical laughter made his whole body shake. The irony of it all! There was nothing worth all this stupidity and violence. We must have been out of our minds to go to all this trouble and for what? We could have solved the whole immigration problem by sitting down quietly, rationally examining the issues and coming to some kind of compromise. Brady was surprised by his own thoughts; they were so unlike him that he couldn't imagine where they had come from. Must be that blasted fog somehow, he thought and then burst out laughing again. "We have been fogged into sanity! I hope it will last, I don't want to be full of hate and fear again. It wasn't very pleasant. Maybe I'll go home, have a nice cup of tea and then call Sam and arrange a meeting where we can discuss all this shit." He left his own weapon on the floor and started to follow his soldiers out of the compound.

~

Hopkins and Zack watched the news, not quite believing what they saw. The image captured from a helicopter by the news cameras showed soldiers emerging from Brady's compound, without their weapons, side by side with their earlier enemies. The reporters on the ground surrounded them and asked the usual stupid questions reporters always ask, like "How do you feel about it" and other inane clichés, but the answers were not typical at all. Most of the soldiers seemed surprised to be there at all. Some said that it didn't make any sense to play soldiers when there was so much work to do at home. A farm boy from Iowa said: "It's harvest time, I should be on my farm to help my father with the crops and I'm wasting my time here." A local soldier said: "I must be out of my mind; my wife is eight months pregnant and I am not there to support her. I must be crazy – I'll go home right now and ask her to forgive me."

One of Brady's ex-soldiers commented on his reason for joining Brady's troops: "I thought I was helping my country by stopping those migrants, but they need help too! They are human beings, just like me and they have families and children and they have lost everything, and they are asking for our help. How can we refuse?" What was even stranger, the reporters agreed with the interviewed soldiers; made encouraging comments, and wished them good luck. None seemed to find any of this strange as if it was the most natural thing to do: stop in the middle of a battle and walk away to help others in need.

Hopkins had his demonstration. He was convinced that the procedure worked. When he switched to another channel, some TV reporters, far away from the action, sounded a different tune. Gone was the tone of comradery and fellowship expressed by the on-the-scene reporters and all he could hear was endless speculation regarding who was responsible for drugging those soldiers to make them abandon their duty and leave all their weapons behind and walk away with some flimsy excuse of wanting to help someone.

He had no more doubt about what he had to do. He could hardly wait for the next day when he would ask Ivo to apply the procedure to all of Washington. Once that was accomplished, he would contact the President and pass on the technical specs he would receive from the aliens. He was sure that Sam Triden, once subjected to the treatment, would make the right decision for all concerned.

Washington DC woke up the next morning to a thick fog enveloping their city. After the previous day's events at Brady's compound, many of the residents worried that the country was under attack with chemical weapons. They tried to escape, jumping into their cars and heading out of the city. They couldn't get very far because the highways were already jammed with panicky residents. They just had to sit in their cars, windows tightly rolled up, waiting for help to arrive from somewhere. However, their cars weren't airtight, and, after a while, the fog seeped into the interior and surrounded them as before, forcing them to breathe it in. Apart from a feeling of slight nausea, they didn't suffer any negative effects. After a while, they started feeling relaxed and hopeful. This wasn't a chemical attack: whatever this was made them feel good. What were they doing here? The congestion slowly started to ease up as cars close to a ramp or an exit moved off the highway and headed back home.

John Curtis, known in his circles as the 'weasel' looked around in the living room of the affluent home he had broken into an hour before. The owners were away on vacation and he had thought this would be a good opportunity to help himself to some valuables that he was sure he needed more than the occupants. Now he wasn't quite sure what he was doing here. He had never felt this confusion before. Must be the damn fog he had to breathe in on his walk to the back door. He looked at the broken window of the door he had forced open and idly thought that he would have to fix it before the owners returned.

Paul Harris was still mad at his wife. He had been yelling at her for the last hour, haranguing the frightened woman about her spending habits, threatening to cut up her credit cards if she didn't stop wasting their money on frivolous entertainment like concert tickets and video recordings. The thick fog pouring in through the open window made him cough and he felt mild nausea, but it soon faded. He was confused, and could not quite remember what the fight was about. Why did he mind her interest in classical music? Just because he preferred rock, that didn't mean they couldn't enjoy both. Looking at her cowering before him made him feel ashamed. She had to know that he loved her and wouldn't do anything to hurt her. What gave her that crazy idea? It wasn't right that she should be afraid of him. He hugged her to his chest and apologized for yelling at her.

Jolene Roberts sat at her desk in the bank, wondering why she was transferring that large sum of money from one of their client's accounts to an offshore bank where she had registered during her visit there last year. That didn't feel right, it wasn't her money and, even though she was sure that the transfer could never be traced back to her, it felt somehow wrong. She didn't even know who the client was. Maybe they needed the money to help a sick child with an operation, maybe it was someone's life-saving. How could she think of stealing it from them? She must have been out of her mind to dream up this mad scheme. She carefully signed out of the account and closed her computer. There had to be a better way to buy her dream home than stealing from clients.

Scott Watson was ready to empty his trailerful of garbage, used tires, and half-empty paint cans into the creek flowing through the vacant property a few blocks from his house. He was doing his yearly yard clean-up and had a lot of junk accumulated over the winter. Taking it to the dump would be a long drive and he would have to pay for the hazardous waste. He had thought it wouldn't bother anyone and soon the creek would carry it off to wherever it flowed. When the thick fog surrounded him, he was even pleased that no one would see him doing this illegal dumping but then started feeling bad about the whole idea. What did the fish do to deserve all that garbage dumped on them? They would surely die. Besides, he had heard so much about the environment being poisoned, he couldn't possibly make it worse. On second thought, he should take all this trash to the dump and pay the fee. Once he decided to do that, suddenly he felt much better. Maybe he would also spring for his son's summer camp. A nice kid deserves a treat from his old man.

Thousands of episodes like these played out all over Washington all day. Apparently, nobody escaped the effect of the fog they were forced to breathe in. Nobody knew where it had come from and how it worked but all the people in the city knew that something profoundly important had happened.

Sam Triden, sitting in the oval office was staring at the reports that had been coming in all day about the fog and its inexplicable effect on people. Of course, the top story he had been mulling over was the outcome of the battle between Brady's people and the army he had sent to arrest them. He was surprised, even shocked, by the way it ended but he also felt relieved. When he received a message from Brady that he wanted to talk, he thought that it would be a good idea, even if he didn't have a clue as to what Brady wanted. However, he agreed to see him this afternoon, after he had met with retired Senator Hopkins whose request for a meeting surprised him. Hopkins wasn't in the government anymore but, when Hopkins told him that he had an explanation for the fog and the strange effect on people, he couldn't say no. He was actually burning with curiosity about what had happened.

Hopkins was ushered into his office and extended his hand cordially to his president who had once been in the enemy camp.

"Sir, I'm sure you are aware of what's been happening all over the city since that fog yesterday."

"Yes, Mr. Hopkins and I agreed to meet with you because you promised an explanation. Not that I believe anything could explain this miracle of people acting suddenly sane all over town."

"The explanation will take some time and it will stretch your credulity beyond anything you have been asked to believe before. Nevertheless, this is the truth and the only one that will explain everything."

"I have the time if you can convince me that you are telling me provable reality."

"This is a long story that starts with a young techno-whiz kid finding a device that enabled him to observe events anywhere and at any time in the past. This device was invented by an ancient technological civilization that left the Earth 50,000 years ago and migrated to another planet."

"Senator, are you telling me a science fiction tale, or are you going to give me a rational explanation? Was it the Russians or the Chinese that dumped all that fog on us?"

"Sir, before I came here, I looked at the device that we call a 'Time Scope' and checked out what you were doing last night in the Secret Parrot restaurant with that actress. I did it because I knew that you would need proof that the device was real."

Sam Triden was shocked. Nobody knew about his secret rendezvous with Miriam Shanna, a very attractive young actress he had dated for the last few months. He had gone to a lot of trouble to make sure it was their secret for the time being. He did not need the inevitable speculation from the tabloids.

"Are you telling me that you have been spying on me?"

"No, Sir, I am telling you that the Time Scope is real.

"OK, let's assume that this fantastic device is real. How is it related to what we are talking about?"

"If you are willing to believe me for the moment, I will tell you exactly how the two are connected."

It took Hopkins over an hour to explain everything about their remote cousins, living on another planet,

50,000 years ahead of them in technology. By applying their superior biotechnical knowledge, they were able to fix some genetic brain disorders in the minds of people in Washington.

"This treatment included the fog we all had to breathe in as well as radiation from space. The only effect of this treatment was that everybody affected by it became more peaceful and cooperative, with a lot more empathy toward others."

Sam Triden was reeling from this fantastic tale. Hopkins didn't seem delusional and, with his reputation of personal integrity, it was unlikely that he would want to tell him a bogus story.

"I want to see this Time Scope device, Senator. Please arrange its transfer to the White House so our scientists can test it and make sure you are telling me the truth.

"The device, unfortunately, is no longer available. The last thing the aliens did before returning to their planet, was to burn out the circuitry. They told me that it doesn't belong to us. It was invented by their ancestors and they decided that it would be a very dangerous instrument in the wrong hands. However, before they did that, they downloaded all the detailed specs of the treatment they used for the demonstration so that we could duplicate it and use it to treat everyone else if that's what we want. Now that everyone in Washington is cured of the genetic brain disorder, and that includes you, me, all members of the US Congress and Senate, as well the entire staff of the Pentagon, I'm sure that we will make the right decision."

Hopkins handed over the memory card that contained all the data he had received from Ivo before the Time Scope was disabled. He still winced when he remembered Zack's face when the kid realized that his plans for a detective agency went up in smoke, but he didn't regret what had happened. It was necessary for everyone's benefit, including Zack's in the long run. The kid had too much brain to waste it on playing detective.

"Very well, Mr. Hopkins, leave it with me and I'll have our scientists study it and see if we can make any use of it. Too bad about that Time Scope, I would have liked to see a demonstration. I have always had some curiosity about past historical events and now that curiosity will have to stay unsatisfied. Thank you for coming in and telling me this fantastic tale. Now I have to say goodbye because I have a meeting with, you'll find this hard to believe, General Brady. Maybe we can come to some understanding after all."

Hopkins left the President, hoping that he would come to the right decision and use the information he was given by Ivo and his people. He felt more hopeful than ever before in his life, at the same time relieved that the drama was firmly out of his hands.

Time to return to Vermont, Muriel and their dogs, surrounded by the beautiful forest for the rest of their lives. He was done with drama and intrigue, hopefully forever.

The End